EAGLES MANOR

TERRY BARRETT

To Brian
Good Wishes
Terry.
Barrett.

Eagles Manor

© Terry Barrett

Cover design: Tobi Carver
Cover image: istock

First Edition published 2010

Published by:
Palores Publications,
11a Penryn Street, Redruth, Kernow, TR15 2SP, UK.

Designed & Printed by:
The St Ives Printing & Publishing Company,
High Street, St Ives, Cornwall TR26 1RS, UK.

ISBN 978 1 906845 17 9

EAGLES MANOR

Terry Barrett

Dedicated to Angela

Chapter One

TERRY BOND, WHO answered to being called T.J., was pounding away on a running machine he called a treadmill. God! he thought, in few more minutes I'll have done five miles. T.J. would like to have been running outside. Today however, it was raining. He did not mind keeping fit, but not getting wet at the same time. Normally he ran about five miles, twice a week, but never on a Saturday. Saturdays were like a holy day. T.J. supported Crystal Palace, a first division football club, known locally as 'Palace'. He could not see them getting much better than they were. They often had some good players, then they would sell them and the weaker team would wind up in the second division.

With five miles completed, T.J. had a shower and dressed before going for a cup of tea in the cafeteria. He found tea more refreshing than water. T.J. was relaxing, enjoying his drink when in came a man, who like T.J. was in his early twenties. The newcomer went to the counter, got a bottle of water and sauntered towards T.J. whilst drinking from the bottle. Pointing to the other chair at the table, he broke off from drinking and said, 'Do you mind?' with that he sat down, leaned over and held out his right hand.

As they shook hands, he said, 'My name is Stan, most call me Checker, on account of I always have my hair cut short. I like it. Anyway, this is a much better style and you never know it might be all the rage one day!' He smiled.

T.J smiled back, 'I'm Terry, known as T.J. I've seen you here before, on the treadmill or in the weightlifting room.'

'You come here often?' Checker asked.

'I do, it helps to let off steam, relax and it's away from the office.'

'That's funny that's exactly what I think. I am a quantity surveyor: I completed my finals over six months ago and got my diploma. It's alright, I go out on sites, take all the measurements, check the levels. Before, I go back to the office to collect the drawings from the technicians. Then sit down bill out all of the quantities, write out all of the specifications, drawings, collate them all together, which are then sent out to all of the contractors for estimates! Sounds simple, but it can take months, just on a proposed building site. Working out here keeps me sane.'

T.J. nodded his understanding.

'What do you do?' asked Checker.

'Oh me, I am a solicitor, well almost, I graduate within the next three months. Although I have worked on some cases, mainly on small claims courts, or magistrates, mind you I was the junior, just learning.' T.J. responded.

Checker smiled, 'Good, now I know a good Brief if I need one!'

'And I know a surveyor if needed.'

They both chuckled, finished their drinks before saying, 'Cheerio, see you next week.' in unison.

T.J. walked to the car park, got in his car and headed towards home. His thoughts strayed to Checker, he seemed a decent sort. T.J. had been looking at property. It would not be a bad idea to keep in touch, it would pay to have your own surveyor. His thoughts changed to Monday's work and starting on his final papers. Everyone at the offices believed he would walk the examination. He hoped they were right.

T.J. drove into his parents driveway.

His mother was potting around in the garden, she shouted out, 'I hope you have left enough room for your Father, you know how he likes to drive straight into the garage.'

T.J. walked over to her, gave her a hug and a little kiss on the cheek. She asked if he wanted tea and he replied, 'Yes.' and they walked into the house.

That evening T.J. went to Granada cinema with Rita, his current girlfriend. She's great, likes a good laugh and sex! Mind you that came after a month of trying! T.J. would always remember the first night he took her out, funny enough it was to Granada. They sat in the back row and after a while he slipped his arm around her shoulder and very slowly worked his hand down to her breast. He thought his luck was in, there was no resistance. All of a sudden, she pushed his hand away.

'Wait a minute.'

Rita started to undo the top button of her blouse, put her hand inside pulled out and placed a sponge false cup in his hand saying,

'If you so much want to play with it, there you go!'

T.J. got very hot and embarrassed, and just sat there looking at it and then he looked at her. She had a smile on her face and they both broke out into uncontrollable laughter.

T.J. and Rita did not see the film. They left the picture house and went to have a cup of hot Bovril and a sausage sandwich at Smokey Joe's stall by the 'Pond' at Thornton Heath roundabout. It was a stall known to people who work in theatres and nightclubs in London, and if you were there after midnight, you would see them pull up in their cars and go to Joe's for refreshments, on their way home.

Monday! Back at work and T.J. needed to start on his final papers.

He worked for a legal firm call Bowen, Bowen & Bowen. Senior Bowen is father and two sons. There are other legal teams there, as for T.J. he is the junior, which involves a lot of gopher work. T.J. owes the employment to his father, as he is the golf partner of Mr Bowen senior, at an upmarket golf club, which encourages people of good repute and the Masons! T.J.'s father is a Mason, he once asked him what it stood for and of what benefit does it offer the public?

After his father tried to explain without revealing the purpose of the Masons.

T.J said, 'So it's a male dominated club, who maybe collect funds to help the poor, but we never hear of their deeds, unlike the Salvation Army or Cancer Relief and so on?'

This brought an angry response, 'When you grow up you will understand.'

Further discussion was cut short by mother saying quite strongly, 'Be quiet both of you!' When mother spoke like that no more was said, as both her husband and son respected and loved her dearly.

Anyway, back at the office T.J. had been informed to devote his time to the paper and that all his usual work would be completed by others. T.J. was invited to ask any questions and to get guidance from others as they all wanted him to succeed.

Tuesday was College all day.

Sometimes T.J. found it a bore for most of the questions and essays were what he had already learnt at the office. He always went to the sports centre on Tuesday nights and he wondered if Checker would be there. T.J. thought he appeared 'streetwise', anyway Checker was a good laugh. T.J. decided to drive there, as normally on dry nights he generally ran there. As T.J. walked into the weight training room, Checker was pounding away at the punch bag, he looked as if he hated it, and was trying to knock the stuffing out of it. When Checker saw T.J. he stopped, waved and came over. Checker looked as if he had just stepped out of the shower. T.J. nodded towards the bag and said, 'It looked as if you didn't like him; anyone I know?'

Checker laughed and said, 'The next bloke that calls me 'skinhead'!'

They both laughed.

After a period of training they both showered and went to the cafeteria, Checker had water and T.J. had tea.

Checker looked over and said, 'You like that tea?'

'It is more refreshing than water alone, if you go out to North Africa tea is drank more than water. By the way I will not be working out on Saturdays now, as I support a local football team, and I will be watching their matches.'

Checker smiled, 'I was about to say the same to you, what team do you support?'

'For my sins, Palace.' T.J. answered.

Checker said, 'Great! I do as well, I've never seen you there, where do you stand? We will go together, I will meet you outside the gym, say 1.30.'

'Yes okay but I sit up in the old stand. I have a season ticket, my Father buys me one every year.'

'Cor! He must be well off, I always go at the Holmesdale Road end! Anyway it's much better than stuck up in the stands. You get the proper fans around you, shouting the likes of 'the ref needs glasses, chuck him off, it was offside!' All the shouting and laughing, it's great, you ought to try it Terry! Unless of course it's raining.' Checker laughed, 'Give it a go!'

'You get a lot of fighting in there and a lot of pushing and shoving sometimes, I watch them from the stands.' T.J. Stated.

'Instead of the football.' Checker laughed. 'You only get that when the games a load of rubbish, or some of the opposing fans have come to cause bother, but it's great fun, you will enjoy yourself. Anyway there are a couple of mates I meet there, with them around the four of us would be too heavy for anybody.'

After some thought T.J. said, 'Okay, I will see you here at 1.30 alright.'

Checker grinned, 'You will enjoy it.'

With that they both left and went out.

That night T.J. took Rita out to the local pub, they both only drank a couple of half lagers, then went on to a fish and chip restaurant; Chinese run. They went in and sat down, ordered a meal. Just for fun T.J. always said, 'Sore finger', as if you say it quickly it sounds like salt and vinegar. Rita and T.J. both laughed but the waitress did not, she was used to the jokes and said quite angrily, 'One day you will have a sore finger!'

Rita and T.J. looked at each other with raised eyebrows and smiles.

On Saturday T.J. met Checker outside the gym and they caught a bus to Thornton Heath High Street, got off at the stop at the bottom of Whitehorse Road and walked up to the ground. The atmosphere was great. They got up to the stand and walked around to the Holmesdale Road end, got their tickets and went in. It was electrifying, the buzz, the noise of thousands of people all around.

Checker said, 'Come on there's my two mates over there.'

As they pushed their way over, there were a few remarks, 'Oi careful who you're pushing of!'

Checker didn't stop and T.J. just followed behind. T.J. admitted to himself that the noise and buzz of conversation around them was far more exciting than sitting up in the stands. They reached where Checker's other friends were and Checker introduced them.

'This is Terry, T.J. to his mates,' he said. 'This is Clifford, we call him Cliff.'

T.J. shook hands with him and thought, he's aptly named, Cliff stood about six feet two inches, with broad shoulders, he looked like a cliff.

T.J. shook hands with Checker's other friend and was told, 'This is Gordon, but he gets called Curly. You could see why when you looked at his hair.'

Checker then started to point a few people out, as he did so he said, 'By the way, see that lot over there on the right, that tallish bloke with all the teenagers around him, sixteen and seventeen year olds, there are often more. Down further they are older and they call themselves 'The Eagle Mob', well if they start trouble? Don't look at their hands, they all wear steel toe capped boots! Their favourite trick is to stamp on your feet and before you can say ouch, they kick the other leg. But they won't come over here, they have already been taught a lesson.'

'Well!' T.J. said to Checker, 'I think you have got it wrong because the big ones coming over here.'

Checker's reply was, 'Very nonchalant ho'yer. If you look at Cliff he is calling him over.'

When he came up to them, he looked a bit worried and said, 'Me?'

Cliff said, 'Yes' he turned to T.J. and said 'This is T.J. a very good friend of ours, and if his toes get stamped on you will be held responsible and you will get a bigger slap than last time! And you had better get yourself a pair of crutches, because you will need them alright!'

He said 'Yes okay, don't worry I will make sure.'

As he turned to go away Cliff's reply was, 'You'd better!'

With that Cliff turned towards T.J. and said, 'They are no bother, but it's always good to remind them,' he laughed. 'Let's hope we get a good game today!' Cliff seemed to have forgotten the incident already.

There was a big roar of noise and excitement as the players ran out on to the pitch.

T.J. looked at Checker, he just nodded, smiled and said, 'You looked surprised, forget it, you are one of us now. You can say we are four, 'The Just Four'.' T.J. started to watch the game, but in his mind he was thinking, I hope none of this gets out of hand.

All of a sudden the noise that erupted around the ground was tremendous. Palace had scored! The excitement, the waving of the scarves, fists punching the air. T.J. found himself jumping up and down, cheering along with the rest of the crowd, and feeling the ripple of adrenalin course across his back. It was like something he had never experienced before.

T.J. looked at Checker, he was all smiles and said, 'Great isn't it? I told you so! Take a look at the stand where you used to sit.'

T.J. looked and there was the usual clapping of hands and cheering but nothing to what he was experiencing at the moment.

Checker was right, T.J. nodded and gave the thumbs up sign. He looked towards Cliff and Curly, they were the same, cheering and shouting encouragement for more goals.

The game ended, Palace had won 2-0 and all the home fans were walking away from the ground. You could hear the buzz of happiness and the fans discussing the play and the goals.

There were some bad things, the 'Young Eagles Mob' were running down the road and grabbing at car windscreen wipers and breaking them. That was why T.J. never drove his car to the matches.

As they all walked along down to the High Street, Curly suggested going to the café. In the café T.J. ordered tea, the rest had coffee and they got a table by the window. Everyone started talking about the game.

After a while Checker said, 'By the way T.J. is a solicitor.'

All talk about the game stopped. The three of them looked at T.J.

'No, not yet, I have not taken my final papers yet!'

Both Curly and Cliff said, 'That will come in handy!'

T.J. asked 'You're not criminals are you?'

Checker, Cliff and Curly all burst out laughing, and between fits of laughter Checker said, 'No way, Cliff is a designer for a publicity agents office, and Curly has his own garage for car repairs and paint spray shop with two staff. So you can see we are all hardened criminals!'

They all enjoyed the moment. A waiter came over with their drinks and asked if they wanted anything to eat. Cliff and Curly ordered cheese rolls, Checker and T.J. had bacon sandwiches.

As they sat eating their food Curly said, 'I am sorry we laughed, but you had ought to have seen your face when you asked if we were crooks! Tell you what, when your car requires a service I will do the first one free.'

T.J. said, 'I will keep you to that!'

Cliff interrupted and said, 'The second one will be twice as dear!'

Cliff and Curly lived in West Croydon, whereas Checker and T.J. lived in Norbury about four miles away, which is not far more or less in a straight line like the London to Brighton Road. During the talking about football and other topics such as dislikes, likes and girlfriends, it appeared all had girlfriends but none of the girls liked football. By the time they had finished it was seven o'clock in the evening and they realised that they were taking their respective girlfriends out. T.J. was lucky, Rita always went to his home and talked to his mother, who was always pleased to see her. Mother always teased T.J. saying, 'It is good to see another woman about the house, when are you going to settle down?' On which his Father would say, 'Leave the boy alone.' Mother would answer back with a little laugh, 'Only teasing.' Father would reply with a little, 'Hmph.'

That night Rita and T.J. drove over to Epsom Downs to a pub called Tattem Corner. There they had the set meal, chicken, chips and a drink. During the meal T.J. told Rita about his new found friends, Palace football supporters and other things, and she sounded pleased for me.

'I hope this does not mean I will be seeing a lot less of you?'

'No.' T.J. replied, 'In fact they all have girlfriends, we could organise a group night out now and again.'

Rita said, 'How good, your description of Checker and Cliff sound scrummy, I will look very much forward to seeing them in the flesh!'

T.J. playfully grabbed hold of her hand and said, 'I'm the only one you are going to be seeing in the flesh.'

With that, 'What are we waiting for?' Rita said, 'Get them off!'

Later Rita laughed at T.J.'s antics of trying to get his jeans off in the car, while she lifted her skirt to show she had no knickers on.

'Come on I'm waiting!' she said.

The sight of which made T.J.'s efforts more frantic which caused her to giggle.

Monday this week is college for finals. Hopefully, by Thursday the results will be final, as T.J. had already passed most of the exams and first diploma before he had left college and joined the Bowen, Bowen & Bowen firm. Although they say the last one is the hardest exam as a lot fail, because they go there thinking they know it all and fail and have to take them again. T.J. was warned about this by Mr Bowen senior. T.J. dreaded it if he was to fail.

T.J. took most of his studies seriously. By Wednesday 3pm the exam papers were finished, the next two days left him to fret and worry about the results, of which he would be notified by Friday. T.J. telephoned Rita for a night out of which she said, 'you know

I always stay in on Wednesdays to wash my hair and then relax, anyway you always go to your snooker club Wednesdays, what's up you been barred or something?'

T.J. said, 'I have finished my exams and I won't know until Friday the results and I cannot relax.'

There was silence for a minute then Rita said 'You are lucky, my parents have gone up town for a show and a meal after. They won't be back before 1am, so come on around and I'll be waiting, and by the time I have finished with you, you will not know what year it is!'

By the time T.J. left Rita's that night he felt as though he had been turned inside out and was walking on air. T.J. was as happy as a sandboy as the saying goes, he was not thinking about exams, only about the most beautiful and exciting way they had made love and consumed each other.

Thursday at the office T.J. tried to stay calm, reading up on a case which would be coming to court soon, of which he would be helping Mr Bowen junior. But T.J. was anxious, worried and unsure what the results would be. At 4pm the secretary of Mr Bowen senior came over to him and said that Mr Bowen would like to see him in his office right now. T.J. looked at her, at first a bit worried, she looked at him and said, 'It's alright he does not bite you know!' T.J. got up and followed the secretary into Mr Bowen senior's office.

Mr Bowen senior was sitting there behind his big desk, 'Come on in and sit down,' he looked over to his secretary and continued, 'can we have some coffee Mrs Blake?'

She said, 'Of course' and turned and asked 'Terry do you like coffee white or black, and do you take sugar?'

T.J. sort of stammered, 'White with sugar please.' With that she left. T.J. was alone with Mr Bowen in his office.

He was looking at T.J. with a little knowing smile on his lips, he did not say anything. T.J. sat there, and felt like a small schoolboy who was about to be reprimanded, or a frightened rabbit about to be killed by a stoat, although it was only a couple of minutes.

Mrs Blake came back into the room carrying a small tray with the coffee, cups and some biscuits. T.J. thought is this the last rites supper, then thought has he heard the results. T.J.'s mind was in turmoil. The silence was broken by Mr Bowen saying 'Thank you

13

Mrs Blake, you may serve.' As she was pouring the coffee she said, 'One lump or two lumps Terry?'

T.J. spluttered, 'Two please'.

She looked at him and smiled.

Mr Bowen intruded on T.J.'s thoughts as he said to Mrs Blake, 'Everything alright?' She nodded and said, 'Yes thanks,' and left the room.

Mr Bowen looked across at T.J. and said 'I suppose you are wondering why I have called you in to see me? Well Terry my boy, I had a telephone call from the Principal of the John Ruskin College and he has informed me that you have passed all your final papers, with the highest marks for quite a long time. Well what do you say to that young man?'

For a moment T.J. could not believe his ears and something had seemed to have taken his breath away. He was stuttering and could not speak.

Mr Bowen was congratulating him. 'Well done Terry, well done!' Then he got up from his chair, walked around the desk and said, 'Come on my boy, I will show you to your new office.'

T.J. followed on behind him, in a bit of a daze. He then saw the staff who had gathered in the general office and had started clapping and saying, 'Well done!' Mrs Blake came over and handed Mr Bowen and T.J. a glass of wine.

Mr Bowen smiled, 'Here's a toast to our new addition of solicitors,' and continued, 'Your office Terry is the large storeroom, all stores have been removed and the room has been refurbished.'

T.J. said, 'Thank you and I will try never to let you down.'

That day ended in a daze, T.J. didn't remember going home, for when he got home both his mother and father were there to greet and congratulate him with a little tot of sherry.

Mother held up her glass and said, 'You have made us both very proud of you, and we hope you will go on to be the best Q.C. in the country.'

T.J. thanked them both for all the help they had given him. 'I will never forget, but mother on a lighter note, could you make do with a poor solicitor at the moment?'

She said, 'Of course for the moment, but later?' They laughed.

Mother said, 'Now father is so pleased for you and he wants to show his son off for he is so proud of you. He has booked a table at his private club for all of us and that's including Rita, who I have already telephoned and she will be here at 8pm. A car will be here to take us there, so off you go upstairs and get ready, and don't forget it is dress suit and bow tie.'

The evening was a great night out, the meal was very tasteful, both mother and Rita in their evening gowns looked a million dollars. T.J. did wonder where Rita had got enough money to buy such a dress, but thought mother might have given a helping hand. Rita stayed the night at T.J.'s home but alas in the spare bedroom.

Friday after breakfast, mother told T.J. that they were all coming with him to college to see him collect his final diploma and graduate. She said 'Also when you have your photograph done I would be grateful if father and myself can be with you.'

T.J. said, 'Of course mother, I would be delighted, it is my wish for without yours and father's help I would not be here.'

Father gave his usual 'hmph' and mother wiped away a tear. T.J. had often noticed when father made that noise it was to cover embarrassment.

'Well come on,' father said, 'are you not going, I'm not waiting about all day, it is time we should be off.' All four of them piled into father's car and away they went to the college.

All went well. T.J. received his diploma all tied up in a red ribbon, then after a few words he received a small plaque for the best graduate for year 1971. Outside in the college grounds the local photographer was taking photos of fellow students in their gowns and mortas. T.J. had one taken with his mother and father and one taken with Rita. As it was a nice summer's day he walked around with Rita and his parents showing them the sights of the college.

Friday Checker rang asking T.J. how he got on, did he pass? T.J. told him he graduated with honours. Checker said, 'Great, how about a drink tonight to celebrate?'

'Right okay, T.J. replied and asked, 'where shall we meet?'

'Norbury Hotel public bar at 8pm.'

T.J. agreed. Checker said he would telephone Cliff and Curly to see if they could make it.

'Great! See you there.' T.J. thought it would be good to see them all together again, as he had been so involved with exams he had lost touch.

T.J. got to the Norbury at five minutes past eight and they were all there, propping up the bar. Curly ordered a lager for him and said to the barman, 'You can get the bottle of Champers out now our guest has arrived!' They all looked at T.J. and Curly said, 'it's alright you are our guest for tonight.'

'But,' T.J. protested, 'I thought we were mates, not a guest?'

'We are,' said Cliff, 'but you have achieved a degree far greater than our qualifications!'

'Ah!' T.J. said, 'But your trades are far more useful and in more demand to the greater public than mine.'

They all looked at T.J., and then Cliff said, 'He is going to make a bloody good brief when we want one! When you get your introduction cards we will all want one, or a few each, so we can give them to our clients, good idea?'

On that note they all drank to that.

After they had seen off the champagne Checker said, 'Come on, I have booked a table for four at a nice little club in Streatham, just passed the ice rink. It has a small dance floor, a stage with a band and some singers. Excellent food and the entertainment is very good!'

Curly said, 'How do you come to know that club?'

'Well,' Checker said, 'I did a bit of a survey for them, and helped with their plans at cost, so they made me a member of the club and it doesn't cost me a penny. It just comes through the post every year, I take Jean my girlfriend now and again it's great.'

'Well,' Cliff said 'come on, what are we waiting for let's go!'

T.J. said, 'Hold on, I would like to make one thing clear, from now on we all pay equal shares. After all we are the 'just four' as Checker says, agreed?'

'Agreed.'

'Good then let's go!'

The club was great, the entrance was through a door in between a row of shops which went down some stairs and at the bottom it opened into a very large club room. At the far right hand side was a stage and looking to the left, way back was the bar, and a door to the left of that led on to the kitchens. Spaced all around the club was something like thirty tables and not near each other, some just for two diners and some for four.

Their table was slightly to the right and as they all sat down a man came over to them and said 'Stanley, how nice to see you again.'

16

Checker went a bit red in the face. He said to the man, 'I would like to introduce you to my friends.' He said their names and then said, 'they would like to become club members, but can we have four lagers for now please, and of course the menu.'

'Four lagers coming up, it is nice to see you lovely boys. I will also bring you some club membership cards to fill in,' and off he went to the bar.

They all turned and looked at Checker, who looked back and said, 'Hold on, don't start thinking or getting funny ideas! I am not! Yes, he, the owner is, and his boyfriend is the chef here, who will be cooking our meals.'

Cliff who was sitting on the same side of the table as Checker winked at Curly and me and said, 'As if we would think such a thing, would we mates!'

At which both Curly and I said in unison, 'No!'

Cliff said, 'See Stanley!'

Of which they all looked at each other and burst out in uncontrollable laughter, and just at that moment over came their drinks. The man said, 'The first drinks are on the house, and if Stanley has not told you yet my name is Brian.'

'Thanks Brian,' was returned by all.

As he left them to ponder over the menu and fill in their membership cards, Checker said very quietly to them, 'My day will come.'

Curly laughed, 'Oh, yes please!'

This caused further merriment.

They all ordered sirloin steaks and Brian seeing that they had completed filling in their membership cards and stopped reading the menu came over to take the orders, and membership cards. He thanked them and as he went to leave Cliff said in a deeper voice than normal, 'Can we have another four lagers, and the wine list please Brian?'

'Of course,' as Brian turned to go away he said to Cliff, 'Oh haven't you got a lovely deep nut brown voice.'

Cliff made a noise like clearing his throat and said, 'I . . . I sort of had a frog in my throat, I am sorry about that.'

As he left, Brian said, 'That's alright Clifford!' He then stopped and said to them all, 'You all have nice names I noticed as you gave me your membership cards.'

17

Brian went off to the kitchens to place the orders, and as he passed the barman he indicated four more lagers for the table.

Checker all of a sudden started a sort of noise like clearing his throat, of which Cliff made a playful pat on his head and they all started laughing again.

The barman came over with their drinks, when he left they all started to talk about Palace's next match which was tomorrow, Saturday, at home against Brighton. This was always a needle match, can also get a bit of trouble as it always causes a lot of fighting. They were all talking and anticipating the score and who would win, when Brian came over to the table with the wine list, and without looking Cliff said, 'Champers please Brian.'

Brian looked around the table at them, looking for their agreement they all nodded. 'Well this is nice, are you celebrating something or other?'

Cliff said, 'Yes, Terry has just passed his final papers and is now a full blown solicitor, with honours I might add.'

Brian looked at T.J. and said, 'Well done Terry.'

'Thank you,' T.J. replied.

Brian continued, 'I could do with a good solicitor, our other one we use is getting a bit pricey!'

T.J. said, 'I am not that cheap, anyway I work for a very upmarket firm called 'Bowen, Bowen & Bowen.'

'Oh it's not that sort of thing,' Brian said 'it's just that now and again my partner and I sometimes need legal advice about getting money owed from bad debts.'

'Well if that's all you need give me a call.'

Brian said, 'thank you' and went away to get the champers.

Checker said to Curly, 'It only leaves you to start servicing their cars and you Cliff a logo for them and we will all be working for them.'

Cliff then said, 'I like it here, how about fetching our girlfriends here?'

He looked at them, they looked at each other and nodded in agreement. 'How about tomorrow after the match?'

Checker replied, 'We will see if Brian can, after all he might be fully booked for tomorrow.'

Brian came back with their meals on a heated trolley and served them as the barman left the champers. Brian looked at them and said 'enjoy your meals' and was just about to leave when Cliff asked, 'Is it possible that we could book a table for eight people tomorrow night, for us and our girlfriends?'

Brian said, 'Girlfriends! What a pity, alas,' with a smile.

They all laughed.

Brian continued, 'Of course even if I have to pinch a bit of the dance floor for my new friends, why not! Say eight to half past,' and as he walked away he looked at them all, sighed and said, 'What a waste,' winked and then laughed and they all laughed with him.

The food was first class, not one of them left a crumb and as they drank their wine they talked about everyday things, tomorrows match, their girlfriends and girls. Then T.J. suddenly thought, 'Hold on! I know your Christian names but not your full names, surnames.'

They all looked at each other.

Curly said, 'You are not a spy are you?'

Cliff tapped the table and said in a knowing manner, 'You could be right Curly!'

Unfortunately he could not keep a straight face and this caused further laughter.

Curly said, 'Well my full name is Gordon King, garage owner.'

Cliff stated, 'I am Clifford Preston.'

Checker said, 'I am Stanley Wolf (lay about) then!'

They all looked at T.J. with raised eyebrows and enquiring looks. T.J. decided to have a little game and instead of saying his full name he said, 'thank you,' with a smile, 'now I know you all.'

Checker said, 'Well!'

T.J. said, 'Well what?'

With that Cliff stood up from the table, 'I think he wants to dance lads!'

And as one they all crowded around T.J. and lifted him up into the air.

Curly said, 'How old do you think he is?'

Checker said, 'At least one hundred!'

'You sure?' said Cliff.

'Ask him.' said Curly.

T.J. replied, 'Five'.

All of a sudden Brian came hurrying over and said, 'Everything alright?'

19

Checker said, 'It's alright Brian, just playing a prank on Terry.'

'Put him down, he looks a mess up there and I don't want my solicitor damaged just yet.'

T.J. was placed back on the floor, and they were all laughing.

Brian smiled and said, 'You naughty boys!' and walked off.

They all sat down and T.J. said, 'My full name is Terence Jack Bond and for that information you will all be receiving my bill in the post soon.'

'Bang goes my free service for his car.' Curly raised his hand and smiled.

'You will be alright Curly.'

Checker interrupted, 'What about me and a free survey? And both Curly and me are great mates of Cliff.'

With that they looked at each other and then T.J. and said, 'Well?'

T.J. smiled, 'Well, it looks like it's checkmate,' he continued, 'It looks as if the musketeers saying goes for us, all for one and one for all, but in our case it's four for one and one for four!'

Checker said, 'Where did you get that saying from? I've never heard of it before.'

'Nor me,' said Curly.

'Or me,' said Cliff, 'But it sounds just right for us all, what do you say mates?'

They all placed their right hands in the centre of the table on top of each other.

Cliff said 'Say it again T.J.'

T.J. repeated the saying of which at the end they said 'all for one' then there was silence for a minute and all of a sudden Curly said 'Come drink up, we are not at a funeral.' Of which they all laughed and started drinking again.

It was past one o'clock Saturday morning when they all decided to call it a day as they would not be fit to go to the match. Brian was called over and asked for the bill.

'I hope you do not think this account is too expensive, I have tried to cut it a bit.'

Curly took charge and received the bill, looked at it and passed it around the table. Cliff was last to see it, he looked across at them nodded his head and said, 'Thank you Brian.'

The bill came to £180 which came to £45 each. They considered that was a fair price for what they had all gorged themselves on.

Everybody was of the same mind, they divided up their share of the cost, and thanked Brian and his partner for a very nice meal and sociable evening. He thanked them all, also for joining his club and said, 'I will be looking forward to seeing you tomorrow night, or should I say tonight. I will order a taxi to take you all home and I will pay the fare.' As he left he said 'After all I cannot have my lovely boys trying to drive home.'

They did not tell him all their cars were in the Norbury Hotel car park. While they waited for the taxi they all talked about Brian and his partners club, and they all agreed that they had made them feel welcome even though they were gay! They had joked about it, made fun of themselves really and Brian was a very good host.

The taxi driver all of a sudden appeared at their table. They said they were ready, bid Brian and his partner farewell and followed the taxi driver up the stairs out of the club to the car whereupon Curly said, 'Bloody hell, this is some taxi, an Austin Princess.' It was parked by the kerbside and glistened and reflected from the street lighting with a very high polished surface.

Curly said, 'This is no taxi, it can only do about 25 miles to the gallon.' Curly looked at the driver and said 'Is this car really yours?'

The driver smiled and said 'No it is Brian's car and I am the second chef, but I also look after the car and drive Brian about when he does not want to drive himself. And I might say you are the first guests to ride in this car, Brian must really like you. Now would you please get in the car as I would like to get back home to sleep. I live in one of the flats above the shop there,' he pointed to a window above the shop. 'So if you would please.'

The four friends climbed into the car, Checker sat in the front to guide him to where Checker and T.J. lived. When they both got out of the car Curly carried on to give him instructions to where they lived in Croydon.

T.J. and Checker got to the junction where Checker turned off but before T.J. started to walk on Checker said, 'Do you know I checked the bill and the food only came to three pounds and fourteen shillings each, it was the drinks that cost the most!'

T.J. smiled, 'That's all your fault, you kept ordering the best champers.'

'No I did not, that was Cliff, but it was a bloody good night though.'

With that they laughed and bid each other a good night.

Checker said, 'Don't forget I will pick you up at 1 o'clock to collect the cars and then go pick up Cliff and Curly at his garage to get their cars from Norbury.'

T.J. shouted out, 'Right,' then walked on. He looked at his watch, it was almost 2 o'clock, and thought not much sleep tonight.

Chapter Two

T.J. HEARD A faint voice saying, 'Do you want this tea or not? I don't know what or where you were, but I heard you creeping in at 2 o'clock.'

He suddenly woke up and his mother was standing beside the bed holding a cup of tea.

'Well,' she said with one of those looks which could freeze the deserts.

He sat up and said, 'What is wrong mother, what is wrong?'

'You came in at 2am. I heard you, and if your father had heard you well, he would have been very annoyed. I would like to know next time if you are going to be very late, and where you are most likely to be. I know you are over twenty years of age but while you still live in my house I would very much like to know, as I do worry about you.'

'I am very sorry mother it was most disrespectful of me. I promise I will let you know that if I am going to be late I will tell you, who I am with and where. I realise that you would worry as I know it is for my welfare and that you love me as much as I love you. But I went to this nightclub in Streatham and it was fantastic, the food was very nice and so was the entertainment. It was a very discreet and private club, members only, no riffraff. I believe if I took you there you would not be displeased.'

'Thank you, but I don't think your father would approve. Next time you are going to be late I want to know.' With that his mother left him with his thoughts and the tea.

T.J. wondered how he was going to explain going to the club tonight and he thought he would get Rita to tell her, saying how he had told her about the club and she wanted to see it for herself. He thought good thinking T.J. and didn't feel a bit guilty.

Checker came around at one o'clock as promised. T.J. had often mentioned him to his mother however this was the first time they had met. T.J. said, 'This is Stanley who I go to the football matches with.'

Of which mother said, 'Hello,' and shook hands and then the inquisition started. T.J. interrupted after a few minutes saying, 'Mother!'

She looked at her son with a smile, 'I was only getting to know Stanley, and making him welcome.'

'Alright I understand he is not a villain ... I hope!'

With that they all looked at each other and chuckled. As they went out of the door they both said goodbye to mother.

Walking down the road Checker said, 'Your mother is nice and good looking.'

T.J. laughed and said, 'Down Rover she is married!'

They got to the main road and turned right to walked up to the Norbury Hotel to retrieve their cars. As they were walking T.J. told Checker he wanted to telephone Rita to explain that he had already told her about the nightclub and was taking her there tonight, if mother was to ask her. And he would be taking her there as she had asked.

T.J. said, 'I hope Rita will understand, for it sounds like double Dutch to me.'

Checker said, 'She will understand if she is anything like my Jean she will be alright especially if she knows you are taking her there tonight and don't forget what time!'

'That will be alright Rita always goes to my house at about 6.30pm every Saturday and waits until I get home from the match.

'There you are, there is a phone booth and it's empty.'

T.J. went inside to telephone Rita, he came out after ten minutes and said to Checker, 'Rita understands and is looking forward to going tonight.'

They got their cars from the Norbury car park, drove around to T.J.'s home, dropped his car and then both carried on to Curly's garage in Checker's car to pick up Cliff and Curly as arranged. By the time they retrieved their cars and getting to meet the other two the time had gone by very quickly. It was decided to have lunch at a good café Curly knew and afterwards go to the match. It was going to be some match against Brighton which was almost a derby match, there was always trouble, fighting in the ground and in the streets before and after the match. T.J. had been assured by the lads that they would be alright of which he replied, 'I hope!'

The four friends left the café and made way to the ground. Walking along Whitehorse Road, the noise was electrifying and the police were riding horses to keep both sets of supporters apart, guiding the Brighton supporters to the visiting fan's end of the ground. All the time each section were shouting insults at each other.

T.J. believed he was told twice that he had no Mummy or Daddy, or words to that effect. However he must admit it was exciting, also a bit frightening. In the ground at the Homesdale Road end there was a buzz with the crowd chanting 'Eagles! Eagles!' Added to the noise of both sets of fans trying to shout the others down.

While this was going on all around the ground, T.J. was looking around, he looked up into the old stand where you could see it was a bit subdued. T.J. looked at his old seat and could see someone sitting there. He then thought, I would have been a bit safer there. He broke off his morbid thoughts and turned to the others who were in high spirits, shouting along with the rest of the crowd, T.J. joined in, it was great!

He looked to either side of the enclosed area where they were, and there was quite a lot of Palace's security staff and police making sure there would be no disruption or opposing fans trying to reach each other. It made him feel a bit safer, it had been said before that Palace had the best security there was, and if there were any problems the troublemakers were quickly evicted from the ground. T.J. looked around and it seemed there would be no more room, everyone was standing shoulder to shoulder, it was packed!

All of a sudden, the crowd roared; the players came onto the pitch, it was tumultuous. T.J. looked towards Checker, who said something but he couldn't hear him. T.J. just gave him the thumbs up, to which he nodded.

Play had started and the game was starting to get aggressive, there was no inspiration about the play, the players were getting the ball and passing it before they were kicked up into the air by the opposition. There were fouls galore, the referee was whistling every few minutes. The crowd was getting very restless shouting abuse at the referee and the opposing fans. Tension in the crowd was rising.

T.J. looked towards the security staff and the police who were deploying along the barriers and getting ready to ward off and control any problems. He saw there was a large group of police and security, in all about twenty of them standing ready to reinforce areas where needed. You have got to praise the Palace directors, for the security and the control. T.J. had been to other grounds where Palace were the visitors and the home crowd got out of control and ran onto the pitch to spoil the game, especially if they were losing. At the moment it was very noisy at Palace, but under control.

Half-time the players were leaving the pitch to a chorus of booing, yells of rubbish and chanting of what a load of rubbish and laughing. Curly, Cliff, Checker and T.J. were laughing at the antics of the Eagle Mob. They looked like a load of deranged animals running around but doing nothing. Then T.J. noticed the big bloke that seemed to control them point to somewhere to their left.

He said to the others, 'That mob of eagles are making their way over here just pushing and hitting out at anyone who gets in their way. The crowd are just getting away as fast as they can.'

Cliff, Curly and Checker said, 'Yes we are watching them.'

T.J. said, 'Hell they have got some big lumps of wood!' They were using them like cudgels. 'How did they get them into the ground?'

Checker said, 'I don't know but I would bet they had them hidden in their jeans or trouser legs.'

Suddenly the mob turned towards them.

Curly shouted, 'Quick let's make our way to the fencing at the top, that way if we keep our backs to the fencing they can only come at us from the front and not one of them will fancy a bent nose.'

They hurried to the fencing.

Cliff said, 'Right you three stay put, I am going off to the right, they will still come after you and they will believe I am doing a runner. But I will be making my way around behind them to get that schmuck, and when I have finished with him he will not be going to any football matches ever again. When I do get to him his little army will try to help him, so you keep them busy!'

Before Cliff or any of them could do anything, some of the Palace security and police pushed passed. One of them said, 'Don't worry lads leave it to us, we know how to deal with this lot and they won't be watching the second half.'

With that they went after them with their truncheons. Within a few minutes it was all over. Some of the mob got away into the crowd but they had got most of them including the big bloke. As they marshalled them over to the entrance to evict them out of the ground T.J. noticed that the police were taking their names. The crowd were cheering and clapping the police for their work.

T.J. noticed that the teams had come out to play the second half. He turned to Checker, 'Cliff called that big bloke Schmuck, is that his name or what?'

Checker smiled, 'No, the name he goes by is Hookey, I don't know his real name but that is what everybody calls him, and he answers to it, but I heard Cliff call him Schmuck.' Checker laughed, 'Well I don't know the origin or the meaning of the word Schmuck but it is used in the cockney language which is a make up of Eastenders and part Jewish and part Italian. I believe it means Prick! I am not certain but it sounds about right.'

T.J. nodded his head, 'I suppose that is about right but what does Hookey stand for?'

'Bloody hell T.J. where have you been all your life, have you not heard of the words about stolen goods, like bent, dodgy, hookey gear, and the rest? Well he is a very dodgy person. Nobody of his age or older will have nothing to do with him, that is why he has got the name Hookey. The only people who hang around him are sixteen and seventeen year olds, they think he is a big man, it is only when they get older that they find out he is not a nice person to be associated with.' Checker continued with a smile, 'Well that is enough of lessons today. I'll continue after the football game is finished.'

'Sorry Checker!'

Checker gave a playful punch on T.J.'s arm, 'Don't be daft.'

They watched the game, it was going on at the same tempo as the first half and it ended a draw. The crowd started to leave the ground. T.J. noticed that the police were still holding the trouble-makers inside a small enclosure, they were looking a bit sorry for themselves. The four friends made their way down towards the coffee shop, went in and sat at a table by the window. They talked about the days events. Checker did tell the others how he had to explain what Hookey and Schmuck meant of which they all three had a good laugh at T.J.'s expense. He had to join in as he took it all as a learning curve which might come in handy in the future.

After the merriment and the tea and sandwiches were consumed they started to talk about the club that night. It was arranged that they all meet at the club at eight o'clock. They left the coffee shop with a cheery 'see you later,' goodbye.

When T.J. got home at about 6.30pm, Rita was already there chatting to his mother in the lounge. Mother asked T.J. if he wanted a cup of tea.

He said, 'Yes please mother.'

As she got up to get another cup from the kitchen, she turned to Rita and said, 'He never says no to a cup of tea.'

Mother left and Rita looked across at T.J., smiled and gave him a wink, of which he thought, ha ha plan A has been put into action. Mother came back into the lounge as Rita started to ask me how the match went and what the score was. Or had Palace lost as normal.

T.J. tried to look indignant and said, 'No, it was a draw score and it was a good game!'

Rita said, 'I heard on the radio.' There was a lot of trouble and she wondered if he was alright?

T.J. told her there was no problem. The Palace security and police had it under control within ten minutes.

As mother gave him his cup of tea, she said that Rita had told her that he was taking her to that club tonight that he was at last night.

T.J. stammered, 'Yes I told Rita about it on the phone and Rita said she would like to see the club and what it was like. I'm sorry mother I wanted to tell you myself, but it appears I am too late.'

Mother said, 'Good I have asked Rita to tell me all about it and if it is as good as you make it out to be. And as Rita will be with you I will have no need to stay up tonight and worry for you!'

'Thank you mother, but I am a big boy.'

'But to me you are my little boy and you always will be.'

All went quiet for a while. Then T.J. said, 'Thank you mother, I will always remember what you just said, always.'

Mother replied, 'Come on drink up your tea and stop all this silly talk, more tea Rita?'

While mother was pouring Rita more tea, she asked what time they were leaving to go to the club? T.J. said he had booked a table for 8pm and then mother looked at the clock and said, 'You will have to get your skates on it's nearly 7pm, you best be getting yourselves ready. And Rita, as you are both most likely to be late I will get the spare bedroom ready for you, and also you should telephone your parents to say you will be staying the night here.'

Rita thanked her, got up to telephone her parents and get ready. She had brought her dress and other nick-nacks with her.

T.J. got up to go to his room to get ready and his mother came over to him and pressed a fifty pound note in his hand. He said, 'No thank you mother I have enough money.'

Mother replied that the night was on her and that she insisted as he was taking her spy with him!

'Besides,' she said, 'if all the reports are favourable I myself will in the future consider my son and heir will invite me to accompany him to this club.'

'Of course I will after all you are the first lady in my life.'

'Then that is settled,' mother said, 'but I do not believe your father will go. Go and get yourself ready and I will order a taxi for 7.45pm.'

When T.J. came downstairs he found Rita waiting in the lounge talking to mother. He said to Rita, 'You are looking very elegant, is that a new dress?'

Rita replied, 'Yes, you never know I might meet a very charming young man... in the meantime I'll settle for you!'

Mother and Rita laughed and mother said, 'Don't tease him!'

T.J. said, 'That's alright I did rather fancy the girl singer last night!'

'Touché, that's my son!'

The taxi arrived and Rita and T.J. left.

As they were travelling in the taxi Rita said to me, 'You are a right old smoothy, you are!'

'What do you mean?'

'Well the way you talked to your mother about your love and how you feel about her. I must admit I was a bit jealous.'

T.J. said, 'That was unkind, I love my mother like any son would. Don't forget she carried me within her and when I was born she gave me life and hope! You know my father was a Q.C.

and most of his work was for C.P.S. and then he went on to be a Crown Court Judge, so you see I only saw my father most weekends. I would not have seen him that much if he was a High Court Judge, which I know he refused. Most of my weekday life revolved around my mother.'

Rita apologised and T.J. said, 'That's alright but next time I will have to report you to C.T.T.J. society.'

They got out of the taxi and walked to the club entrance. Rita said, 'What does that society do?'

T.J. said, 'Don't worry I will tell you later.'

They walked into the club. Brian came over and guided them to the table where Cliff and Curly were with their girlfriends. As they sat down Brian asked what drinks they wanted. They ordered and Brian left.

The friends introduced their girlfriends. Cliff's girlfriend was called Sue, Curly's girlfriend was named Mary.

Brian returned with the drinks and enquired where young Stanley was. Curly said that Stan had telephoned him to say he would be a bit late.

Just as Brian turned to leave Checker and his girlfriend came into the entrance. Brian turned to them and said, 'Ha, Stanley has arrived and with his lovely lady.' He brought them back to the table and enquired what drinks they would like. He returned with Checker's drinks and the menus for them to peruse.

Later as they were talking T.J. noticed that there were more staff on than last night. There was an extra barman and two extra waiting on the other tables of which were slowly filling as people were coming into the club. The band on the stage was playing soft music.

Suddenly T.J. got a dig from Rita's elbow and she said, 'I was talking to you!'

'I am sorry but I was just looking around the club, what did you say?'

Rita smiled, 'That's better now you are back with me.'

T.J. looked across the table and Cliff and Curly were looking at him. They were quietly laughing and making the thumbs down sign with their hands on the table, more or less enquiring if he was under the thumb.

Sue and Mary said, 'Don't worry T.J. they are as well!'

They all looked at each other; the girls as one all raised their hands and then put their thumbs down on the table and started laughing, then they all joined in.

Brian came hurrying over and asked if anything was wrong, they said no and told him what had happened, and that the girls had implied that they were all under the thumb. Brian said, 'No, never,' with a little smile, 'are you all ready to order your meals?'

They said, 'Yes please.'

They had told the girls that they had steak the night before and it was cooked just right and the taste was beautiful, so everyone ordered steak. The girls had jacket potatoes whereas they had chips. Brian enquired if they wanted starters and they chose the soup of the day.

With that Brian said, 'I will give your orders to the chef and will be right back to take your order for the wine, but I can recommend the red Bordeaux. I am rather partial to it so I always make sure I get the best. I will leave you to decide and will return in a moment.'

They discussed the wine with each other and decided on the Bordeaux, and decided they needed another round of drinks when Brian returned. But just as they were talking one of the other waiters came over to their table to see if he could take their order for drinks. Just as Cliff was about to tell him their order there was quite a bit of soft clapping noise. They turned to see where it was coming from and who was clapping.

It was Brian hurrying over to the table saying to the waiter, 'Raymond, I told you before. You and Basil are to wait on the other sixteen tables, this is my table and these are my friends. I shall wait on them personally.' Of which he then turned to us, sighed and said, 'You can not get the staff these days,' and with a bit of a grin on his face said, 'You wanted another round of drinks?'

'Yes please.'

'Have you settled on the wine yet?'

Cliff said, 'Yes the Bordeaux please.'

Brian said, 'Ha! You have chosen well.' With that he went off to get their drinks.

Rita turned to T.J. and said, 'That Brian is a lovely and polite person but he did seem a bit effeminate.'

T.J. answered that probably waiting on people and trying to be nice makes them sound like that and he said it with crossed fingers. Checker who was sitting next to T.J. made a noise like clearing his throat and across the table Cliff nodded and said, 'Well put!'

Brian returned with their drinks and as he served around the table, he said the meals would not be long and he would bring the Bordeaux just before.

Checker's girlfriend Jean leaned across the table and said to Rita very quietly, 'He is very effeminate', turning she asked Checker, 'Is he one of those?'

Checker replied, 'One of what?'

'You know,' Jean said.

'No it is just like T.J. said, it comes from waiting on tables.'

Curly said, 'Oh leave it out we are not here to discuss other people, we are here to enjoy ourselves.'

Cliff said, 'Yes come on forget the silly talk and let's live a bit, fancy a dance Sue?'

With that they both got up to go to the dance floor.

Rita turned to T.J. and said, 'Well?'

He joked, 'I have got a bad foot.'

Before he could continue Rita said, 'You will have!'

With that T.J. got up to take Rita to the dance floor.

T.J. looked around on the dance floor. He was not one for dancing, a slow waltz or foxtrot and that was his lot, none of the fast stuff, throwing each other around the dance floor. He was thankful that Rita understood and never asked him to dance other than a waltz.

The music ended and as they returned to the table Brian appeared with the wine and started to fill their glasses. When he had finished he said, 'I will now bring your meals', and within five minutes Brian was back pushing his heated trolley with the help of Raymond one of the other waiters.

With the meals served Brian said, 'Bon appetite my friends, enjoy and I will be back to pour more wine for you,'

Curly called Brian over to him. He lent over to Curly to listen, and all at once said, 'Of course Gordon, right away,' and off he went towards the bar.

Cliff looked across at Curly and said, 'Champers?'

Curly nodded, 'Of course.'

Everyone started to tuck into their food and it was beautiful! Every particle of food was so delicious. T.J. looked around the table and everybody was so intent on eating, not one word was said. He thought they were like pigs at the trough.

When everybody had finished they looked at each other. They nodded each voicing compliments of such a sumptuous meal cooked and presented with care. Brian and his partner had treated them like royalty.

Brian saw they had finished their meal and came over with one of the waiters to clear the table. As he was clearing he asked if they were happy with the meal. They all complimented him on such a delicious meal, which pleased him, the smile on his face was a pleasure to see.

T.J. was about to take a sip of wine when Rita gave him a playful punch on the arm. 'I know what it means!' At first he did not know what Rita was on about, then she said, 'C.T.T.J. society.'

Everyone around the table was looking at Rita and T.J. He laughed and said, 'It's just a joke.'

She hit T.J. again, 'No sex tonight for you!'

Curly looked at T.J. and made an 'ooh' noise, laughed and said, 'Who's been a naughty boy then?' Afterwards T.J. had to tell them all about the joke. Rita just sat there smiling and then kissed him on the cheek, all of them cheered and applauded.

The night was great, after Rita had made a hint of no sex, it seemed to relax everyone, especially the girls. They all started to talk more and left the men at the table while they went out on the dance floor, dancing in a circle laughing and talking to each other just like they had known each other a long time.

Curly signalled to Brian at the bar for another bottle of Champers, which was brought over by Brian. He opened the bottle at the same time gestured towards the girls on the dance floor and said, 'I am pleased they are having a good time.'

Checker said, 'The girls had all said that they had never had such a night, the food was excellent and the whole ambience of the club was beautiful.'

'Thank you, I must tell my partner, I am sure he will be as pleased as I am, thank you again!' and off Brian went into the kitchens.

The girls came off the dance floor slightly out of breath. T.J. turned to Rita to ask if she was enjoying herself, he received no reply for the girls were talking to each other and swapping telephone numbers. He looked towards Checker who smiled.

T.J. said, 'I fancy a lager,' he looked towards Cliff and Curly and they nodded in agreement. Just as T.J. indicated to Brian at the bar.

Rita and the girls turned and said, 'Yes please.'

T.J. Laughed. 'You did not answer when I asked you if you were having a good time!'

Before he could say anything more Rita said, 'Ha, you did not ask me if I wanted a drink then?'

At that moment Brian came over and T.J. said, 'Four lagers please, and whatever the girls are having.'

Rita turned to T.J. and said, 'Thank you.'

Well the night out had ended, they all agreed that it was a fabulous time. Brian brought the bill over and the cost was divided four ways. T.J. thought, I am glad mother insisted I took that fifty pounds, I would have just afforded it myself, but I would have had to go to the bank for more cash. I must admit I will have to curb my expenses. The club would be just once a month until I start earning a lot more.

As they left the club Checker and T.J. with their girlfriends got in one taxi and Cliff and Curly and girls left in another. Brian had ordered them, this time however they paid.

Sunday, T.J. went downstairs to the dining room. Mother and Rita were there having breakfast, and mother enquired what he would like for breakfast? T.J. said, 'Tea please' and started to help himself from the heated trolley. He made a full English breakfast with some toast.

Mother looked at his plate and said, 'Are you going to eat all that?'

'Why not I am quite hungry.'

'With what I have been told I would of thought it would be just a cup of black coffee.'

T.J. laughed and said, 'Mother, I am a growing boy and need plenty of sustenance!' He looked at Rita and said to his mother, 'What else has your spy said?'

Mothers reply was that the club was very nice, the food was excellent and on the whole, she said with a smile, 'My spy had a very enjoyable night. She also noticed that the club did not only cater for the younger generation, so it appears it could be the kind of club I would like to visit, with you and Rita as my guests of course.'

T.J. replied that he would be delighted, in fact honoured.

Mother replied, 'Don't get carried away my boy, I am not royalty as yet, although if your father had accepted the post of High Court I might have been a lady!'

With breakfast things cleared away, Rita stayed in the house with mother and T.J. volunteered to mow the lawns, and to sweep the patio and garden paths. By 11.30 he was hot and thirsty, so it was a welcoming sight to see them both come through the French doors from the conservatory onto the patio carrying a large jug of fruit juice and glasses. The first glass of juice he drank within a minute, then sat down on the garden bench savouring the next glass of drink. Mother then interrupted T.J.'s thoughts with a little smile on her face. She mischievously pointed over to the far corner of the lawn and said, 'you've missed a bit.'

T.J. answered with a little bow, 'I will see to it at once madam!'

Mother replied, 'If I have to point out bad workmanship again I will have to dispense with your services!'

'Promise?'

Monday, back at work. For the first hour T.J. looked around the office that he had been allocated. It had been completely redecorated. There was one filing cabinet, one tall wooden cupboard, a large desk, a large swivel chair which he was sitting in and another two chairs on the opposite side of the desk. As he was revelling in the opulence of his kingdom, T.J. was suddenly brought back to reality with a sharp knock on the door.

In walked one of the girls from the main office saying, 'Young Mr Roger would very much like you to assist him at Croydon Crown Court.'

'Thank you, er what is your name please?'

'My name is Doreen', and with that she left the office.

T.J. untied the cord around the file and the first thing he noticed was the date of the trial. It was tomorrow, which only left him with little time to relax!

He started to read the files and thought, I have been thrown in at the deep end already. It was a case about a junior partner of a local company who had been accused of misappropriation of some of the company funds. T.J. read through the documents carefully, it looked very much like a case of litigation of which each person is accusing the other of misappropriation of the company's funds. Mr Roger, it appears, believes he can win the case. T.J. read through the documents a number of times, testing himself with questions, then looking to see if he was correct. T.J. knew that it was possible Mr Roger would ask for some information from the documents in the duration of the court case.

Tuesday, Croydon Crown Court. T.J. found himself sitting beside young Mr Roger Bowden, who was looking at the case notes, and preparing to do battle in defence of the junior partner of the company, a Mr C Crust. It appeared that the company chairman, who was not present, signed four of the company cheques but they had to be countersigned by another partner of the company to become valid. This appeared to be normal practice as the chairman was often away. There was one cheque missing and it had been cashed with an illegible signature.

T.J. sat there listening to the opening references to the case and he had come to realise that Mr Roger was brilliant. As the questions and answers went along T.J. could see that Mr Roger would definitely win this case. He just sat and learned.

Wednesday, back at the office. T.J. have been given four small cases to defend. But first he was to make himself aware of the clients and gain more information from them. The application for court hearings had been lodged and were awaiting trial dates.

As T.J. was reading some of the papers the telephone rang. He answered and reception said that there was a call from a Mr Stanley Wolfe. T.J. said, 'Yes put him through.'

The unmistakable voice of Checker said, 'How are you getting on?'

T.J. answered, 'Fine, is there anything you want?'

'No, I just wanted to see if you were going to the match tonight? Don't forget it's a cup match.'

'Yes, but to be truthful I had completely forgotten about it, with so much going on.'

Checker said, 'That's alright I'll call around to your place at 6.30pm.'

'Right, see you then,' T.J. said.

As promised Checker arrived on time. As T.J. walked down to the car, mother called from the house, 'Hope you enjoy the match.' He looked back and waved.

'Are you driving up to the park near the ground?'

Checker replied, 'No, I was going to park in Wilfred Road, it's about ten minutes walk from the ground and it will be safe to park there.'

They went in the Homesdale Road end, although it was a midweek game there was quite a crowd.

Checker said, 'There is Cliff and Curly over there. I thought they would be here.'

As they came up to Cliff and Curly, Cliff said, 'What a great night Saturday was. It was brilliant. Sue and I thoroughly enjoyed it! We must do it again some time, right?'

T.J. replied, 'Yes it was great but probably in a month's time, as that's when I receive my monthly cheque.'

'What?' Cliff replied. 'I thought you lawyers made lots of money!'

T.J. laughed. 'In about a year's time, ask me then. You have forgotten I am just a junior at the moment.'

'Well, anytime I need a lawyer you will be my choice.'

'Thank you,' T.J. replied. 'Who are we playing tonight?'

'Everton, and it's going to be a hard match, those Scousers don't take any prisoners.'

Well as usual the crowd became excited as the teams came onto the pitch. Just down in front of them a fair section of the crowd were shouting and booing at some of the Everton players. T.J. looked at Checker and said, 'What are they booing for, the game hasn't started yet?'

Checker's reply was, 'The big fellow is their centre-half, and a nasty piece of work. Last time he was here, he punched our little winger and broke his jaw, all he got was a caution from the ref.'

T.J. thought to himself, this is going to be a very hard game and I hope Palace win.

The teams lined up and with one long blast of the referees whistle the match was on. The game flowed from end to end, you could see there was no quarter given. T.J. was proud of Palace, they gave everything they had and more! He had watched Palace play many times but today they fought for every ball. Every tackle was crunch time. By the end of the ninety minutes T.J. was drained of all energy, he was hoarse from shouting. T.J. looked at the lads, they were the same but were all smiling. Palace had done them proud, they had won, but what a game! Cliff looked at the others and made a sign like drinking a pint. As they left the ground to find the nearest pub T.J. was feeling very pleased that he had not missed the game.

Thursday, in his office reading up on one of the case files. T.J. had asked the client to come into the office at 10.30am so he could gain as much information from him and also hear his side of the argument. As T.J. read through the case papers again, Mr Roger Bowden came into the office and asked if everything was alright?

T.J. replied, 'Yes thank you', and at the same time enquired about Mr Crust's case.

Roger said, 'Yes I am pleased that you have asked about that, we carried the day. But did you learn anything from being there?'

'Yes and I am very pleased that you invited me, thank you.'

Mr Roger said, 'Good, well done,' and turned to the door, as he left he said, 'Don't forget, any problems ask!'

T.J. returned to reading the case papers, and as he read kept making notes on questions he wanted to ask the client. After all T.J. believed Mr Bowen senior would know if he made the grade or not.

This was his first case and he was determined not to let his father down for recommending him to Mr Bowen or the firm and most of all his mother! By hook or by crook he was going to win this case.

T.J.'s client arrived at 10.30am. He went to down to the reception area where there were two men. T.J. asked for a Mr Clarke. They both stood up. He said it again but with the Christian name, Mr George Clarke. They both said, 'Yes', then one of them said, 'I'm his brother, do you mind? You see he gets nervous when seeing someone like you.'

T.J. answered, 'No, but only he does the talking and not you sir, for he your brother is the person who is in the court, not you.'

He replied, 'Yes of course.'

T.J. led them both to the office where they sat down. T.J. said, 'Now the problem, as I have read from your case files is that you

Mr Clarke are charged with causing affray, i.e. fighting in the street, Stanley Road, with a Mr Brown, who is accusing you of a provoked attack on his person.' T.J. asked Mr Clarke, 'Is there any proof in this man's claim?'

Silence.

'I also have a copy of the police statement saying that you left the scene of the incident.'

Silence.

'Mr Brown made a statement to the police and signed the statement. Police say that they went to your home and found you were not there. But they arrested you at your home later that day at 18.30 hours. You were released on bail to await a court hearing. Is that all correct?' T.J. asked Mr Clarke.

Silence.

He thought, hell this is like talking to a bank manager about a bank loan. Well, at least he would say no!

'I say again Mr Clarke . . .'

Then his brother spoke up, 'Can I tell you what happened that day?'

T.J. asked the other Mr Clarke, 'Has your brother George an impediment in his hearing or speech?'

'No,' he answered, 'it's just that he is so upset, you see he did not do it he was at work. He told the police that but they arrested him, he just went quiet and that is when they charged him as they did not believe him.'

T.J. pondered for a bit then said, 'Is what your brother says true?'

Silence.

T.J. Thought, bloody hell, he would make a good monk in a vow of silence. Once again he said, 'Mr George Clarke is the statement your brother made true?'

The other brother nudged him and said, 'Tell him, if you don't; you'll go to prison as sure as little apples.'

At last Mr George Clarke nodded his head and said, 'Yes it is true what my brother said, I was at work.'

'Good, have you any witnesses to that effect like your employer or workmates?'

He replied, 'I suppose so, I never asked them.'

T.J. turned to the brother and said, 'Well at least we have one witness.'

He said, 'Who is that?'

'You sir,' T.J. replied.

George's brother said, 'Oh no, not me. I won't be going to court, that Mr Brown is a nasty man. If you prove that my brother is innocent and he sees me in court he will tell the police that he has made a mistake and it was me who hit him.'

'Did you?'

There was no reply. T.J. sat for a moment just looking at both of the brothers. Now he believed that George Clarke was innocent but the other brother was the guilty one!

'Can you tell me please who do you work for and what kind of work you carry out for your employer?'

The other Mr Clarke started to say, 'When . . .'

T.J. stopped him, 'I am asking your brother, now that he has gained his speech and hearing I would like him to answer. Right Mr Clarke what is the name of your employer? Where do you work and what kind of work do you do for your employer?'

For a minute there was silence then he looked at his brother who said, 'Go on then, I don't want to be here all day!' T.J. thought, any more of this and you won't be here all day as I will show you both the door.

At last George Clarke started to give him the information he required. His employer was a Mr Taylor, who owned and ran a builders supply company. He employed Mr Clarke and one other person named Bill, who ran the supply yard. They worked together in the yard loading and unloading lorries.

Mr Clarke had also informed T.J. that the company had a time-card machine where they clock in and out of work. At last he had concrete evidence. T.J. passed what information he had onto the research office.

'Right Mr Clarke I will inform you of your court hearing, until then I advise you to keep clear of Mr Brown.'

As T.J. showed them both out he thought, I hope the next case will be more simple. As he returned to his office he asked one of the receptionists if Mr Roger Bowen was in his office.

She replied, 'Yes.'

T.J. knocked on his door and went in, he said, 'Problem?'

'No, I wanted you to hear my first case history, the proceedings and taking the right course of action.'

When T.J. had finished, Mr Roger remarked that T.J. was doing everything right and that he wished him good luck, and when the case came to court he would like to be there.

'Thank you,' T.J. said and left the office and returned to his own.

As T.J. was about to leave his office that night he picked up the Clarke file and put it into his briefcase. He was going to take it home to discuss with his father, he was sure his father would guide him right.

That night sitting in the study with his father they discussed how he should proceed with the defence of his client in court. His father made it quite clear at the outset, if the research office findings agree with your clients alibi your client would be acquitted and almost likely be awarded costs, that is of course if you have applied for them. T.J. thanked his father for the guidance and made a note about the costs.

Friday, in the office reading through the paperwork of T.J.'s next case, there were claims and counter claims from the client. It appeared T.J.'s client had installed the complete plumbing materials to a bungalow on a small building site. The main contractor had asked his client if he could wait for payment as he had no monies to pay for the work or materials until he could sell the property within a few months or longer. T.J.'s client who worked for himself could not afford to wait for payment and also believed that he would never be paid for his work. So he returned to the site over the weekend and removed all the fixtures and fittings, which included copper pipe work, storage tanks, heating system and finally a complete bathroom. The contractor, a Mr Roach, claimed he had informed T.J.'s client to return to the site and reinstate all of the materials that he had 'stolen' from the building site. He should do this within fourteen days or risk being arrested for theft. Mr Roach had employed legal aid who had supported his claim, T.J. was informed.

T.J.'s client, Mr David Barton, arrived in reception. T.J. went to meet him and invited Mr Barton into his office. After preliminary talks with his client T.J. read out all of the charges that Mr Roach had made against him. T.J. asked, 'What part of Mr Roach's statement do you disagree with?'

Mr Barton disagreed with the whole statement. Firstly Mr Barton was asked by Mr Roach to give an estimate for all of the plumbing work to the bungalow, which Mr Roach had accepted. His estimate was to carry out the work as soon as possible. There was no mention of waiting for payment. If he had mentioned it Mr Barton advised he would not have agreed to carry out the work. Being that he was a small plumbing contractor trying to build a bigger company to employ staff not carry out work for no payment.

T.J. replied, 'Mr Barton, you should have requested an interim payment to cover the costs of materials. Now I will outline your course of action. Firstly, Mr Barton, you will have to return to site and reinstate all of the materials as you did commit an offence against the law. The law states once anybody delivers materials to a site, whether it be a factory, site or private house then the materials become the property of the owner of the premises. I know this is unkind, but you have got to return to site and reinstall all of the materials.'

'Now, if you want me to act for you it will cost, but understand that you will not be able to claim these costs from Mr Roach. Once you have replumbed the property you can take legal action, which could force Mr Roach into bankruptcy which would not help you get the monies you are owed. All the loans made to him by banks, his builder suppliers would be paid first and there may be nothing left for you. However I can suggest that I write to Mr Roach to inform him of your intentions, and that if you have not received full payment within fourteen days you will instruct this office to make presentation to the small claims court. If payment is not received in full then you will instigate proceedings for bankruptcy within thirty days of receipt of the correspondence.'

T.J. looked at Mr Barton. 'Is that what you would like me to carry out? You would have to pay this office the cost of my services, plus the typist which would amount to sixty-five pounds. You would not be able to claim these costs from Mr Roach. There would of course be further costs involved if you went to the small claims court. However, there is a possibility that at the small claims court you could recover all of your costs. Now Mr Barton, do you wish me to send the correspondence hoping it might worry Mr Roach into making the payment, or to also instigate proceedings to go to the small claims court?'

Mr Barton replied, 'Just send the letter for now.'

T.J. replied, 'Fine I will send the correspondence, could you please make a payment for sixty-five pounds to my secretary in the other office.' T.J. then said, 'Thank you and I hope that you will receive payment from Mr Roach.'

T.J. looked at his watch and was amazed the time was nearly five, so he decided to call it a day and go home early, as it was gym night. T.J. was going training and meeting Checker, he thought, I could do with a bit of light relief, talk and a laugh with a good friend and hear of any news from Cliff and Curly and talk about the football!

Chapter Three

WHEN T.J. GOT to the gym Checker was already there. He stopped the machine he was training on and came over. T.J. said to him, 'You're early tonight!'

'I thought I would try and get it out of the system!'

'Same here, so I thought I would come here and get rid of the dissatisfaction and end the day on a lighter note.'

Checker replied, 'Sounds like you have had a good court case?'

T.J. said, 'No just paperwork, collecting all of the information and case building in readiness for the trial.'

'Right. When we have finished training we can relax in the cafeteria and you can tell me all about it. You never know I might be able to help you!' Checker said.

T.J. replied, 'It is about a non payment of monies for work, and G.B.H. and that is all I can tell you. Have you not heard of client confidentiality?'

Checker said, 'Yes, but you can tell me, we're mates, you know I won't tell anyone!'

'I will make a deal with you, I will take you to the court, you can sit right behind me and look as if you are my team. Now which case would you choose to come to?'

'I don't know I'll take the one that takes the longest!'

'Right,' T.J. said, 'let's get on with my training. I came here to wind down from work, not to talk about it.'

Checker replied with an 'ooher' and with a laugh and said, 'Sorry darling.'

T.J. threw his sweat towel at him.

They finished training, showered and went to the cafeteria, sat at the table enjoying their drinks. Checker informed T.J. that Cliff and Curly wanted to see them both at the Norbury Hotel tomorrow night about 8pm.

'What about?'

Checker replied, 'Cliff was a bit vague. He said something about property and he has had some warning from a friend who goes to Chelsea matches, and that was it. He'll tell us more tomorrow night.'

T.J. looked at Checker who said, 'I don't know.'

T.J. laughed and said, 'Come on let's go to the Norbury and have a drink!'

At the Norbury having a quiet drink talking about travelling over to West Ham on Saturday for Palace's next match, Checker said, 'It would be better if we went by car. We'll park about two miles from the ground and walk the rest. It's easier than public transport, changing trains. It will take about one and a half hours where as using our own transport will take half that time.'

T.J. replied, 'We will see what Cliff and Curly think. They'll be going I believe.'

Checker said, 'Right but it still puzzles me what Cliff spoke about, property, oh well we'll see tomorrow night.'

Then he stopped, looked at Checker and said, 'You do know tomorrow is Saturday, it was tonight they were talking about meeting them!'

Checker looked and all of a sudden he said, 'Yes, yes it is tonight they said!'

T.J. replied, 'What time?'

He looked at his watch and said, 'Now!'

With that they both looked towards the door, T.J. Paused, looked at Checker and said, 'I don't know I think you should see a doctor!'

'My day will come!'

About five minutes later in walked Cliff and Curly. Checker ordered a round of drinks. Cliff asked if they had been waiting long. T.J. replied, 'We may not have been here,' pointing at Checker. 'Mastermind got his days mixed up and only just realised it was tonight!' T.J. ducked a playful punch from Checker.

The bar waiter brought over the drinks. When he had left T.J. said to Cliff, 'Checker tells me you want to talk about some property plus a warning you have had from a friend.'

Cliff replied by saying, 'I will tell you about the properties, there are two in number and they are a pair of four storey high buildings in good repair. The owner wants to sell both as a job lot. They have very large gardens at the rear with small gardens at the front. One of them is a corner plot to a cul-de-sac, the other is adjoining. The owner wants eight thousand pounds for both. I believe we could split them into four good sized flats, what do you think?'

T.J. said, 'Well, if you are going into the property market Cliff, I would gladly do the legal work free, no doubt Checker would also do the survey free.'

Cliff's reply was, 'No, you have got it all wrong, I am talking about all of us buying them as partners! Curly agrees.'

Two thousand pounds each, T.J. looked at Checker. He could see he was quiet, thinking about how he could raise the cash or thinking is it a good idea? T.J. turned to Cliff and said, 'You certainly have taken the wind out of our sails.'

'Well?'

T.J. said, 'I would like to see what I am going to invest my money into, secondly if all parties are in agreement legal contracts would have to be drawn up to protect everyone's welfare and investment. If any of the investors wanted to sell his share then the other shareholders would have first refusal, there's a lot of legal work involved!'

Checker said, 'Great if T.J. can do the paperwork I will do the survey, but like T.J. said let's have a look first.'

'Good, how about Sunday?'

Checker said, 'You are in a hurry, have you been given the red card at home?'

'No, but this is a golden opportunity that does not pass by often. We should take it as this is something that later on in life when we get married and sell, will give us a good start for the future.' Cliff looked at them.

Curly said, 'I'm in!'

Checker nodded

T.J. said, 'Okay, but there is a lot of paperwork to be done to bind us in and protect all of us.'

'Right, let's drink to that!' Cliff said.

They all lifted their glasses and drank to it.

'Right, let's all meet at Curly's garage 10am on Sunday.'

They all agreed.

'What's the other thing you were referring to, something about a warning from a friend?' Checker asked.

Cliff said, 'Yes' and pondered for a few minutes, then said, 'Tomorrows match at West Ham.'

'Yes,' they queried in unison.

'Whose car?'

Checker said, 'Mine.'

Cliff said, 'Right, in the future we don't wear any of Palace's scarves or hats especially tomorrow!'

T.J. asked, 'Why?'

'Well, it's because of what a friend has told me,' Cliff stopped talking then looked around the bar. 'They said they were going to come here tonight. Well maybe later.'

'Why?' T.J. asked again.

Cliff replied, 'Well, my two friends who were coming here tonight would have shown you. You know most of the fights start outside of the grounds, in pubs or shops before or after the games.'

They all replied, 'Yes!'

'Well the West Ham mob call themselves 'the Intercity', I am not quite sure of the last word but anyhow they play rough! There are a few knuckle dusters, knives and one I have not heard of before. It is small about four to six inches in length of bike chain, which is attached to a piece of strong cord. The chain has been sharpened on all four edges. They carry it around the neck under their coat collars, and then start swinging them about! They can make a mess of anyone's face, I know I have seen it. Now if my friends come tonight you will see what I am saying. If they do, just look at Bomber's eyes and nothing else, just treat him casually, smile, and laugh alright?'

By now they were all looking at each other thinking, what?

Curly broke the sombre quietness by saying, 'Who wants a drink?'

'Four of the same!'

Cliff said, 'Make that two more lagers, Bomber and Sticks have just come in.'

Cliff shouted, 'Bomber over here.' Then he said to Checker, 'Pull those two chairs over.' Bomber and Sticks came over to their table, then Cliff introduced them.

As T.J. looked at Bomber he remembered to look into his eyes as he shook his hand and said, 'Nice to see you.' Then he was shaking hands with Checker and T.J. got a full view of about a six inch jagged scar running down the right side of his face. T.J. thought a plastic surgeon would have a hell of a job to cover that.

Introductions over, everyone was talking to each other like old friends. Of course the main topic of conversation was football, mind you Bomber and Sticks were asking why they followed a team like Palace when Chelsea are much better. To prove it they are higher than Palace in the division.

They were all laughing. Bomber turned to T.J. and said, 'Cliff tells me that you are a solicitor.'

'Yes that's right.'

'Any good?'

'I hope so.'

T.J. looked at Cliff and said, 'It's OK T.J., Bomber could possibly like a solicitor who knows about football, for if they catch the nutter who did that,' pointing at his own face, 'he would like all the accesses in his hands!'

T.J. said to Bomber, 'I came out for a night out, but it seems I got to do some business. Well to cut it short, did you look for a fight and come off worst or did it just happen, and if it was the latter I promise you, you will get the best Q.C. in the country and it won't cost you any money!'

'Blimey T.J.' Checker said, 'You did not tell me that you had that much pull!'

'I have not, but I know someone who has.'

By that time everyone was around the table looking at T.J. He spoke to Bomber and said, 'If you are telling me the truth, no porkies, I mean it?'

Sticks interrupted the conversation, he pointed at Bomber and said, 'Bomber has not lied! Bomber and I were walking away from the Chelsea match against West Ham. We got about one mile away from the pitch when a group of lads, about six of them, came running towards us. We stepped aside to let them pass, then I heard Bomber cry out. I looked at Bomber, he was holding his face and the claret was running through his fingers. I looked at one of the blokes, he was just standing there looking at Bomber. Then he saw me looking at him, he swung at me, I ducked and put my left arm up for protection.'

Sticks then pulled the sleeve of his shirt to show them his arm. It was deeply scarred. They all sat there in silence looking at his arm.

'Have the police done anything about it?' T.J. asked.

Sticks answered, 'Yes, I have given them a drawing of the person and they are looking for him.'

'Is it a good drawing, you know likeness?' Checker asked.

Bomber answered, 'Yes it is. Sticks is a cartoon artist for a mag, but he is a quick draw man so the police have a good description of him. But it won't do them any good if I get to him first!'

'And me,' added Sticks.

The quietness around the table lasted for about three minutes when it was broken with Curly saying, 'Drink up mates, another round?'

While waiting for the bar waiter to bring the drinks over the conversation got around to football and tomorrows match against West Ham. When Bomber asked, 'Do you mind if Sticks and I tag along?'

Checker answered, 'No, we don't mind but it won't be like the Chelsea lot, Palace plays a less aggressive game.'

Bomber replied, 'That's alright we know what Palace play like when they come over to us!'

Curly said, 'Cheeky, you wait until they meet again, Palace will show you how to play football!'

The drinks waiter brought over the order and left.

Cliff enquired, 'Why do you want to watch Palace? Chelsea is playing at home.'

Sticks replied, 'Bomber and me are going to look to see if those blokes are there or not, also to see if they are West Ham supporters or not. You can help if you want?'

T.J. asked, 'How, we don't know what they look like?'

'Easy,' answered Bomber, 'Sticks, show the lads those drawings you've got.'

Sticks pulled out some papers from his jacket pocket and passed one to each of them around the table. The drawings were a profile and full frontal of a man, they were good. T.J. wondered why the police had not picked him up by now. They all agreed to keep a look out for him.

'If we see him there, what then? Do we phone the police or what?' T.J. asked.

Bomber said, 'We will follow him to his home.'

T.J. said, 'Then tell the police?'

Sticks answered, 'Yes we will phone the police but after we have paid him a visit!'

T.J. thought he did not want to know this. He made up his mind that if he did see the man he would not point him out to anybody.

Curly said, 'Yes, we will help you Sticks, but we will not help you to damage him. We will wait for you somewhere nearby, but that's all.'

Bomber replied, 'I appreciate what you are saying Curly and that is all we ask, no more or no less. All Sticks and I are going to do is give him some of his own treatment, kind of payback time!'

With that Bomber put his hand in his pocket and pulled out a small parcel, unwrapped it and lying there in the middle was a small length of bike chain about five inches attached to a piece of cord, the edges of the chain looked as though they had been sharpened.

T.J. had a slight shiver just looking at it knowing the potential of the weapon. He informed them that if Bomber and Sticks promised that none of the four of them knew of their intentions or to help them, but only to look for him and to report to the police if they found him. If they were found to be implicated in their intentions, they could become involved and he knew it would not help his career!

Bomber replied, 'I appreciate what you are saying T.J. and if Sticks and myself are caught not one of you will be implicated.'

Cliff said, 'You can't ask for anything fairer than that, can you?'

T.J. nodded and confirmed what had been said, 'I agree.' But mentally he thought if he sees the person he will not point him out!

Checker cut across T.J.'s thoughts by saying to Curly, 'Transport will have to be your small eight-seater bus, six will be too many for my car.'

Curly replied, 'O.K. we will all meet here at say 11 o'clock tomorrow, all agreed?'

They all agreed.

Checker said, 'Right, now all the chat's finished, let's get on with some serious drinking time.'

Saturday, they all met at the Norbury. It appeared Curly had picked up the others in Croydon, Checker and T.J. were the last. They set off and started travelling to the West Ham match. The mood was ambivalent, laughing and cheerful, mickey-taking each other and Palace and Chelsea teams. Somehow when they got within five miles of the West Ham ground the mood changed, there was very little talking. When they got within three miles Curly parked the bus up near to a police station. They all got out, Curly locked the bus doors and they started to walk towards the ground. Being that they were a group of six they kept a wary eye out for any trouble that may have come their way.

They got to the ground as it was filling up. There was the usual buzz going around, a lot of talking, the acclaim of fans shouting from opposite sides. Normally T.J. would have been enjoying the atmosphere but today he found himself looking around at faces thinking that if he sees the guy what should he do, say nothing or point him out to Bomber?

T.J. looked towards Checker, who noticed T.J. was looking at him. Checker leant over and said, 'Don't worry, just enjoy the game, that's what I am going to do. Anyway if that bloke was in the vicinity Bomber and Sticks would have seen him by now.'

T.J. looked to where they were standing. They had gone! He asked Cliff if he knew their whereabouts. Cliff just shrugged his shoulders. 'I don't know, they were here a minute ago. Why worry, they'll be back, enjoy the match!'

T.J. started to watch the match but just could not get in touch with what was going on. He was not enjoying the game and kept thinking what would happen if Bomber and Sticks found that man? T.J. thought of the scar on Bomber's face, saying to himself, so what there is an old saying: 'an eye for an eye, a tooth for a tooth.'

T.J. was very glad when the game had ended. There was still no sign of Bomber and Sticks as they walked out of the ground and for once there was no banter saying what a match it had been.

Curly broke the sombre mood by saying, 'There is a café over there, come on let's have a cuppa!'

The four went into the café. Sat in the corner were Bomber and Sticks. Bomber had his back to them and just as Checker was about to speak Sticks put his finger to his lips and looked away. T.J. thought straight away that the man they were looking for must have been in the café.

Checker interrupted T.J.'s thoughts saying, 'Tea?' T.J. nodded and sat down with Curly and Cliff at a table for four.

Whilst Checker got the drinks T.J. tried to be nonchalant, saying, 'Let's hope it is not raining tomorrow when we go to look at those houses.'

But just as Curly was saying, 'I hope not,' T.J. saw the man in Stick's drawing. He was sitting on the next table facing him. T.J. looked towards Cliff and Curly. Cliff looked at him, smiled, winked and said, 'Don't worry we will be with you.'

T.J. replied, 'Great.'

Checker returned with their drinks and then he saw the bloke. Before he could say anything Curly motioned to him with a shake of his head. Checker very quick on the uptake turned to T.J. and said, 'That's right T.J., you did not want sugar in your tea?'

T.J. replied, 'No thanks,' and started to drink his tea.

As T.J. drank he looked at the man. He was clean shaven and had good clothes. He did not look like a nasty person, he looked as though butter wouldn't melt in his mouth! T.J. wondered if Bomber and Sticks had made a mistake.

Just at that moment the young man and his friend got up from their table, made their way to the door and left. Moments after Bomber and Sticks followed.

They sat drinking their tea when Curly said, 'Drink up mates I think we should keep a close and careful watch!' As they left the café they could see Sticks and Bomber roughly a hundred yards away to the left looking in a shop window.

Checker said, 'Hold on, if those two have stopped it must mean the others have too.'

T.J. looked beyond Sticks and yes there they were. The two men were standing at a bus stop. T.J. pointed them out to the others.

Curly said, 'Right, come on you lot let's get the bus, it's only half a mile away. Cross the road here and see if we can get the motor before their bus comes along. We could even be ready to follow the bus if we are quick enough!'

They got to Curly's minibus a little out of breath, trying to keep up with Cliff striding out in front of them, he practically had them running behind him. Once in the bus Curly started the motor up and then proceeded to drive to the next turning so they could reverse into it and then drive out to get to the other side of the main road. They then stopped about half a mile in front of the bus stop where the men were waiting.

They had been waiting about ten minutes when a bus came into view. When it got to within a few yards one of the men put his arm out to signal the bus driver to stop. The men boarded the bus, and as the bus drew away T.J. noticed Sticks and Bomber running towards them.

As they got in the minibus Bomber started to laugh and yelled out, 'Follow that bus, driver!' They all looked at him, and then joined in laughing. To T.J. it showed that although how badly scarred he was he still had a sense of humour.

As they followed the bus Curly asked, 'Did anyone see where the bus was heading for?'

No one had noticed.

Curly said, 'It's going in our direction for home anyway, we are on the Barking Road. Keep a good look out on the bus, I will try and get a bit closer as we will be coming up to a big roundabout and flyover. I only hope he goes straight on into East India Dock Road and then into Commercial Road. If they do Bomber, your man is not a West Ham supporter, for at the end of Commercial Road you turn left to be going down to Towerbridge and within easy reach of half a dozen football clubs in London.'

As the bus carried on it's journey it looked as though Curly was right. Then the bus stopped and the two men got off. According to Curly they were in East India Dock Road. The bus they had been travelling on turned off to the right, but the two men just stood at the bus stop. It appeared they were waiting for another bus. As they drove past them both Bomber and Sticks ducked down so that they could not be seen. They went on for about a mile further and stopped.

Curly said, 'Right, I'll get out of the motor, lift the bonnet up and pretend to be doing something. If they do get on the next bus, have a look at the front of it to see where it is going to.'

As they were watching the men, two other men walked up to the bus stop and joined the queue. Within two minutes a police car pulled up at the bus stop. Two police officers got out of the car, our two suspects looked as though they were about to run, when the two men standing behind them grabbed hold of them, the two from the police car put handcuffs on them. As all of this was going on a police van pulled up, but before they were bundled into the van the police officers were searching them. T.J. could see them take something from around their coat collars. As they were being put into the van the two plain clothes policemen started to walk towards their minibus.

Curly said, 'Sit tight and see if they walk past.' As the two men came up to the bus they stopped and one of them tapped on the window.

Cliff wound down the window and answered, 'Yes?'

The police officer said, 'Police sir, we did observe you tailing those two young men, could you tell me why?'

T.J. leant forward from the back seat and said, 'Excuse me officer, my name is Terence Bond. I am the solicitor representing these two young men, pointing to Bomber and Sticks. I believe they gave the police a drawing of the young man you have just arrested. They did this to his face.' T.J. pointed to Bomber and he turned his scarred face so that the police officer could see.

The police officer looked at Bomber's face and unconsciously uttered, 'Christ!'

T.J. ignored the remark and said, 'We were here to watch the football when my client saw the man and we decided to follow him to find out whereabouts he lived so we could report him to the police. My clients will make themselves available to the C.P.S. when required and so will I.'

The police officer said, 'Sorry sir, I hope the C.P.S. with your help make sure they get about ten years!' With that they both walked back to their car.

Cliff turned around and said, 'Well done T.J., I did not know how to answer him.'

Bomber uttered, 'Bastard, damn I wanted to get to him first, still no matter how long it takes I will get to him!'

Sunday, Checker and T.J. arrived at Curly's garage at 10am on the dot. But no Cliff and Curly as of yet, so they started talking about the events of the Saturday. T.J. told Checker that he was thankful that the police had caught them before Bomber and Sticks had.

Checker agreed and said, 'How can I help them?'

'If the C.P.S. are going to prosecute,' T.J. replied, 'I must ask Cliff if he could get a photograph of Bomber's damaged face and Sticks arm, then I could show them to a person who would make dam sure they would get the maximum penalty.'

Checker said, 'Who? You can tell me, I won't tell anyone!'

T.J. said, 'I know, because we are mates.'

They both laughed, at that point Cliff and Curly arrived. T.J. and Checker got out of the car and walked up to Cliff and Curly and asked them if they could walk or would they need to take the car?

Cliff said, 'It's not far, you had better lock your car Checker and we will walk there. Anyway it will do us a bit of good.'

'How far is it?' T.J. asked.

Cliff said, 'About three miles, it's in a road called St James.'

As they walked along talking about what had happened yesterday, Checker said to Cliff, 'T.J. wants a photograph of the damage to Bomber's face and Sticks arm.'

'Bomber and Sticks!' Cliff queried, 'What for T.J?'

T.J. replied that he wanted to show them to a person who would make certain that they get their just desserts for the terrible damage done to them.

Cliff replied, 'I will ask them then.'

They arrived at the properties, two large four storey high buildings. T.J. noticed they were both double fronted, then Cliff led them around into the cul-de-sac. It was about two hundred yards long and at the bottom was a six to eight foot high wall right across the road. Cliff told them there was a steep embankment the other side leading down to a railway track. On the other side of the road was a large three storey high bakery where they make bread for the supermarkets.

Checker turned to Cliff and said, 'I like it, does the back garden go all the way down to the embankment?'

'Yes, why?'

'We could get a row of garages down here in the first garden and still leave a garden at the rear. We would have no trouble about planning as the local government want off-street parking. We could even rent some out!'

Cliff said, 'Well that's Checker and Curly sorted, what about you T.J?'

T.J. said. 'I am pleased about the outside, the roof looks good but let's see what's inside?'

Cliff had a smile on his face as he turned and said, 'You will be surprised T.J.!'

They walked back round to the front and Cliff pulled a bunch of keys from his pocket. 'Come on then!' Cliff stopped at the front, there were about eight steps leading up to the front door. Then he walked to the side of the steps to another lot of steps going down. 'Follow me' he said.

Down the steps there was a front door. Well they toured all over, both houses were vacant. The terraced house had already been turned into three flats comprising of basement, first, second, third and fourth floors.

All the time Checker had been sounding floors, walls and windows. All he was saying was, 'Perfect, I'm in!'

They all looked at T.J., he said, 'So am I!'

It was decided, they would buy! They needed to meet up with the owner and get his solicitors details so T.J. could exchange contracts and complete.

T.J. arrived back at home just in time for Sunday dinner.

Mother said, 'I am glad you are home as I can now serve up.'

It was roast beef, T.J.'s favourite!

Father came in, 'Not too much for me mother, I will be off to the club this afternoon.'

'What time?' Mother asked.

He replied, '3.30.'

Dinner served they all tucked into the meal, afterwards they had some wine, T.J.'s mother had cleaned the table.

T.J. said, 'Leave the dishes to me, I have a bit of news I would like to talk to you both about.'

Father's usual reply was a little grump and mother looked concerned.

T.J. continued, 'Firstly father, I have a couple of friends who when walking home from a football match were set upon and savagely attacked. One is disfigured for life with a jagged scar right across his face. The police have caught the men. The question is do they have to rely on the C.P.S. or can they have their own solicitor to get the maximum penalty and who would be the best solicitor?'

Father replied, 'The Crown have quite a lot of competent Q.C.s but I can think of one who would suit your friends of course if he wants to, that is if they are innocent and did not cause the affray themselves?'

'They are,' T.J. replied.

Father said, 'I'll talk to my friend to see if he will handle the case, no promises though!'

'Thank you father. Now I am going to venture into the property market! Before you ask I am not leaving home, but I am thinking about going into partnership on two four storey high houses. Stanley, as you both know, is a surveyor and he has inspected them and said they are a good buy. To cover my investment I will be drawing up contracts to cover all investors, my friends. The contracts I draw up father, I will need your help to make sure there are no loopholes in the document. This partnership I look upon as an investment for the future. They say that investing in bricks and mortar is a wise one as the cost of housing keeps rising.'

Father replied, 'I will help you with your documents, but you know mother and I will be passing this house over to you when we pass over.'

T.J. interrupted, 'Father, I want you and mother to live for a good many years yet, so if I get married and have a family in the future I will have a place to live. The properties will be turned into four large flats. Also when you have passed over as you say, I will live here until I do as well, for I have too many fond memories in this house.'

Mother said, 'Good, now let's have tea and father you will help him with those contracts.'

Father replied with his usual, 'Hmph.'

Monday, back at work, but with so many things going on T.J. found it difficult to concentrate, but concentrate he must! He started to read through a case file about a young man who had used a bike chain as a weapon on a person and claimed it was used in self-defence. The young man was on remand at Brixton prison. I have to see this person T.J. thought, so he phoned Brixton prison to see if he could see the prisoner, a Mr Ronald Bateman. The answer was yes. T.J. managed to book an appointment for 2pm that day. T.J. wondered if it was the one that had attacked Bomber and Sticks or an associate of theirs. T.J. got an early lunch and proceeded to Brixton prison.

When T.J. got to the prison he was shown into a room, the prison officer said, 'Mr Bateman will not be long sir, one of the officers have gone to get him.'

As T.J. stood in the room the light came in a window which was made of glass bricks. The room was cheerless he felt a cold shiver coarse through him. T.J. thought he would never want to be incarcerated in such a place! He sat down at a table and waited.

After two or three minutes the door opened and into the room walked a young man in his twenties accompanied by a prison officer who stated, 'Mr Ronald Bateman sir.'

T.J. stood and offered his hand to shake, saying at the same time, 'I am Mr Bond of Bowen, Bowen & Bowen solicitors, I believe you have asked us to represent you in court?'

Mr Bateman nodded his head and mumbled, 'Yes please.'

They both sat down. T.J. looked towards the officer but before he could say anything the officer said, 'It is alright sir, I have to stay.'

T.J. looked across the table at the young man and was thankful he was not the one who had attacked Bomber and Sticks.

'Right introductions over, I want you to tell me all that happened on the day prior to your arrest and I will listen and take notes. I want to start at the beginning and also how you came into possession of a bicycle chain, which you used as a weapon? I have not received a statement from the police yet.'

Mr Bateman looked and said, 'Now?'

T.J. nodded his head, 'Carry on Mr Bateman.'

Mr Bateman stated he had a bicycle chain attached to a piece of cord which he carried in his coat pocket. It was for self-protection as there is a gang, about eight of them, who all have these bike chains. They call themselves the 'Borough Boys'. They go around and give anyone a slap and if they retaliate then they give them the chain.

T.J. interrupted him and said, 'Are they football fans, support a certain team and have they got a leader?'

Mr Bateman replied, 'Do you know them then?'

'No, I am just trying to get a picture of them, carry on Mr Bateman.'

'They don't support a football team, but they wait outside football grounds when football matches have finished. They mix with the fans as they leave the ground. They pick a man out or two men and follow them and when they get clear of the crowd that's when they attack them! So you see it is easy for them because one set of football fans believe it is the other fans so then it's a war!'

'Right, Mr Bateman. I am going to show you a drawing of a man. I want you to see if you recognise him or not.' T.J. took the drawing Sticks had drawn and showed it to Mr Bateman.

'Blimey, that's the man! How did you get that?'

T.J. asked, 'Do you know him Mr Bateman?'

'Yes that is the man who leads the gang.'

'Do you know him and are you a member of his gang?' T.J. asked.

'No!'

'Well, Mr Bateman I am very sorry but I do not believe I can help you. I am going to pass on all of your information to another solicitor who will come and see you. If you tell him what you have told me and more, I believe he will be able to help you more than I can.'

Mr Bateman looked across at T.J.

'Don't worry, Mr Bateman. It will be alright, the solicitor will be a Queen's Counsellor, 'the best'.' T.J. did not tell him it would be from the C.P.S.

Tuesday. T.J. attended a general meeting at the office between all solicitors to discuss forthcoming court cases, offering views, opinions and helping each other with suggestions.

He sat there and listened. T.J. had never been invited before to these office meetings, it went on for more than three hours. Although he had nothing to offer up for discussion T.J. found it very informative and it gave him a lot of information which would be a great help in the future. T.J. had often wondered in past years why these office meetings were held every three months and what they were all about and now he knew, and also why the firm was reputed to be one of the best.

After lunch, about 2.30pm, the receptionist phoned to say a Mr David Barton was in reception wanting to see T.J. He went out to meet him and invited him back to his office.

'Well Mr Barton, how can I help you? Has Mr Roach paid up or are we to go to the small claims court?'

Mr Barton smiled and said that Mr Roach had paid his account in full, plus more for all the aggravation he had caused him. He also said that if he needed any more plumbing work carried out then he hoped that he could call on his services.

T.J. said, 'Great! Well I wish you all the best Mr Barton and I hope you get to make that company.'

Mr Barton replied by saying thank you for the help and offering T.J. a bottle of wine which was all boxed.

T.J. said, 'Thank you' and with that walked with Mr Barton to the outer hall and said goodbye.

As T.J. got back to his office he wondered if he had been wrong to accept that gift from Mr Barton. He walked back into the main office and asked Mr Roger's secretary if he was in and if he could see him for a moment?

She replied, 'He is free at the moment.'

T.J. knocked on the door and walked in.

Roger looked up from what he was reading paused and said, 'Come on in Terry, problem?'

T.J. said that he had accepted a bottle of wine from a satisfied client and asked if he had done wrong?

Roger smiled and said, 'Of course not, but you must never ask for it, as this would not be adequately acceptable and could be seen as misconception by others.'

T.J. said, 'Thank you,' and left Roger's office. T.J. thought, I did not ask for the wine so everything is alright.

As usual Tuesday night was gym night. T.J. met with Checker for an hours training, then a quiet drink at the Norbury, a chat, a laugh and football talk. What a break from work, although T.J. used to look forward to going into work. Since he had met up with Checker it had taken the boredom out of the other side of life, streetwise! Checker sort of made light of everything, it helped T.J. to relax more especially with his cockney sayings!

It was 7.30pm when T.J. walked into the gym, he was early as they normally met at 8pm. T.J. changed into his training clothes and shoes and went into the treadmill machine room, when he saw Checker he was pounding away on one of the machines. T.J. thought, hell he is early! T.J. walked over to Checker, who stopped the treadmill and both of them simultaneously said, 'You're early!'

'Lost your watch?'

Checker smiled and said, 'No I was going to telephone you at your office, but when I phoned your office before your telephonist wanted to know who's calling and what for. She ought to work for MI5! So I thought I might see you before I left tonight and here you are!'

T.J. replied, 'Why are you early then, any troubles or are you meeting Jean or another female? I could blackmail you, I could do with some extra cash!'

'No nothing like that, but mind you!' Checker laughed, 'No I had a telephone call today from an old friend from way back. When we were both about eight years old we met at Oldfield Farm in Tonbridge, Kent. I used to go there every September with my parents hop-picking. We used to stay there for about a month, I loved it! Sometimes we would stay longer apple picking, it was great! My parents were not well off then and you could earn a lot of cash especially being 'tax free'.'

'Where did you live on the farm, in the barns?'

'No. They had specially built sheds all joined together, in each shed was about six bunks, just enough room for a family. Outside about twenty feet away was a big shed, it had no sides and was about fourteen feet high. The middle was a huge stone built around a fire place, there were lots of logs there, and that was where all the hop and fruit pickers used to cook their food. It was great fun!'

'And that is where you met your friend?' T.J. asked.

'Well sort of, he is a true 'Romany', not like the Didicoys.'

T.J. said, 'Romanys, Didicoys, what's the difference?'

'Well the Romanys are what you would call Gypsies. You would often see them in the country, in their horse-drawn homes on wheels. They worked around some of the farms in Kent, 'Hedge bumping'. Before you ask, it is cutting halfway through saplings and other trees and bending and weaving them together to make good stock-proof fencing. Also with the cuttings you would see the women and children fashioning and making wooden pegs, and when they had made a lot they would go around the town selling them. They also used to go to racetrack meetings in the autumn selling lucky heather and telling your fortunes. They don't so much now but they still work on the farms. The Didicoys have taken over the racetracks and pretend to be fortune tellers. They have also taken over the name of the famous gypsy 'Rose Lee'. There are so many of them now conning Joe public.'

'Where do the Didicoys live then?' T.J. asked.

Checker replied, 'In houses, council estates, some of them even own their own homes, and they are very up market properties. The Romanys, before you ask, come into towns mainly December to March. Quite a few of them have got big yards, well in Mitcham they have, they're completely closed in, high fencing. They stay there carry out a few repairs or do a bit of 'rag and bone' work. I like them, they are honest, hardworking, it's the Didicoy's that give them a bad name. Well that's the history lesson over T.J. I think I will go and get changed to meet my mate 'Manty', you can come if you like? But you will miss your training session.'

T.J. said, 'No problem, I'll get changed back to street clothes and wait for you in the cafeteria.'

'Right, won't be long!'

As T.J. sat in the cafeteria having a drink of tea, he thought, Checker must have had a wonderful childhood, growing up and mixing with all kinds of people and different nationalities. Learning some words that are not in the Oxford dictionary and a few dodgy characters, Chancers, as Checker calls them. What a colourful life. He must ask him more about Manty!

Just then Checker came into the cafeteria, got a bottle of water and walked over and sat down at the table.

T.J. said, 'Your mate Manty sounds a bit of a lad, do you keep in touch much?'

Checker answered with a smile and said, 'I have not taken the oath yet my Lord, so I don't have to answer that question!' He then continued, 'You can make your own mind up about Manty, we are going to meet him at the Nag's Head in Mitcham, and yes we see each other now and again, that's when he has not gone to Kent. He is a good friend and useful.'

T.J. said, 'Sorry mate, I must have sounded nosey, but I was only being a bit inquisitive as I have not been around, as you say, that's all!'

Checker said, 'Never mind T.J.' stick with me and you will see a lot of people and places that I don't think your mum and dad would approve of. You see they are all hardworking people, colourful and they enjoy life to the full, they don't think of tomorrow as just another day. Come on then let's go, I told Manty I would see him about 8pm.'

As they left the gym T.J. saw Checker's car. They got in and made their way over to Mitcham. T.J. had never stopped in or walked around Mitcham, just driven through. They drove past the cricket green on the left, and then turned left about a hundred yards on the right and parked outside The Nag's Head.

There were some scruffy looking kids outside the pub, Checker asked them if they had seen Manty, and if he was in the pub? They shook their heads and one of them said, 'No, not yet!'

T.J. looked at Checker and said, 'What did you ask them for, they are only kids?'

Checker winked, 'It's an insurance that they won't mess about with the car now that they know I am a friend of Manty's.'

'Would they?'

'Too true, they are Didicoy kids, but they won't mess with the gypsies,' replied Checker.

They walked into the pub, it was a bit dark although the lights were on. They got a couple of lagers and went over to the side of the room and sat down. As T.J. sat he was looking around the bar, there were some right nasty looking people. There were a couple of blokes to one side of the bar, one of them pulled his hand out of his pocket, he had a fist full of rolled up bank notes, must have been a couple of hundred or more!

Checker gave T.J. a nudge and said quietly, 'Don't stare at people, you could get yourself into a lot of bother in this place.'

'Sorry Checker, but I could not help but notice all that money that man had on him.'

Checker laughed and said quietly, 'That was nothing, there are some blokes in here that have enough money in their pockets to choke a donkey! They need it for they are all at it, you know wheeling and dealing! If you sit there long enough some geezer will try to sell you a dummy.'

T.J. looked at him.

'Only kidding!' Checker said, then he looked over to the door, a tallish swarthy looking person was looking around. Checker shouted, 'Over here Manty.'

Everyone in the bar looked around, Checker did not seem to notice.

'Checker me old China, thanks for coming over.'

Checker said, 'Think nothing of it, what are mates for? Now want a drink Manty?'

Manty said, 'No,' then looked at T.J. then Checker.

Checker said, 'It's alright Manty, T.J. is straight, pucker, and he's a mate!'

Manty did not say anything.

Checker said, 'Look I would not have brought T.J. with me but he's close, he's gold alright? You know me Manty, remember, we are blood brothers, that oath we took when we were at Oldfield Farm, you remember cut our palms of our hands and shook hands, then we were blood brothers. Well that still stands with me, nobody will come between us, alright?'

Manty smiled and said, 'Yes, it's alright, I know we were only kids, nine years old when we did it but it still stands.'

'Do you want a drink now?'

Manty said, 'No, not here, too many ears and the olden sent me he wants some advice.'

Checker replied, 'How is your father, is he alright?'

'Yes, but it's my grandfather who wants to see you.'

'Is he still about?' Checker asked, 'I thought he would have been dead long ago.'

'No, he still gets around, he's 87 years old you know and he still goes out with the cart, logging or selling bags of horse manure.'

'Christ, I hope I live to see that age and be as fit. I remember him, he used to be the pole man on the hop vines.' Checker continued, 'He used to be good to my father, he always picked the best row of vines, and he always cut our row of vines down first, he was good. Well if I can help him I will. Let's go, drink up T.J. we are going to see a grand old man,'

T.J. downed his drink.

'Come on Manty, show us the way I can't remember, I've only been there once and that was with you when we were kids.' Checker said.

Manty smiled and the three of them walked out of the pub.

Outside T.J. stopped, he said, 'Look at that there!'

It was a beautiful pony and trap, it was gleaming under the street lighting. He had only seen one before in London's Hyde Park, but this one was the best, T.J. was gob-smacked.

Checker and Manty started to laugh.

Manty said, 'Haven't you seen a pony and trap before?'

'Yes, but this close.'

T.J. walked up to the two young boys who were looking after it, they looked about ten to twelve years of age. He said, 'Yours?'

'No, Manty's,' one of the young boys answered.

T.J. turned and both of them looked very pleased with themselves. The two young boys went off with Checker and T.J. sat in the pony and trap with Manty driving. It was great sitting up there, T.J. was enjoying every single minute. He could not explain the emotion, just sitting high up on the trap, the horse just trotting along, it was great!

They arrived at the yard, the gates were open, they drove in. The two young boys were there and they closed the gates. They got off the trap and the boys took the horse and as they walked to a big beautiful caravan, Manty turned to the young boys and said, 'Give her a good rub down before you feed her.'

T.J. and Manty went up some steps to the caravan and walked in. Checker was talking to a man. If this was Manty's grandfather he did not look 87 years old to T.J., more like 67. They stopped talking and Checker turned to T.J. and said, 'Meet Manty's grandfather.'

T.J. said, 'Hello and what a big caravan you have.'

The old man smiled and said his name was Ruby.

'Checker tells me your name is Terry.'

'Yes, and I am pleased to meet you Ruby.' T.J. turned to Manty and asked, 'Is that his real name?'

Ruby answered, 'It is my real name, us Romanys call our children names by what we please, my mother loved rubies and that is how I was called Ruby.'

T.J. sat down at the side window and looked out into the yard, it looked about a good half acre maybe more. There were two other big caravans, not as big as this one though. There were some sheds down the bottom which looked like stables. T.J. could not see the trap but there were three horse carts there. He was looking out into the yard to try and not listen to the talks taking place between Checker, Manty and Ruby.

Then T.J.'s thoughts were interrupted by Checker saying, 'This is more up your street T.J., it's legal work.' Checker turned to Ruby and Manty and said, 'It's a good job I brought him along, he is a solicitor.'

Manty said, 'Is that right?'

T.J. nodded and said, 'I have not been listening to your conversation so I do not know what it is you want. So if you care to tell me I will see if I can help you.'

Checker said, 'The local council want their land, this yard. They have threatened to take compulsory purchase of the yard. Ruby owns the land, his father purchased the freehold in 1902. Can they stop the council and if not what can they do?'

T.J. pondered for a moment, 'Well I know very little of land values or the procedure you have mentioned, but leave it with me and I will have an answer by tomorrow night, I promise. I can see several ways but I will not tell you them now until I am certain, alright?'

As they drove home Checker asked, 'What do you think of my friends?'

'Well they are different, but they seem alright. I suppose if I got to know them a bit more I would probably see them in a different light. Anyhow Checker, I want you to measure up the yard, then go to see some very big speculator builders and an upmarket estate agent and try and get an estimate for development of the land for building for I am sure that is what the council will have in mind. So if they do enforce the purchase they would have to pay the full price or else your friends could sell it to whoever offers the best price. Don't just go to one go to a lot.'

Checker said, 'Blimey, you want a lot, what are you going to do?'

T.J. replied, 'I will be looking into the legal side of the problem! But tell Ruby and Manty that it is only an exercise to cover their backs so they are not to worry.'

'Alright, I suppose so, after all they are my friends. Did I tell you T.J. that the locals in Mitcham call the area Red Skin Village!'

'You are kidding now, are you not?'

'No, but don't ask me why, maybe it's because of the Romanys there, a few of them, well a couple hundred or more.'

'Mind you Checker, if they forced a sale where would they go? Also who would rent them land to settle on?'

Checker said, 'No problem! They bought four acres of land years ago, about eighteen years, down Bedington Lane, for the grazing of their three ponies. They have got mains water there for the water troughs plus a toilet which the local council gave them planning permission for. In the winter they take their ponies and one van and stay there, mainly the kids you know! The one's who were looking after the pony and trap tonight. You know being a true Romany means they have to grow up fast!'

'Well Checker, you paint a wonderful picture of the Romany way of life, but it is not for me!'

Checker said, 'If I had the courage and the full Romany knowledge and know how on their kind of life I would do it tomorrow. Well I think I would!'

'Come on Checker take me home!'

As they were driving home Checker said, 'I fancy a nice cup of hot Bovril and a sausage sandwich at Smokey Joe's, how about you T.J.?'

'Yes, I was wondering what to have for supper, that will just about hit the spot.'

Chapter Four

THEY DROVE TO Smokey Joe's. Checker parked the car and as he and T.J. were walking to Joe's they saw Curly and Cliff. They were talking to a person in his early twenties and another young man about seventeen or eighteen.

Curly saw them and waved. 'Hello you two come to see the night life?'

They both laughed, told Curly and Cliff they had been to Mitcham and decided to catch a hot drink and a sandwich.

'What are you and Cliff doing?' T.J. Asked.

Cliff replied, 'Just had a drink in the Wheatsheath and came over to Joe's for a nightcap, when we bumped into Slim here and his mate J.J.'

T.J. and Checker shook hands with them and Cliff said 'They have just been telling us of what has been happening to them and the sequence of events of tonight.'

Curly said, 'You tell them Slim. Tell them what you told us.'

'Well', Slim said, 'Me, J.J., Billy King, who everyone calls "Kingy", and Big Sammy went to the White GDS tonight for a lark and to see if there was any decent bit of skirt going spare, anyway it turned out most of them were occupied! The loose ones were not worth entertaining mainly (Bow wows!). Well J.J. here clicks with a young bit of skirt and he's out on the dance floor with her. There was us having a drink at the bar and Kingy noticed this bloke going up to J.J. and the bird he was with. He said to me that the bloke had a cut-throat in his hand, you know one of those open razors. Well Kingy said to me to get J.J. and he would see us at Smokey Joe's. He told me that he would see me later and that he would look after the bloke and accommodate him. Well, me and Kingy went onto the dance floor, I grabbed hold of J.J. and told him to follow me, at the same time Kingy and Big Sammy got hold of the bloke with the razor and here we are waiting for Kingy.'

T.J. turned to Curly, 'Is this Kingy any relation of yours being his name is King?'

Curly said, 'Well in a way he is, my grandfather is the brother of his grandfather. I believe he is what you say a second cousin or something like that. We have met, mind you he is a strong boy although he only stands about five foot six. He is strong and he knows no fear, he has these piercing blue eyes and they seem to widen when he is annoyed with someone. I have seen him fight much bigger blokes and seen him knocked down on the floor yet still get up for more, in the end the other blokes loose heart and that is when Kingy comes in and shows no mercy.'

'What? Blokes as big as Cliff?'

'Yes and bigger!'

Then T.J. noticed two men walking towards Smokey Joe's and he knew straight away it was Kingy and Big Sammy, the smaller one had a jaunty look about him, as he came up to them he was all smiles. Slim said to them, 'Everything alright?'

Big Sammy said, 'Yes but look at my hand, the mad sod hit me as well,' pointing at Kingy.

Billy King laughed and said, 'You should not have left your hand in the way when I hit him!'

T.J. looked at Big Sammy's hand. It was badly swollen, he said, 'Is it broken?'

But Kingy said, 'It's just bruised, he can move his fingers.'

Curly said, 'Bloody hell Kingy what did you hit him with?'

Kingy turned to Sammy and said, 'You tell them I will get the drinks and sausages sandwiches.'

Sammy explained, 'As we escorted the man off the dance floor to the corridor leading to the main entrance, as you know the corridor is about fifty yards long and fixed to the walls about halfway along are the fire fighting gear in glass cases. Well I was holding the bloke by his collar at the back of his neck and I was holding his left arm while Kingy was holding his right arm. All the time we were talking to the bloke telling him that it was naughty to threaten people with an open razor. Then all of a sudden Kingy said 'Wait a minute' and as we stopped Kingy smashed the glass cabinet window with his elbow and reached in and took out the brass hose pipe nozzle and turned it around and hit the geezer and my bloody hand! Well I let go and called Kingy a daft bastard but he did not hear me and he hit the bloke once more as he was falling. Then he put the hose nozzle back in the cabinet. I looked at the geezer, he was just lying there with claret on the back of his head. Kingy said, 'Come on, job done let's go and catch up with

Slim.' Well we have been in a few barneys in the past but it's the first time I have seen him use something, it's always been his fists.'

At that moment Kingy turned round from the counter, gave Sammy his sausage sandwich and at the same time said, 'He's always moaning!'

'Did you call for an ambulance for this geezer?' T.J. Asked.

Checker said, 'Leave it out T.J., somebody in the dance hall would have done that and called the wooden tops no doubt!'

Then Billy King turned round, 'Blimey Checker, I didn't see you there, how have you been?'

Checker said, 'Likewise, you alright? I see you have been keeping your hand in!' Kingy just laughed.

T.J. said to Billy King, 'Are you Australian?' Then realised he was Curly's cousin!

'Who are you?'

As he said that T.J. noticed his eyes start to widen. T.J. thought bloody hell I have not been introduced to him, I was just a nosey bystander.

Checker quickly said, 'It's alright Billy this is my best mate! My fault I should have told you.'

Billy King gave a small laugh and said to T.J., 'You've been quick to notice my accent, you see I went to New Zealand for nearly four years and you sort of pick up the lingo. Then my old man died so I came back home to live with my mother, I couldn't let her look after herself.'

Checker asked, 'How is your mum Billy, is she OK?'

'She's fine, she wants for nothing I give her everything', he said. 'When I go out for the night my sister's daughter stays the night. She likes it as they have no telly in their house, anyway they only live next door but one.'

Suddenly Billy turned quickly to J.J. and said, 'You, you schmuck! Next time a geezer comes up to you with a razor and offers you a stripe don't argue like tonight! Run cos next time Slim, Sammy or me might not be around.'

J.J. said, 'Sorry Billy, I did not think and thank you.'

'That's alright, but next time think!'

Then all talk of the night's events was forgotten.

Most talk was then about girls, jokes and football. T.J. soon learnt that Kingy was not a football fan. In his sort of nasal slow drawl he said, 'I can't see what you blokes see in seeing a load of nancy's running about all chasing a leather ball, if you want to see real football you lot ought to see Australian Rules, now that is a man's game!'

Cliff said, 'Our English rugby is just as hard maybe more!'

Everyone laughed. Billy said, 'Fair enough, there are men's games but not those nancys!'

Well the night ended on a good note and just as Checker and T.J. started to leave Cliff stopped them and said he wanted to meet at the Norbury tomorrow night about 8pm. The deal had almost been done on the houses, all that was required was exchange of contracts and money! As Checker and T.J. drove home T.J. asked, 'You alright about the properties?'

'Yes, but a full survey has to be done which I will do but you have all the legal work to do, to see that there are no restrictions or council planning in the area. That might blight the properties, we will talk it over with the others tomorrow night in the Norbury.'

Next day at the office T.J. received notification of the date set for the trial at the Crown Court of Mr Clarke. T.J. got the file papers out and noted that the research office had completed their search and their findings. They had agreed with his client's statement that his employer Mr Taylor backed Mr Clarke's statement. He was at work and also his yard foreman, a William Snow, stated he finished work and clocked off at the same time, at 5pm. He also noted the clock card Mr Taylor had allowed them to have, but had requested it be returned after the trial.

T.J. had checked with Mr Roger that his client had a watertight alibi, and one that would make the Crown Prosecution Service make a fool of themselves. His reply was, 'Not the C.P.S. but the police as they had not done their homework properly, and I believe Mr Brown of which their case was founded would not be in their good books! Also the police that are involved would not be happy and will more than likely be reprimanded. But you must carry on as your client, although he would be cleared and proved innocent, must charge for court and own costs plus his reputation!'

T.J. wrote a letter advising Mr Clarke of the date of the hearing and asked him to come in to the office the day before at 11am to go over the court proceedings and inform him that we would be pressing for all costs and some remuneration for himself.

That night as arranged Checker and T.J. got to the Norbury at about 7.50pm. Curly and Cliff were already there. Checker went to the bar to get the lagers and T.J. went and sat down at the table along with Cliff and Curly. When Checker came over to the table Cliff said that he had called the meeting as the owner of the properties had asked if they were still interested in buying? Cliff looked at them and got the answer of 'yes' from them all.

'But,' Checker said 'before contracts are exchanged I would like to carry out a full survey which would involve a search for damp, subsidence, woodworm, nail sick of roofing material, dry rot and many other problems. Also T.J. has got to do all the legal side of it to see if there are any restrictions like property listed, future planning by local council which could blight the property. Have you got anything to add T.J.?'

'Yes, first I must have the solicitor's name who is acting for the owner, the full address of the property to enable me to carry out the search and of course the monies to enable me to exchange contracts. Plus it is going to be a shared ownership, therefore we would need a company name and all four of us would need to be joint directors of equal holdings. I have drawn up contracts that will safeguard all of us, and if one of us wishes to sell his holdings he has to give the remaining shareholders first refusal to purchase his share. If anyone wants to rent out his flat the other shareholders have the right to vet the people who it would be let to, and last of all any improvements or refurbishment costs are to be shared equally between the shareholders. Now while we all drink our lagers would you all like to think of a possible name for our company?' T.J. concluded.

Cliff said, 'Blimey you two, we are not buying Buckingham Palace! We don't have to go to all that palaver surely, after all we are mates?'

Curly said to Cliff, 'They are both right, yes we are mates but whose to know say in five or ten years time we could have all gone our different ways, married with kids! But like as we are now T.J.'s saying goes, we are one and what you said when you first suggested it was a means for our futures.'

There was silence for a minute, then Cliff said, 'Yes you are right, my mistake I got carried away but as you say we will buy them but we must make sure we are not buying a pig in the poke and regret it afterwards. Right, who's come up with a name?'

Checker replied, 'How about Marchant Buildings?'

He was greeted with laughing and the only repeatable saying was, 'On your bike!'

T.J. said, 'I did consider using all of our initials, I thought about B.M.K.W. Holdings Ltd but that is my suggestion we must consider everyone's views and agree on a name for the company. For if we do buy our letter heading must have a name?'

Everyone agreed to think on it.

Curly said, 'Now that we have got that out of the way the next and most important subject is Saturday's home game. It's the next round of the cup and I took the liberty of getting four tickets for the day and believe me they are like gold dust! You are very fortunate that I have an in at the club.'

T.J. said that he had forgotten about the match. Checker and Cliff said that they would be able to get them at the gate on the day of the match.

Curly said, 'Not likely. They will all be sold out by Friday morning. It's a big match, top team Birmingham, and those Brummies won't roll over easily but I know we will beat them.'

They all started talking football, what players should be in the team and who should not be, what the score would be and so on right up to closing time, which they had not noticed until the last bell rang and the barman called, 'Time gentlemen please.'

As they all stood up at the bus stop with Curly and Cliff waiting for a bus to take them towards Croydon, T.J. said, 'Now don't forget a name for the company!'

As Checker and T.J. walked home Checker said, 'I like the idea of using initials, I go along with that.'

'Thank you!' Then T.J. said to Checker, 'What I am about to say don't take it badly, it is only, well I come from a reasonably well off family. When I was born my family set up a trust fund for me to mature when I reached the age of twenty one. Then when my grandparents passed over I received a benefit from their will and the rest went to my parents. My other grandparents on my mother's side are still alive, so you see I have been very well provided for.'

Checker interrupted and said, 'You want to pull out of buying those houses then?'

T.J. said, 'No what I am trying to say is if you have to borrow your stake of the properties don't. I have enough for both of us and you can pay me back when you get rich.' Checker tried to interrupt but T.J. said, 'Wait a minute, I am nearly twenty two and you have been the first person that I can honestly say is a mate. I have learnt a lot from our friendship. Alright now you can talk and have your say. Call me an idiot if you like but I hope I have not insulted you, I hope you understand where I am coming from?'

Checker said, 'Bloody hell T.J. you have certainly taken the wind out of my sails. I don't know how you knew, I was going to borrow off my parents. I know they have some monies but not a lot, I know they would not refuse me, but I felt guilty by doing so as they did support me through my tech. It is good of you to offer me a loan but you know the saying T.J. "lend a friend money and you lose a friend" for there is always the thought that the borrower is always beholden to the lender and the lender feels the borrower owes them favours! Thank you for your offer T.J. but I do not want to lose you as a friend, so I will go to my parents. But I promise if they cannot afford it I will ask you but on a purely business contract the same as the bank but I know you would not charge interest.'

T.J. said, 'Fair enough, but I promise it will never break our friendship.'

As they said goodnight to each other T.J. said, 'It's my turn to drive to the match on Saturday, I'll call around to your house at 1.30pm alright?'

Checker replied, 'Okay see you then.'

T.J. lay in bed that night thinking about the proposed purchase of the properties, and also wondering if it could jeopardise the relationship of the four friends. For since he had met the other three it had opened up a whole different way of life which he would not like to lose. T.J. told himself he must try and get to sleep as he had a big day tomorrow in court helping young Mr Roger. He liked helping him as he always gave an air of confidence and he had never known him lose a case.

Thursday in Croydon Crown Court, it was brilliant listening to Mr Roger tearing the defence of the opposition apart. T.J. wished that some day he would be like that. The case lasted two days and T.J. found it very informative but very weary but enjoyable.

Saturday: T.J. telephoned Rita to apologise for not going out with her the previous night, for he talked over the contract with his father that he had constructed for their consortium. T.J. told him they did not have a heading for the contract but he thanked him very much for all of his help.

After an early lunch T.J. got ready, drove over to Checker's house to collect him to go to the football match. Checker was there in the front garden helping his mother with a bit of gardening. T.J. got out of the car and walked over to where Checker and his mother were.

Mrs Wolf said, 'Hello Terry how are you?'

T.J. replied, 'Fine thank you and yourself?'

'None better Terry, but he is glad you have arrived,' she pointed to her son, 'he hates gardening!'

'I'll go and drive around the block a couple of times if you want me to Mrs Wolf, I am in no hurry?'

'No that's alright he is getting itchy feet already, you had better be off and enjoy the match, I hope they win!'

As they were driving to the match T.J. said to Checker, 'Shall I park at Wilfred Road, it will be safer there.'

'Nowadays it is, but in the twenties and thirties and right up until the war it was a very rough area. It was called "Bang-ole", the police never went there unless they were mob handed'

T.J. asked, 'How do you know?'

Checker said, 'I had relatives that lived there. I often heard some of the older people of the family talk about those days mind you I believe they are all dead by now, it was the slum area of Croydon you know. There was one uncle to my mother I think well the oldens used to talk about him a lot. There was a time when he was a young man he and his friend put a wooded top in one of the storm drains in the middle of the road, then went up to the phone box and phoned the cop shop and told them, then they sat up further and watched the wooded tops come down to rescue him. The whole street was out watching them. They say there was about fifty of them with their horse-drawn paddy wagons, when they got their man out of the drain they say the whole road did a lot of clapping of their hands, shouting insults at them. But they didn't take any notice they just got into their paddy wagons and drove off. But the older part of the family were very proud of him, as when the war came he joined up, he landed up in the Desert Rats, the eighth army in North Africa. Because of his upbringing his way of life, also he was strong and had no fear. He was quickly made Sergeant, he then joined the L.D.P. and went on long range desert patrols behind German lines. Anyhow just before the British army's big push against Rommel he got captured by the Arabs that backed the Germans. Well because of the advancing British army the Arabs just staked him out in the desert, cut down both of his arms and just left him. Fortunately he was found by some of his L.D.P. mates out scouting in advance and he was saved. He was sent back and hospitalised and when he returned to duty they awarded him with a Military Medal.'

'Poor bastard,' T.J. said, 'that was it.'

'I'll tell you another day, park over there and let's get up to the ground, Curly will be doing his nut waiting for us! Don't forget he has got the tickets.'

When T.J. and Checker got to the ground Cliff and Curly were waiting in the queue at the entrance which was slowly moving through the turnstile to get in.

Cliff said, 'You are lucky, if we had got to the entrance before you got here you would not have been able to get in, we told you to be early!'

T.J. and Checker muttered, 'Sorry!'

They all went through the entrance turnstile and made their way up to where they always stood. They were very lucky as most of the crowd that had got in before them had gone to stand at the bottom of the slope. Where they stood was about a third back from the goal area. From there they could get a good view of the whole pitch and the game. The noise around them, in fact the whole stadium was alive with people talking, some laughing and shout-ing, it was electrifying and it was getting louder and louder as the ground filled. There was about thirty minutes to go before the game was due to start. The whole of the stadium and standing areas looked to be full to the maximum capacity.

The ground staff were out on the pitch checking the goal area and netting. There was about ten minutes to go when the teams came out onto the pitch to start warming up before the game started. Some of the players were by the rails where most of the young supporters were talking to them and getting autographs. Then the referee and linesmen came out on the pitch checking the goal netting. The referee called both captains of the teams to the centre of the pitch, the ground staff left the pitch and a spin of the coin decided who would kick off.

The game was started by Palace who had won the toss. Their wing man went down the pitch like a greyhound, a long ball was played down towards them, it became obvious that Palace were going for a quick goal, and they got it! The roar of the crowd was tremendous! And as once before T.J. just jumped up and down punching the air with his fist and feeling the exquisite ripple of adrenaline coursing it's way through his body. This was the second time he had felt this feeling, T.J. had heard that the feeling was better than sex. It had come very close. That goal got the home crowd roaring for more, the excitement had spread to the players, they were chasing for every ball, they were like terriers. The Brummies looked like they did not know what day it was.

The home crowd were roaring for more goals, T.J. was tingling with the excitement and joining in with the shouting. The referee blew his whistle to signal half-time and T.J. was glad for he was exhausted. T.J. looked at the others they were just as happy.

Checker put his arm on T.J.'s shoulder and said, 'What a game, I am knackered, what a game! We should have had at least a couple more goals, we can't let up! They have got to keep the same tempo going, if they let up those Brummies will creep back in.'

About ten minutes had passed and T.J. started to get on edge, he was getting a bit agitated and could not wait for the match to restart. Checker had noticed and said, 'Calm down, you'll give yourself a coronary!'

T.J. laughed and said, 'Well that's the first time I have heard it called that.'

By Checker saying that it seemed to break T.J.'s agitation, he started laughing, 'This bloody football game is getting to me! It's all your fault. When I used to sit up in the stands I never used to get wound up like this!'

Checker replied, 'Ah, but you never used to enjoy the game as much did you?'

They both laughed, Cliff turned to them and said, 'What's the joke?'

Checker said pointing, 'T.J. here has slipped a couple of gears, nearly given himself a coronary.'

This had them all laughing.

Cliff said, 'I don't know Checker, you may of got your R.I.C.S. but you sure did not get the full marks for your English!'

'I might have come up the hard way, and I'm thankful for it. I learnt a lot about life the colourful and the dark side, not like you college boys, but I still got my dip!'

Curly said, 'Hold on Checker, he was only joking, I for one like your attitude and your nonchalant look at life'

'And me,' said Cliff, 'Don't forget we are mates one and all and no one will break that, alright?'

Just at that moment the cry went up for the teams had come back onto the pitch. The crowds started clapping and shouting for more goals.

Checker leaned over to T.J. and said, 'Sorry mate.'

'What for, you've done nothing wrong?'

All of a sudden a roar from the crowd went up, Birmingham had nearly scored.

Checker said, 'I told you they are no pushovers. It looks as though their manager had a go at them at half-time and they were now starting to play good football.'

The Palace manager started to wave at some of the team and it looked like Palace started to reform their defence, but still left two forwards up front and using the long ball tactic, which made their defence stay back instead of supporting their attack. But the Brummies were playing good football! All of them were on tender hooks right to the end of the game and what a game. There were no more goals scored so Palace went through to the next round.

At the usual café they stopped at, no-one could stop talking about the game and wondered who would be their next opposition. Cliff brought the football talk to an end and brought out of his pocket an envelope.

Cliff gave it to T.J. and said, 'This is the solicitor's name that is representing the bloke who is selling the houses. His name is

Frank Bashford and the address of the properties is in full so it's down to you two now!'

Cliff put his hand in his pocket and pulled out a bunch of keys and gave them to Checker. 'Now if either of you two want any help don't forget we are all in this, and by the way me and Curly both like the title or the heading of the contract you suggested using our initials, what say you Checker?'

'Yes I'm all for it.'

T.J. said, 'It looks like we are doing all the work mate, we ought to charge these two our fees!'

This caused everyone to start laughing. T.J. kept a straight face, looked at Cliff, then raised his eyebrow.

Cliff stopped laughing and said to the others, 'He means it?'

T.J. replied, 'But of course,' looking at each in turn, although when T.J. looked at Checker he gave him a sly wink, who was quick on the uptake and said, 'It's alright for you T.J. your fees would only come to about £150, whereas my fees are a lot higher!'

But after a couple of minutes Checker could not contain himself any longer, for he burst out laughing which was infectious! T.J. also joined in and Curly said, 'You had Cliff going there T.J.' Everyone started laughing.

Curly said, 'I'll get you back T.J.!'

T.J. said, 'Who me?'

Just before they left the café Curly suggested that they should all meet soon for another night at Brian's. All agreed on next Saturday night, that suited T.J. as he was taking Rita out tonight, and Checker believed he said early on that he was baby-sitting at his girlfriend Jean's house for her younger sister whilst her parents went out. It was all arranged for next Saturday.

Curly said, 'By the way you all owe me £2 each for your tickets for the game.'

As they all paid up Checker said, 'You see T.J. they are money mad and us poor little yobs are skint!' Checker ducked a playful punch from Curly.

As they walked down Wilfred Road the houses looked quite modern and nice and clean. T.J. said, 'It takes a lot to believe what you said about this road, what did you call this area?'

Checker gave a little laugh and said, 'Bang-ole, it was a slum area of Croydon, all kinds of people lived here, some good, some bad and some very dangerous.'

'Your uncle then?'

Checker said, 'No not my uncle, my mother's uncle seeing that you want me to tell you about him I will. When he got out of hospital he was a local hero, but when he got back to Wilfred Road it was no more. Hitler had wiped out the whole area about half a mile square. Well he had to try and trace any members of his family. He found a few although not his parents, unfortunately they had died in the blitz. Anyway after a bit of sick leave he went back to his unit, that's where they awarded him the military medal. Well after the war ended he was demobbed like millions of others, the government had no money and a lot of them ended up on the dole. That is those that had no trade. Well Harry, which was his Christian name reverted back to his old ways, a bit of wheeling and dealing and a bit of stealing. He got caught and was convicted of a petty crime, these days you would be let off with a caution. Well, he went to prison and you know what those bastards did in Whitehall, they stopped his military pension which you got when you were wounded in action, and they took away his military medal, the bastards!'

Checker was quiet for a while then on a more cheerful note said, 'That's another thing I have taught you T.J., come on your motor is all safe and sound take me home driver, I've some baby-sitting to do!'

Just as Checker was getting out of the motor he said, 'I just remembered, now how did you get on with Manty's problem?'

T.J. said, 'Fine, have you done what we said?'

'Yes, Manty wants to see us, you free tomorrow?'

'Yes I will pick you up about 2pm.'

As T.J. got home and opened the door he knew Rita was in as usual talking to mother. T.J. often wondered how mother and Rita got on so well, the chemistry between them was so great. T.J. thought that if he ever split up with Rita it would be like starting world war three. He could envisage his mother sending him to Coventry. He shuddered at the thought!

T.J. shouted, 'I'm home!'

Mother called out in the lounge, 'Terry!' T.J. walked in and mother said, 'Tea?'

'Yes please,' T.J. replied.

Rita said, 'Good game?'

'Yes we won but it was exhausting shouting, jumping up and down.'

'Well sit down and have a nice cup of tea and relax as you're taking me out tonight, and I don't want to be dragging a dead duck behind me!'

Mother said, 'Now, now don't be so hard on him, he's had a hard day!' They both looked at each other and laughed.

That night Rita and T.J. went to the Granada Picture House at Thornton Heath. The film that was showing was The Jolson Story. T.J. had seen it before but he had enjoyed it so much he wanted to see it again. When the film had ended they went along to Smokey Joe's. Whilst they were drinking their drinks and eating their sausage sandwiches, Rita joked about eating outside in the cold and what a fine way it was to treat a lady, instead of taking her to a restaurant!

T.J. said, 'Where's the lady?'

She was just about to playfully hit T.J. when a voice said from behind. 'Now, now young lady we can't have anybody fighting in the streets!'

T.J. and Rita turned around to see Cliff and his girlfriend Sue. They both laughed.

'Hello, been anywhere exciting Cliff?' asked T.J.

'No we came out for a Chinese meal but it's closed,' he said and pointed across the road.

Sue said, 'It's nice here, ain't it, what's your chop suey like Rita?'

She replied, 'Not too bad Sue!' This caused a laugh.

After Cliff had got his and Sue's drinks and sandwiches he turned to Sue and said, 'You won't be moaning next Saturday when we take you to the club again!'

'That will be great, are all the others coming as well?'

'Of course.'

Rita looked at T.J. and said, 'What's all this, you never told me?'

T.J.,s lame excuse was that he was going to tell her later. But just before Rita could say anything else along came Kingy, Big Sam and Slim.

Cliff said, 'Whatcha you lot, don't tell me you have been in the dance hall again?'

Kingy replied in his slow nasal like drawl, 'Naw we've been to the Star at Broadgreen jazz night, Kenny Ball, it was great! Slim here won the tickets in a raffle, then we came up here for a nightcap. Where is my cousin is he not with you tonight?'

Cliff answered, 'No it's only me and T.J. out with our girlfriends.'

Kingy turned towards T.J. and said, 'Whatcha T.J., you're the lawyer right?'

'Yes Billy.'

'Good, it's good to know a brief, you never know when you'll need one do you?' He pointed at Rita and said, 'Your girlfriend?'

T.J. replied, 'Yes.'

'She looks a good one!'

Before T.J. could reply Rita said to Billy, 'Thank you for your backhanded compliment, but next time in English please!'

Billy said, 'Blimey mate you got a fiery one there T.J., I like that in a girl.'

Rita said, 'Thank you.'

Kingy said, 'Ha! I got it, you've been watching those nancys playing that girls game!' He turned to Big Sam and Slim and said, 'They did play today did they?'

Cliff said, 'Yes and it was a brilliant game, it was the kind of game you would have liked, a hard fought game.'

Kingy replied, 'No way, I don't mind them chasing a little leather ball around it's when one of those nancys scores a goal, the rest of them run over to the scorer and start hugging and kissing him. I bet when they get home that night it takes them all their time to give the little wife a kiss. They're probably too tired and have to go and have a lie down!'

Kingy, Sammy and Slim had a big laugh, after about twenty minutes Rita nudged T.J. and they bid everyone a good night.

Sunday morning, T.J. went for about a three mile run before breakfast, and returned home to a beautiful cooked full English breakfast. T.J. had mentioned to mother that Checker was coming over to pick him up as they were going over to Mitcham to see some friends, T.J.'s mother had arranged to serve lunch about half an hour early.

As promised Checker arrived right on time, T.J. said cheerio to mother and got into Checker's car. Mother waved goodbye and they were off. Driving towards Mitcham T.J. asked Checker if he knew what had happened to his mother's uncle. Checker said, all he knew of him was that he was so annoyed at the way he had been treated that he had changed his name by deed poll and moved out of the manor. Nobody had heard from him since and he could have been dead or have emigrated. My mother can only remember for about a week, she remembers well, she recalls that he was good looking, cheerful and made her laugh. She was playing in the garden when she fell over and broke her collar bone. When she came home from hospital he had left.

T.J. said to Checker, 'The poor sod!'

Checker was silent for a while then said, 'That is the way politicians think of the people, as long as they are alright, don't serve in the military, in the frontline, they could not care less. My father has a saying about politicians it goes like this "show me a politician and I will show you a liar!" I realised that it sounded about right, they are a breed of people who only go into politics for the money and what they can get out of it for themselves.'

'Do you know Checker the restaurant dining rooms and the bars at Westminster are all paid for by the taxpayer? Also there are cars, not just for the top boys but for all of them. My father has been there often. They like to invite people from their constituencies so they can play the big man, but it's the taxpayer that pays the bill!'

They were quiet for a while, both thinking about what they had been talking about and how they would like to change the system! When they came up to Ruby's yard the gates were open, they drove in and Checker parked the car. As they walked over to the caravan Ruby came to the door to greet them. When they went into the caravan, there were eight already there. Manty made them welcome and introduced them to everyone. They were all Ruby's sons and daughters. Manty said they had all come to hear what was said as they all had a vested interest in the findings.

Checker looked at T.J. to start the proceedings.

T.J. turned to Manty and Ruby and started by saying, 'The information I have is not what I would say is concrete, but I have been informed councillors have requested for an outline plan from their technical planning department. This is for a construction of houses, flats and other suggestions. This is information that I have been given by a friend who was informed by a local councillor at the golf club. I have also been told that the councillors have not had a reply from their planners as yet.'

Checker continued by saying, 'I have notified all interested spec builders, estate agents and property developers. I have told them to send all or any of the interest in the development, plus asked the estate agents for a valuation of the site and to send them to Ruby.'

Checker looked across at Ruby and asked him if he had received anything yet?

Ruby's reply was to go to the cupboard and take out a pile of unopened letters, placed them on the table and said, 'I did not open them as I would not know how to read them.'

Checker and T.J. sat at the table and started to open all of the letters. Most of them were from estate agents who were very interested in selling the plot as a building site for development, but if Ruby could get planning permission for a development himself for a block of flats or other plans they would very much like to be the agent for him. They seemed to be in agreement that to just sell as a plot of land would be in the area of about ten to fifteen thousand pounds, but with planning permission for a development this could be considerably higher, and not one of them would hazard a guess! The speculator builders of those that were interested wanted to buy the site and develop it themselves. This also applied to the property developers who were on the same lines as the builders.

There was quietness in the caravan, some spoke among themselves.

Ruby looked at T.J. and Checker and said, 'Well?'

Checker looked towards T.J., 'I think we have hit a brick wall mate! I cannot see what we can do.'

T.J. said, 'Let's think for a minute, don't give up so easily. There must be a way we can solve this problem.'

T.J. began to think what Mr Roger would do. T.J. believed he would try to create confusion by giving his opponents a problem. He pondered for about five minutes or more then looked at Checker, who was just looking defeated. T.J. had an idea, he didn't know how or where it came from.

T.J. said to Checker, 'When you apply for a planning project do you give the whole drawing or just a rough outline of the project?'

Checker replied, 'A rough outline would be sufficient, why?'

'Could you draw up a plan consisting of twelve apartments, six ground floor and six first floor? I have seen some similar to what I have described, I will show you if you wish. Then take a photostat copy of the drawings along with all the necessary paperwork. Get one off to the council requesting permission to build for the housing of Ruby, his children and grandchildren. They will more than likely be refused and that is when I will ask for the reasons of refusal on Ruby's behalf. My solicitors firm which Ruby will have to pay are as you know a well known firm and very respected. I believe the council would have to think carefully and would offer Ruby a very respectable sum of money if they want to develop the site or drop the whole idea. The correspondence from our firm would cost roughly one to two hundred pounds, but it could be a very strong case for them. What do you think, and what does Ruby and his family think? You tell them in your own words Checker alright?'

Checker turned to Ruby and Manty and outlined the plan of action and asked them to consider whether they wanted to go ahead with the idea. Meanwhile Checker and T.J. stepped outside whilst they talked over their plan of action. After about ten minutes Manty came to the door and asked them to go in. Ruby appeared to be happy, there were a few smiles from some of the others. Manty appeared to be their spokesperson, he said that they were very happy for T.J. and Checker to go ahead with the plan of action and hoped the council would not purchase the land.

T.J. said to Checker, 'If you can deal with it as soon as possible, like by Tuesday! Then send them by recorded delivery as it has to be at their offices before any official correspondence is sent to Ruby making an offer for a compulsory purchase of the land.'

Checker said, 'I will do my best, it would help if I could look at the other property you spoke about.'

T.J. replied, 'That's alright the porter there is an old friend of my uncle, my mother's brother, he's a contract gardener. He looks after the grounds there, we can go now if you want?'

'The sooner the better,' Checker replied.

T.J. directed Checker towards Streatham Vale then up to Crown Point and into a small private estate. There were six small compact blocks of flats built in about four acres of land, each block was in the shape of the letter "T". T.J. got out of Checker's car and told him he would find the porter and let him know why they were there and he wouldn't be long.

T.J. got back to Checker after about ten minutes and told him it was alright to look around and the porter said that if any of the residents asked why they were there they were to tell them they were looking around the grounds as they were thinking about buying the apartment that is up for sale.

Checker got out of the car and started to walk to one of the blocks, taking a small pad and pen from his pocket he said, 'Come on, show me around then!'

When they got back to the car Checker remarked that he thought these flats must cost a lot?

T.J. replied, 'Yes, the one up for sale is priced at £160k, a bit more than the two houses we are going to buy!'

'But they will be just as good when I have finished with them,' answered Checker.

'I hope so' T.J. said.

Chapter Five

THEY LEFT THE flats and made their way back to Norbury, so they could call in at the hotel for a lager and to discuss the plan of action.

'Now I want to get on with the exchange of our houses, how is it going with your survey?' T.J. asked.

Checker replied that everything was going fast and so far, he could not fault it. There was no rising or penetrating damp, everything was sound so far! But he still had to carry out the inspection of the loft areas and the roof coverings. But now Manty's work had come up he would probably complete the survey by the weekend.

T.J. was just about to say something to Checker when he noticed standing at the bar with a couple of mates was the one they call Hookey. But before T.J. could say anything this person called Hookey shouted out, 'Look who we got here mates, it's a couple of those wankers that got us chucked out of the footie match the other week!'

Checker turned, looked around and then looked at T.J. and winked. He said out loud, 'Was that the nutter at the bar who just farted or does he always talk like that?'

T.J. said, 'Beats me mate but it does smell a bit!'

Checker whispered to T.J., 'If it comes to it do you think you can handle the other two if I take on Hookey?'

T.J. answered, 'Yes, but the two of us will fight together, the two of us can take them out.'

Hookey once again shouted, 'Oi you two!'

Checker laughed and said, 'What's up mate, have you lost your dummy? If you want something to suck on I'll give you my fist!'

With that Checker and T.J. both stood up and waited for a reaction from them. It went all quiet and seemed to be quiet for a long time, but it was about a minute before Checker started to walk towards them. T.J. followed but before anyone could say anything Checker moved fast like grease lightning. He got to Hookey and hit him right on the jaw, he must of hit him on the button or the point two points of the jaw bone, a knockout punch, Hookey's legs buckled. Checker hit him again and Hookey collapsed in a heap. Hookey's two friends, like T.J., were just staring at what had happened. Checker looked at them and they just ran out of the bar. T.J. looked at Checker, he was white with rage.

'Come on T.J. the shows over, let's go!' Checker turned to the barman and said, 'Sorry about the mess Frankie!'
Frankie replied, 'That's alright Checker the cops will clear it up, they're on the way and thanks I owe you a pint!'

'Come on, across the road. we will watch from there. When the wooden tops have been and gone, I can pick my car up from the parking lot around the back.'

It didn't take the police long to arrive, they went in and about ten minutes later they dragged out Hookey. He was handcuffed and shouting out that he was the innocent party, and that he had two witnesses. He shouted, 'Look there they are,' and he was nodding his head and looking down the road where his two friends were standing looking at what was taking place.

Then one of the policemen said to Hookey, 'Them two?'

Hookey replied, 'Yes,' and at that one of the policemen started to walk down the road towards Hookey's friends, he called out to them. They immediately turned around and started running away very fast. The policeman did not go after them he just returned to the other officers and said to Hookey 'you got some good friends!'

Checker and T.J. watched the police drive off. They stood there for about five minutes then crossed back over to the hotel. Checker held T.J.'s arm back for a minute and said, 'Let's go back into the bar, Frankie will tell me what happened.'

They went into the bar, Frankie saw them and said in a loud voice, 'Hello you two, you missed some fun in here tonight.'

Checker being quick on the uptake said, 'Oh yes what happened?'

Frankie said, 'Well there was these three geezers, they all came in together then they started arguing then two started laying into the other one and knocked him out sparko! Then they did a runner and just left him lying there, just where you're standing now.'

'Where is the bloke now?' asked Checker.

'Oh the police just carted him off, anyway you two want your usual then?'

Checker replied, 'Yes please, Frankie.' Then he turned and asked a man further down the bar that seemed to be writing a book. 'You want the same again officer?'

He replied, 'No thanks, I'm just about finished here, just one more question, you're sure you've not seen these men before tonight?'

Frankie replied, 'No sir, and I am glad I called your station when they started arguing, who knows what damage they could have done. My old regulars over there were quite worried, thank goodness it didn't spread further.'

The plain clothes policeman said, 'Well thank you for your help, I'll be off now goodnight.'

When the man left the bar Frankie said, 'Now my old mate, I owe you one, the drinks are on the house alright!'

As Checker and T.J. made their way home T.J. said, 'That was a close one tonight, but I must say the way you put Hookey down was great! Did you do a bit of boxing when you was younger?'

Checker replied, 'No, as I told you before, when I was a kid about twelve I lived in an area which was a bit rough by your standards. I was top dog with the other kids, then one day some kids came into the area from another part and there were some words said. Their top man did not say a word, he just hit me and hard, just like I did to Hookey tonight. Anyway I went down like sack load of bricks, I was a bit dazed. He was standing over me and he said 'had enough?' I just nodded my head, picked myself up and they went off. I learnt one thing that day, that the best line of defence is to say nothing and just attack. I also found out later that that kid was training to be an amateur boxer and he was good!

Next day at work T.J. read through some case notes. He just could not stop thinking about how Checker had put Hookey away, and what he had said about the best line of defence is to attack. T.J. Thought, that's what young Mr. Roger does, attack, this is something I must learn to do. He looked at his watch, it said nearly 11 o'clock, it was the time Mr George Clarke was due to arrive as his case was up tomorrow at Croydon's Court. I want to go through the proceeding with him T.J. thought, I hope he has not brought his brother along!

The telephone rang, T.J. answered the call and the receptionist said, 'A Mr Clarke to see you.'

'Thank you, I will be down in a minute,'

T.J. let him wait for about five minutes then he went down to the reception to meet him. T.J. thought, hell he has brought his brother along. T.J. said, 'Good morning.' and led them back to his office.'

Once they were seated T.J. spoke to the elder brother asking him why he was always tagging along and did he not have a job to go to?'

He replied, 'No.'

T.J. said to him, 'This case is about your brother who has been charged with assault on a Mr Brown. You say your brother is innocent yet you don't want to be a witness, so I do not see the relevance of you being here. If you don't mind I must ask you to leave these offices now, at once. If you insist on staying it will leave me no option but to subpoena you as a witness in defence of your brother.'

The elder Mr Clarke got up from his chair and said, 'You are not getting me in that court room,' and he turned and stormed out of the office.

T.J. looked at Mr George Clarke and said, 'If I am going to court to plead for your case I cannot have any interferences from your brother, do you understand?'

Mr Clarke said, 'Yes he does go on a bit.'

'Right now,' T.J. said, 'I would like to run through the court proceeding with you. Your employer has sent me a written statement which is signed and witnessed by his solicitors, stating you were at your place of work on the day in question. I believe you have a good employer in Mr Taylor. I also have a second written statement and witnessed once again from your yard foreman, a Mr William Snow, plus your clock time card which Mr Taylor has kindly lent us. So you see Mr Clarke you have nothing to worry about. When we go into court you will have to stand in the dock. All you have to do is give your name and address, I will look after you and we will win the day. I will ask you if you have been worried about the charge and you must answer yes.'

He then interrupted T.J. by saying that he had been worried and it had put him off his food.

T.J. said, 'Alright I will see you at Croydon Crown Court number two tomorrow at 10am.'

He answered, 'Yes.'

T.J. showed him out, and as he walked back to his office thought about tomorrow and how it was going to be great. His first case and he was going to win!

Tuesday 9am checking with the court clerk for the rota T.J. also met Mr Brown's solicitor, he was much older than T.J. thought he would be.

The solicitor said to T.J. in a false manner, 'I will take it easy as I see this is your first case and of course you are the son of one of the most famous Q.C.s that ever worked for the C.P.S.'

T.J. replied, 'You have no need to be concerned of my well being, I also thank you for the compliment to my father, but I believe I shall carry the day, as the saying goes, "he's a chip off the old man's block!" I will see you in court sir.'

T.J. walked away to the small rest room for staff and visiting legal teams, for a cup of tea before the fun started. T.J. believed he had given Mr Start, Mr Brown's solicitor, room for thought.

Nine forty-five and T.J. saw his client, Mr Clarke had arrived.

T.J. went to him; 'Don't get worried just be calm and I will see that no harm comes to you.'

The court usher came across to them, he asked Mr Clarke his name and then asked him to follow him. They were also accompanied by a police sergeant, they went into a room that backs onto the court room. T.J. went into the court room and took his place in the front facing the bench. He sat down and started to prepare his paperwork ready for the contest. Then out of the corner of his eye T.J. saw his mother and father, at first it took his breath away. T.J. looked towards them, father remained still, T.J. was sure there was a little smile on his face, and his mother gave him a slight wave. T.J. thought I hope I don't let them down. Then a voice rang out, 'All rise!'

The judge came in and sat down. He looked briefly at Mr Start then at T.J. and sombrely nodded. The clerk of the court then started reading out the names of the clients and the charges which were against T.J.'s client Mr Clarke. The judge looked towards T.J. and said, 'How does your client Mr Clarke plead?'

T.J. replied, 'Not guilty your honour and I will strongly present his innocence to the court sir.'

'We shall see Mr Bond,' there was the slightest sign of a smile, at the same time he glanced towards where T.J.'s father was sitting.

He then looked at Mr Start and with an enquiring look, 'Yes?'

Mr Start stood up and replied, 'I am here to prove beyond doubt that my client, a Mr Brown, was cruelly and viciously assaulted on his person by the prisoner, a Mr G Clarke.'

The judge nodded his head, 'You may proceed Mr Start.'

'I would like to call my first witness, Mr Brown.' Mr Start said.

Mr Brown got into the stand and Mr Start asked him to tell the court what happened on the day he was assaulted. When he had finished T.J. only had to ask him one question; could he see the person in court who had assaulted him, he duly pointed out Mr Clarke. T.J. told the judge he had no more questions. As Mr Start rose off his seat he gave T.J. a smurky smile. T.J. thought to himself that very shortly he would be looking pig sick, and then it would be his turn to smile.

Mr Start called his next witness, a Constable Calver, who said he had received a call from the police station to go to a Mr Brown's at number 40 Stanley Road. When he got to Mr Brown's house he noticed that Mr Brown had a swelling to the right side of his face and he was holding a blood stained handkerchief to his nose.

'I asked him if he knew his assailant and he said yes it was Mr Clarke and he gave me Mr Clarke's address at number 51 just up the road. He said they are spongers off the tax payers, they don't know what a days work is. Then D.S. Sandford arrived and took over the investigation. I went with the sergeant to house number 51 and found nobody at home. So the sergeant decided to call back later and that is when we found Mr Clarke at home, that is when we cautioned him, arrested him and took him to the station for more questioning and to be identified by Mr Brown. Mr Brown did identify Mr Clarke as the person who carried out the assault, it was then that Mr Clarke was charged.'

Mr Start said, 'Thank you.'

The judge then asked if T.J. wanted to question the witness to which he replied, 'No my lord.'

By this time Mr Start was looking full of himself, he must have thought he was on the last lap and could see the winning tape. Mr Start stood up and informed the court he had one last witness, D.S. Sandford who had carried out the arrest. Mr Start asked the sergeant had he anything he could add to the constable's statement.

He said, 'No sir.'

It was then that T.J. stood up and asked the sergeant, 'When you arrested Mr Clarke had you carried out a full investigation, checked his statement and checked that he was not at work that day?'

D.S. Sandford replied, 'There was no need sir, Mr Brown had identified Mr Clarke as the person who had carried out the assault and that type of person would not have had a job!'

T.J. replied, 'He could not have had a job, why sergeant?'

'Well sir, you get to recognise people, their habits, their well being and mannerisms, you can tell quite easily.'

'That is all sergeant, thank you,' T.J. replied.

T.J. then turned to the Judge and said, 'My Lord, I could have brought to the court two witnesses to collaborate Mr Clarke's statement but the cost to the court and the Crown would have been very costly so I asked them to make written statements. These were witnessed by Mr Bramble of Bramble and Son solicitors which I am sure the court will know of them. The witnesses are a Mr Taylor who is Mr Clarke's employer and the other is a Mr Snow who is foreman at Mr Clarke's work. Mr Taylor's business is a supply depot, a large store employing two sales staff in the store, three in the depot supplying to the construction trade. He also has three lorries and drivers delivering to building sites. The turnover is approximately two to three thousand pounds per day. If I had served notice on them to appear here today Mr Taylor informed me he would have to close his business for the day as he is a hands on owner and director and also running out of his labour force. So I have here the witness statements and a clock time card showing Mr Clarke was at work on the day in question.'

T.J. handed copies to the usher to distribute to the judge and Mr Start of the C.P.S., T.J. looked at him and smiled.

After they had read the statements T.J. turned to the judge and said, 'My Lord, I will be requesting full costs plus a considerable amount for Mr Clarke for he has suffered considerably, mentally and physically I understand these past few months. From an outgoing likeable person to a very inwardly and at times I am informed he is quite tearful. I would also request that the criminal record and finger prints be withdrawn from police files and destroyed.'

The judge looked at T.J. and said, 'Mr Bond, you have presented a very formidable case, could you please inform the court what kind of costs you will be expecting for Mr Clarke, to help him to full recovery?'

'At least two thousand pounds sir.'

The judge looked at T.J. and then at Mr Start, 'Well has the prosecution anything to say or to offer Mr Start?'

He replied, 'No my Lord.'

The judge said, 'We shall retire and return in two hours.'

The usher called, 'All rise!'

T.J. looked to where his mother and father had been sitting, they had gone, he hoped they had stayed to see the end.

T.J. turned to look at Mr Start. He was packing away his case papers, he looked towards him and came over. He said, 'Well done, but I do believe I had you cornered at one stage.'

'If the police had been a bit more thorough I suspect you would have won the day, that is with a different man in the dock!'

T.J. walked outside the court room just to get a breath of fresh air, for inwardly he was feeling very elated. His first court case, he knew it was very simple but he had won, purely on a case of mistaken identity!

The day ended well, Mr Clarke got a good compensation. Before he left T.J. said to him, 'Now when you receive your cheque do not spend it, put it in the bank or post office for a while as the Crown may reopen the case, and they would want all the monies back! So come to me before you spend any of it.'

T.J. knew very well they would not reopen the case, he only said it to try to keep his brother's hands off it for he was sure he would try!

T.J. returned to the office, there were a few pats on the back and well done's then he put all the paperwork into accounts for them to work out all the costs for the court.

When T.J. got home mother, father and Rita were there, they were all so pleased for him. He had a nice cup of tea and mother told him that father had booked a table at the club for dinner that night.

T.J. said, 'Thank you, but when I had finished in court I looked for you and you were gone, before the findings?'

Mother said, 'No we were there but just watching as it was your day!'

Wednesday night, T.J. met Checker for training. When they had finished they went along to the Norbury to have a quiet chat and a beer mainly to talk about the houses. Checker said everything was sound, so they could go ahead with the purchase of them. T.J. said he would contact Cliff and Curly for their finance plus the name of the solicitor who was representing the seller, a Mr Bashford. For as far as Checker could ascertain there were no planning restrictions or future development in the area which would affect the properties.

Checker said, 'Looks like I will have to ask my mum and dad for a loan!'

He gave a short laugh, T.J. could see he was worried.

T.J. replied, 'Why ask your parents, look I have thought about this a lot Checker and I have come up with a solution to the problem. I have opened a building society account, I will give you the account details which you can give to your employers and they can set up a standing order of £20 per month. You will soon pay the loan off and you won't miss it. There will be no beholding by either of us and only you and I need know about it, nobody else alright?'

Checker was short of words. He did not know what to say so T.J. said it for him.

'Look, we are mates aren't we? I believe if the shoe was on the other foot you would be there for me, I consider you as a brother, a friend and it is a friendship I do not want to lose for the rest of my life alright?'

Checker at last spoke, 'Bloody hell T.J. you certainly know how to shake a person up, I suppose it's all your solicitor training, you have taken a load off my mind. I accept your offer and all I can say is thanks mate!'

T.J. held his hand out and said, 'Come on shake on it, but I am not cutting my hand as well!'

As they shook hands they both smiled and once again Checker said, 'Thanks mate!'

T.J. replied, 'No more thanks alright, the deal is done and forgotten about, no more words on the subject.' He continued, 'Now what about Ruby's problem, did you manage to send off the request and drawing to the council?'

Checker replied in the affirmative.

T.J. said, 'Good, now you may know that we cannot stop the council making a compulsory purchase but we could threaten to go to the highest court or even Europe, they would have to pay the market price or forget it. We would have shown that we want to build flats to accommodate the family which is quite large.'

Checker replied, 'What if the council call our bluff and give us planning permission?'

'Well we would just sell the plot with planning permission to a spec builder or developer for a good price and move on!'

'You cunning sod!' Checker said and then he started laughing and T.J. joined in.

Next day, Thursday, T.J. telephoned Curly and Cliff to let them know that everything was alright with the houses. They agreed to meet that night at the Norbury at about 8pm. With a little laugh T.J. said, 'Don't forget to bring your cheque books with you!'

Curly agreed to meet and celebrate at the club Saturday.

T.J. said, 'Yes fine, see you both tonight.'

That night when Checker and T.J. got to the Norbury, Curly and Cliff were already there. As they walked up to them Curly turned to Cliff and said, 'We'd better get the lads a drink for all their hard work!'

Checker was quick to reply by saying that he would be the one directing work on repairs and painting so he would make sure that they would not miss out on their share of the workload. With a laugh Cliff said, 'Hell we have not bought them yet and we have already got a foreman!'

'And a surveyor as well,' replied Checker which caused a bit of a ragging and laughter.

They all sat down at a table and were talking about their flats and what they would do and what colour the paintwork would be and so on. Checker said he had drafted some drawings on how the flats should be divided. As T.J. got his drawing it showed that the basement flat and the first floor flat were one, and the second and third floor the other flat, this applied to both properties.

As they studied them Checker said, 'Now if we are all in agreement of the design the one thing remaining is who has which flat in which house?'

T.J. thought for a moment and said, 'What if one or two of us fancied the same flat, would it be better for us to draw lots to see who gets which flat?'

All talk subsided as they thought about which flat they wanted, each one of them unsure how to voice their choice in fear of upsetting mates. T.J. wanted the basement of the semi-detached one, he thought this was going to be a big test to their friendship. The all for one and one for all could now be put to the question.

T.J. said to Checker, 'Have you got some spare paper sheets in that envelope you brought the drawings in that I can have?'

Checker answered, 'Yes,' and he gave T.J. two pages of which he tore up into four sheets.

T.J. said, 'Now I will give you all a sheet of paper, write on the paper which flat you would like, and if we all want the same flat we will have to think of a fair way to draw lots. If we do not get the flat we desire then it's bad luck but we will have to accept the decision, what do you say?'

They all looked at each other, looking for some kind of answer. T.J. once again asked but he did remind them that Cliff put the idea to them and they had all agreed it would be a financial steeping stone to their future. As Cliff said, they could have all get married and moved on! Putting into that light and reminding them what they had agreed at the start they all somehow started to relax.

Curly said, 'Right T.J. let's do what you said and put down the flat we fancy and then see the result.'

They all jotted down the flat they wanted on the pieces of paper, T.J. put the semi-detached basement flat, and then they put them on the table. Cliff's was the second flat in the terrace, Curly's was the same flat that T.J. wanted and Checker's was the second floor flat of the semi. So it seemed that Curly and T.J. had to draw for the basement flat. It was decided it would be the highest card from the pack which Frank supplied. Checker shuffled the cards and dealt one to each Curly and T.J. Just as T.J. was about to turn his card Curly reached over and said he had changed his mind and he would have the other basement flat.

T.J. said, 'No we made a bargain and we will stand by it.'

Curly nodded, 'Let's do it then!'

T.J. turned his card it was the ten of clubs. They all looked to Curly who turned his card, it was the eight of hearts.

Curly said, 'The deal is done right, let's do it!'

Checker said, 'I am glad for I would never want to do that again.'

T.J. said, 'Well mates, I have got Checker's cheque, and all I need now are yours, then I can go on a world cruise!'

There was a bit of laughter then Curly said, 'You'd better book yourself a bed in Mayday for at least a year!'

T.J. replied, 'Promises, promises!' he continued, 'You should have been here with Checker and me the other day, Monday I think. We were in here having a quiet drink when who should come in but that person call Hookey with some friends.'

Checker said, 'Leave it out T.J. they don't want to know, that's just small talk.'

Cliff said, 'Come on you've wetted our thirst now, what happened?'

T.J. looked at Checker and said, 'Sorry!'

He nodded, 'Go on then, but don't exaggerate.'

T.J. carried on and told them that Checker had given Hookey a couple of slaps and that Hookey went out like a light, Hookey's two friends had left the bar very quickly. They had it on their toes, as Checker puts it!'

Cliff and Curly looked at Checker, 'You put Hookey away with just two punches?'

Checker replied, 'Yes, I was lucky that's all!'

Cliff said, 'Well if we ever have a meet with anyone we will put you in front.'

Curly said, 'Yes, I won't mind holding your coat!'

The remarks lightened the mood.

T.J. ordered four lagers.

Frank the barman said, 'Coming right up.'

T.J. thought to himself, I hope he doesn't say anything about the other night.

Friday was work as usual. T.J. had handled and won a court case of his own, a lot of his work involved acting as deputy to young Mr Roger. He didn't mind, he was learning new tricks of the trade everyday.

That night Rita and T.J. went to the Odean cinema. It was an oldie film with a gangster called Legs Diamond, in the Capone era in America. Afterwards they walked down to an Indian restaurant. T.J. was not over keen on Indian food especially curries, there's so much curry powder and other hot spices in the dish that you cannot taste the source of the meat you had ordered. Yet Rita and a lot of other people liked it the hotter the better. T.J. liked to taste what he was eating. Rita ordered a vindaloo and T.J. had a tandoori chicken. After their meal T.J. drove home, taking the long route by way of Streatham Common. When T.J. dropped Rita off at her home he reminded her that on Saturday night they were at the club so she needed to be at his house at 6.30pm.

Saturday: T.J. helped mother in the garden clearing all the dead leaves and other rubbish, and digging over some of the garden for her. It was about 11am when T.J. thought Checker should be here by now. They were supposed to be going to Croydon to pick up some shopping for his mother. T.J. carried on digging, thinking Checker was a bit late then he heard his mother laughing. T.J. looked up to see where she was and there was mother and Checker sitting on the bench on the patio. Checker called out, 'Carry on my good man but don't take all day!'

T.J. Stopped and walked over to them and said, 'How long have you been here?'

They both laughed.

T.J. said, 'I'll get rid of these wellies, get my shoes on and we will be off.'

When they were driving into Croydon, Checker said, 'All I have to do is pick up a bit of shopping for my mother, she has already paid for it and I have the receipt so I shouldn't be long. I'll park around the back of the little pub, then pick up the parcel from Kenards store then we will have a lager before we go home.'

As they walked towards the pub Checker said, 'Now do not ask any questions alright? I will tell them you are my mate and we both work at the same office. A couple of them are old school friends but their father did not make them go to night school or tech so they are just labourers on a building site, but they are hard men, some of them do a bit of creeping, bouncers at dance halls and clubs. They'll fight at the drop of a hat so just answer yes or no but don't tell them your job!'

T.J. said, 'OK.'

Just as we were going through the doors T.J. Thought, I hope none of them recognise me. The bar was quite big, it was sparsely furnished with three round tables and chairs and two pinball machines. There was about ten to twelve people in there all dressed as if they were on a building site.

As they went to the bar a voice said, 'Checker my old mate, haven't seen you for a couple of months, where have you been?' He was a thick set person with broad shoulders, he stood about six feet, blond and good looking.

Checker said, 'I looked in a couple of times Trev but you were not around so I thought you might have been on a visit.'

Trev laughed, 'No probably smashed or brassick! I leave the visiting for John and the others.'

'Want a pint?'

'Yes.'

Checker looked at T.J. and asked if he wanted a lager. T.J. nodded. As the barman was serving them Checker said to Trev, 'Meet my workmate Terry.'

Trevor looked and they shook hands, he asked, 'Do you work with Checker then?'

T.J. replied, 'Yes, you won't go far wrong with Checker!'

At that moment another bloke came over to Checker said 'Great to see you mate, how have you been John, pint?'

'Yes,' replied John.

When they had their drinks they went over to one of the tables and sat down. Checker, Trevor and John were talking away to each other just like old friends that had not seen each other for a while, then John looked at T.J.

'You're quiet, you're not the old bill are you?'

Checker replied, 'Leave it out John, he's my mate Terry, he's pure he is gold.'

John laughed, 'Only having a joke Checker, I can smell the old bill a mile away!'

Trevor broke out laughing pointing at John, 'Smell them a mile off, what about last week then?' He turned to them and said, 'John and me, we left here and went up the road for some fish and chips, the law turned up and asked where we were going. They were only yards away.'

John smiled, 'I had a cold that day the laconic way.'

It was then T.J. noticed the tattoo on John's neck right across his adam's apple. He thought Christ that must have hurt. T.J. could not make out what it was and he did not ask.

Trevor said to Checker, 'Still go to Palace?'

'Yes, but we are not going this week as they are away to Leeds so I'll give it a miss.' Checker turned to T.J. and said, 'Trev lives not far from the ground.'

T.J. looked at Trevor, 'You come all the way down here?'

'Yes my mates come here.'

Just at that moment this person came up to the table and said, 'What do you want then?'

T.J. looked at him and then at Checker, he got the message to keep quiet.

Then Trevor replied, 'Beef, how much?'

The man replied, 'Four quid.'

The man wrote it down on a note pad, 'John?'

'I'll have the same but not much fat alright.'

He looked at Checker who said, 'I'll have the same, and the same for Terry here.'

T.J. sat looking at the man who stood there for a minute pulling out shopping bags from his pockets, he said, 'I'll go to Tesco this time.' He put all the bags away except for three Tesco bags which he folded separately, put them in his pocket and went over to the entrance door. Looked up and down the road then crossed over and went up to Tesco's store.

T.J. looked towards Checker, he just smiled and Trevor, John and Checker carried on talking where they had left off.

T.J. heard Checker asking John if he was still a bouncer at this pub, he replied that he was now and again, but he said, 'If anyone starts trouble here they know what they will get!' T.J. thought, a bouncer, he is the smallest of all of them, still he might be a bit hard, it was difficult to tell under that leather jacket he wore.

John said, 'We don't get much trouble, the rockers generally sort it out amongst themselves.'

Checker said, 'They still have the chapel here?'

Trev replied, 'Yes, the Baloon bar is their club room. The only time John is called to settle the problem is when they hold one of their dances and somebody fancies someone else's girl. Mind you when John goes in it is soon over.'

Checker enquired, 'Do you help John then?'

'Sometimes, only when it's two on one, but if it is a crowd then he is on his own!'

T.J. said, 'That's a bit unfair leaving when there is a mob.'

Trevor laughed and said, 'No, when John goes in nobody is a friend, he goes mental. The claret is flying all over, he takes no prisoners.'

T.J. looked at John and thought, they must be pulling my leg, they're having a joke. T.J. shook his head and said, 'No!'

T.J. had read and heard of The Rockers and the Mods when they met up mainly at Brighton, there were always casualties, what with the Mods using their baseball bats and the Rockers chains.

The talking broke as the man who had taken orders for their meat came into the pub. He was going around looking at his list and giving people their joints of meat and taking money from them. He came up to their table and said, 'All beef right? All the same.' He placed a joint of beef in front of each of them, they started to look at the price tags.

Trevor said, 'This one's four pounds and three shillings alright?'

The man said, 'Right.'

Trevor gave him two pounds and two shillings.

John, 'Mine is four pounds,' so he gave the man two pounds.

Checker looked at T.J.'s and said, 'Your's is the same as John's, two pounds.'

So T.J. gave the man two pounds and Checker did likewise. As the man moved on T.J. turned to Checker, 'I owe him more, my joint was worth four pounds?'

They laughed and Checker picked up the meat and Trevor did likewise, 'Be back in a minute!'

T.J. looked at John who said, 'You owe him nothing, the meat is stolen, bent, hookey, so he only gets half the price! Checker and Trevor are putting the meat in their cars out of sight, so if anyone had followed him and called the old bill he's gone. If you look around you cannot see him can you? He's gone out in the street with all the other shoppers, he is watching and if no police come he knows he is home and dry!'

Checker and Trevor returned from the car park. John looked at Checker, 'Your mate is a bit green ain't he?'

Checker nodded, 'A bit, I'm teaching him!'

T.J. Thought, hell here am I buying stolen meat! Trevor looked across the bar and there was a tall, well built man all dressed in leathers, he had long hair. Trevor called out his name and he came over. 'Ha John, I am glad I've seen you. We are having a dance tonight, are you in tonight?'

John replied, 'Yes I know, the landlord Jim has asked me to attend.'

Trevor said, 'Here, our mate is a bit green behind the ears, go on tell him you are a rough lot.'

He turned to T.J. and said, 'No, we all just like riding our motorbikes.' Then he turned and walked away.

Checker said, 'There you go can't be fairer that that!'

T.J. looked at them, 'Why does the landlord want John to attend? Is it only to stop gate crashers trying to get in without paying?'

Checker said, 'Look, before the butcher came you questioned why we don't help John when he goes into a mob.'

Trevor and Checker said to John, 'Go on show him the only friend you want when you go in!'

John opened his leather jacket from the inside pocket he pulled out a large big headed spanner like T.J. had seen being used on the railways. It was about twenty inches long and had a spike at the other end, about ten inches up from the spike it had a rubber like grip around it plus a leather loop attached which he had his hand through.

'You hit people with that?'

'Only those that ask for it!'

They started laughing. T.J. thought, you know some right mates Checker!

As they drove home T.J. said to Checker, 'I cannot give that joint of beef to mother, you can have mine as well Checker.'

Checker replied, 'You sure, I don't mind, I believe I understand, I always tell my mother it was half price in a sale so I bought it.'

'Checker, did you see that tattoo on John's neck?'

He nodded his head, 'Yes, did you read what it said?'

'No, I just could not see it clearly.'

Checker laughed quietly, 'Before I tell you what it says I will tell you why. John was and still is a great mate, we met at school along with Trevor and we always went around together, playing and fighting together. Then as we slowly drifted apart I started working as a trainee draftsman, they went into the construction industry labouring on building sites. Trevor started to learn bricklaying, John just moved from job to job kind of restless, at the same time he started training and doing amateur boxing. Trev and I went to see a couple of his fights, he was good. Well he had a fight on a building site and he knocked the bloke out, broke his jaw and the police were called. John was arrested and he had a witness to say he acted in self-defence. It did not do any good as he had trained as a boxer and it was illegal for a boxer to fight outside of the sport. He went to prison for three months and had to pay a couple of hundred pounds compo to the bloke. That started John on the slippery slope, the next time he went to prison he put that tattoo on his neck. He told me he had done it with a needle and when he had finished and the wound was still open he put boot black or ink on it, I'm not sure which as it was such a long time ago.'

T.J. said, 'He must have been in torment to do such a thing!'

Checker then told T.J. 'The tattoo spelt "FUCK them all!" John has no respect for the law, police, judges the lot. He feels he has been dealt a bad hand, the only people he trusts are a very few and I am glad I am one of the few.'

After a couple of minutes quiet Checker said, 'That's another thing you have learnt of my past T.J. but this time you tell no one alright?'

T.J. replied, 'No one and thank you for showing your trust in me.'

'Don't be so daft and tonight Jean and me will come around to your house and we will share a taxi to the club about 7.30pm, is that alright?'

Checker and Jean arrived on time. T.J. showed them into the lounge and mother made them welcome. T.J. said, 'Rita as usual is always last to get ready!'

Mother looked at her son, frowned and remarked, 'That's unkind Terry.'

'Sorry mother but sometimes Rita just can't get her false leg on straight, sort of back to front!' Before he could say it was a joke, he felt a sharp dig in the ribs. It was Rita looking very annoyed.

'Don't let me ever hear you joke about the inflicted again!'

'I'm sorry, it was meant as a joke, it was wrong and very distasteful.'

Mother broke the quiet, 'Come on you young people have you ordered your taxi yet?'

T.J. replied, 'Yes, it should be here any minute.'

Mother looked, smiled and said, 'I think the taxi has arrived.'

As they left mother said goodbye to them.

They got to the club and as they went in T.J. noticed that Cliff and Curly had not yet arrived. Brian came over and made them welcome. He guided them to their usual table taking the girl's coats and asking what drinks they wanted. The girls left the table to go to the little girl's room. Checker looked at T.J. and said, 'You sailed close to the wind tonight mate.'

'Yes but I didn't mean it to come out so quick, I meant it as a joke and it fell flat.'

'Forget it, but I don't know about your mum she looked a bit naughty at you.'

Just before the girls came back Cliff and Curly with their girls came in. As they came over Brian came hurrying over to make them welcome and take their drinks order. Cliff apologised for being a bit late but they had stayed to get the football results. Palace had lost. T.J. thought, that just about summed up his night, well, it couldn't get any worse.

The girls were chatting away to each other about what they had been doing since they had last met and Cliff asked T.J., 'How's the exchange going?'

'You gave the owner's name, a Mr Bashford, you gave me the address of the properties, but you did not give the name of the solicitor who is acting for Mr Bashford!'

'Are you sure?'

T.J. said, 'Yes of course I'm sure, you gave me the name of the owner, a Mr Bashford but you did not give me his telephone number nor did you give me details of his solicitor! If you had I would have been able to say everything is alright and set a date to sign the papers, for when you gave me some paperwork and Checker the keys. I looked at the paperwork and found that Mr Bashford is in fact the owner and not the solicitor!'

'Not the solicitor, hold on I will telephone mum who will look it up for me.'

Cliff went to ask Brian if he could use the telephone by the bar.

After about ten minutes Cliff came back and apologised, 'I am sorry T.J., you are right the solicitor's name is a Mr Stutters and Dart of South Croydon, do you know them?'

T.J. answered, 'No, but I will telephone them first thing on Monday morning.'

Curly said, 'Right, now that's sorted lets enjoy ourselves, come on Cliff stop looking miserable everything will be alright and by next Saturday we will be the new owners and cleaning them up, that's right T.J. isn't it?'

'Without a doubt and if there is any scrubbing to be done I will get Rita to do it!'

Checker said, 'Yes, that's right I will get Jean to do it as well.'

Curly said, 'What are you two going to do?'

Checker replied, 'Ha, we are the supervisors!'

They realised the girls were looking at them. Jean said to Checker, 'Enough small talk, come on let's have a dance,' and

107

Rita said, 'You too and no excuses, tonight is to enjoy and by the way all of us girls will be out shopping in London next Saturday!'

Cliff looked and said, 'That's put your noses out of joint!'

Both Curly and Cliff laughed and then Sue looked at Cliff, 'Come on you're dancing too!'

As Rita and T.J. were dancing she said, 'These flats you are buying, why?'

'Well it is an investment for my future, it is a calculated risk, the price of property is rising and if I was to get married I would have a home. I understand the other lads are of the same opinion. So you see it is an investment and until the day I need it I will probably let it out on an annual contract and make some money.'

'Oh!'

'Anyway I haven't bought it yet,' T.J. replied.

The music stopped and they returned to their tables and noticed that Brian had brought the drinks over and the menus to peruse. The men all wanted steaks, but the girls had fish, turbot. When Brian came over to collect their orders he was very polite as usual but somehow he didn't have the same smiling confidence as normal. Cliff asked him if he was alright? Was he not well? Brian replied that he was worried about a problem and was not quite sure how to deal with it.

Cliff looked towards T.J. and said to Brian, 'If it's a legal problem maybe Terry can help you.'

T.J. said, 'Perhaps I could.'

They all looked at Brian who said, 'No, it is not that, it is the group of two men and three girls on table number five. They have had quite a large meal and wine and were given their bill over thirty minutes ago but I do not believe they have any money, and I don't think they are going to pay.'

Cliff looked passed them to the table, he said, 'I believe I know them. Well one of them. They have got their backs to us. So it's odds on they have not seen us yet. The one I know, if it's him does this sort of joke quite often. But he will not do it to me, as in the past I have given him a slap and it was a slap I do not believe he will have forgotten!' He turned to Brian and said, 'Follow me and Curly to the entrance hall I have an idea.'

As Brian followed he said, 'I do not want any fighting Clifford!'

'There won't be but you will get paid.'

All three of them went into the entrance hall and about five minutes later Brian appeared going around the tables asking the diners if they were satisfied with everything and if they required any more wine. As he got to the adjoining table to number five, he said to the customers quite loud, 'Ah, here are the new owners.'

In fact most people looked around to the entrance and there stood Cliff and Curly, they had somehow acquired bow ties, they did look good! Brian started to walk towards them but Cliff held up his hand and slowly walked to Brian who just happened to be standing by table number five.

As they came up to Brian Cliff said, 'Hello Brian, everything alright? No complaints?'

But before Brian could say yes, Cliff turned to Curly and said, 'Nip upstairs, tell Razor I want to see him to tell him I have a job I want doing!' Then he turned to Brian and said as he looked at the people on table number five, 'It looks like these good people want to pay their cheque, come on Brian don't keep them waiting.' Then he looked close at one of the men and said, 'Do I know you, you look familiar?'

The man answered, 'No I don't think so.'

So, as he and his mate scrabbled around in their pockets for money to pay the bill Curly came back and said, 'Sorry guv, Razor will be along in a minute.'

As Brian was collecting the money Cliff turned to the people as they were leaving and said, 'Goodnight, thank you for coming hope to see you again sometime!'

He turned to Curly and said, 'Where's your manners? See the people out!'

Brian let out a big sigh of relief, looked at Cliff and said, 'Thank you Clifford, I do believe that those two boys could have caused bedlam, just so we would have asked them to leave without paying. But they would have given our establishment a very bad name, also I think they would have returned again but I don't think they will now!'

As Cliff walked back to their table with Brian, Curly also came from the entrance with a big Cheshire grin on his face. 'They have all gone, I watched them getting onto the bus to Croydon, they did look a bit sorry.'

As Cliff and Curly sat down Brian said, 'I will start your meals,' and turned to Clifford said thank you and off he walked to the kitchens.

Checker, T.J. and the girls had all been talking about what had been going on when Curly and Cliff told them what had happened. When they finished Checker said, 'Well if that had been T.J. and me you would not have frightened us two!'

Cliff laughed, 'Yes we would, you have forgotten Razor!' On that note they all laughed.

After that everybody enjoyed ourselves, the food was excellent, the ambience around them was great. The telling of jokes, the dancing, it was like one big happiness. Time did not seem to matter. Just before they were about to call it a night Brian came over to their table.

'My friends, my partner and I would like to say a big thank you by allowing you to have the last drink of the night on us!' And as he was saying that his partner approached from the direction of the kitchens carrying two large bottles of Champagne.

Cliff said, 'There is no need for that Brian, what we did tonight we did for friends.'

Brian said, 'Thank you I am glad you have said that, my partner and I are glad to be included as your friends, so this drink is a drink amongst friends!'

Cliff replied, 'Well put!'

Sunday: Checker, Jean, T.J. and Rita went to look over the properties in St James Road, they were big old Victorian double-fronted houses. Checker was describing the layouts and the partitioning of the flats and which doorways would be sealed off to give complete separation between the flats. All the floors would have to be treated with a flame retardant sealer, but the bulk of the work will be on the entrance hallway on the first floor. Of course there was the electrical and plumbing works, it would take about four months to complete.

T.J. remarked, 'That long?'

Checker answered, 'Yes and will the council let us have the planning? I think so as we are taking what would be council tenants off the waiting list, that should help persuade them.'

Rita and Jean were going from room to room saying what they would do. T.J. said, 'Hold on a minute we have not bought them yet!'

Jean said, 'We will have by next week won't we Stan?'

He nodded his head, 'By next week Duchess.'

Monday, back to work. Must telephone Mr Stutters solicitor for exchange of contracts for the properties. Just as T.J. was about to telephone Mr Roger came into the office.

'Terry, I would like you to take over a case. Your friend Mr Start of the C.P.S. is for the prosecution. Our client is a Mr Raymond Barker who proclaims he is innocent of all charges; you will see it is all in the file.'

With that he placed the file on his desk and left.

As T.J. read through the file he realised that he could not take the case on as it was the man called Hookey. He had been arrested for causing an affray at the Norbury Hotel! The bar manager, a Mr Frank Weeks, stated that Mr Barker came into the hotel with two other men and within twenty minutes they started shouting abuse at other people in the bar. They started fighting amongst themselves knocking over a table and some chairs. Then two of them picked on Mr Barker, punches were thrown and Mr Barker collapsed on the floor. The other two men ran out of the bar, and a few minutes later the police arrived and arrested Mr Barker.

T.J. thought, he must have words with Mr Roger after he telephoned Mr Stutters to make arrangements for completion of their purchase of the St James Road properties. Mr Stutters agreed a date (next Friday) for the exchange of contracts. T.J. would hand over a cheque and also collect the keys to the property. Then T.J. thought, where did Checker get the keys from for us to view on Sunday?

After T.J. finished reading the file of Mr Barker he went to Mr Roger's office and opened the subject of Mr Barker's case with him. T.J. informed him that he knew Mr Barker who also had a nickname of Hookey. He was a villainous person who led a gang of very disruptive people, who all wore steel toecap boots and who would kick people. T.J. explained, how he came to know him was through supporting a local football team. But at times they spoilt the game for the supporters. He was also at the Norbury Hotel and witnessed the incident that night. He was having a drink with a friend when Mr Barker started a disturbance calling people "wankers". They then left so he thought it would be inappropriate for him to take on the case.

Mr Roger looked at T.J., paused and said, 'You would make a good witness for the C.P.S.'

T.J. smiled and declined the offer. He returned to his office and thought he would give Checker a call and have a little joke.

Checker answered his call, 'Whatcha, mate! What's up?'

'I have been asked to take a case to represent a Mr Barker, you know him as Hookey.'

Before T.J. could carry on Checker said, 'You mean Hookey at Palace?'

'Yes, and I wondered if I could put you down as a witness?'

He laughed and said, 'Do you want me to send Razor to see you?'

They both laughed, and then Checker said, 'Is that Hookey's true name?'

T.J. replied, 'Yes and it's going to court.'

'See you tonight at the Norbury, 8pm OK?'

T.J. replied, 'Yes, see you then.'

When T.J. got to the Norbury not only was Checker there but also Cliff and Curly. T.J. thought Checker must have telephoned them. As he joined them at the table they all said, 'Well?'

T.J. took a sip of lager, savoured it and said, 'Yes!'

Checker said, 'Curly go and get Razor!' The way he said it put them all in a jovial mood.

T.J. said, 'Hasn't Frankie told you anything?'

'No, only that he has to go to court for the C.P.S. as a witness, so come on what do you know?'

Just as T.J. was about to tell them, Cliff turned to Frankie and said, 'Four more pints please.'

'Hold on I've only had one sip of this one!' As T.J. said it, he noticed they all had full pints as well. Frankie came over, put extra pints on the table and sat down. All of them looking at T.J.

'I am not supposed to tell anybody of client's problems and pending court cases.'

Checker said, 'Come on, Frankie only wants to know what Hookey is saying, after all he is protecting you and me.'

Well after it was put like that what could T.J. do?

He told them exactly what Hookey was saying in his defence and that he did not have any witnesses, so Frankie's statement still stands. T.J. asked Frankie if he had a witness to collaborate his statement. He said yes his mother's brother who comes into the pub a lot. He was only coming if needed and the C.P.S. has said he would be needed.

After Frankie returned to the bar all talk returned to the properties and the exchange. T.J. told them everything was fine and exchange and completion would take place on Friday. So they would be the new owners on Saturday, there was a little cheer.

Curly said, 'Not Saturday, Palace are playing at home and it's Millwall, that's a crunch match and I don't want to miss it!'

They all agreed for it promised to be a lively match. After that talk was full of jokes and laughs.

Checker told them about a couple of mates from school he used to go around with. He and his two other mates went over to Tooting one Saturday night and they went to a lively pub.

'It was packed, music playing and a dance area. Anyway, we got our beer, the band was playing but nobody was dancing. So Trevor, one of my mates, said that it would only take one to get on the floor and they would all get on the floor and then they could judge if there was any spare! Trevor said, "Watch my beer, I can see a nice bird over there at that long table. I will go over and chat her up." And off he went. We were watching as he turned away from her and came to us laughing. Both John and I said, "What's the joke?" He said, "Well I was asking her to dance and before she could say anything the geezer sitting on the next table said 'Don't you think you ought to ask me first?' I said "I don't want to dance with you pal!" And all his mates on the table started laughing and taking the mickey."'

Curly said, 'I'll tell you a funny story about my mother's uncle.'

'Your great uncle,' Cliff said.

Curly just ignored him and continued, 'At the beginning of World War Two my mother's uncle and his brother, like a lot of men, did not condone the killing of another man, woman or child, whatever their race. So they were all called conscience objectors, the government gave them three options, either to work in the coal mines to become known as Bevan Boys, to enlist in the army or go to prison.

'Well my mother's uncle did not like any of the options and neither did his brother so they decided on a plan in my mother's uncle's house. The flooring on ground floor had raised about two feet so they took up the floorboards in the kitchen and dug down a further four feet and made a little room with beds in and lighting. Very comfy. For about a year they avoided the police but one day the military police followed his brother to their home and after about five minutes they raided the house. When they got to the kitchen there was the open trap door in the floor and both of them got caught and put into prison. His brother was what you would call a Barrack Room Lawyer and formed strikes and petitions. He got reforms for the improvement of prisoners of conscience objectors, before that they were treated as the lowest form of humanity.'

Cliff said, 'Are you having us on Curly?'

He replied, 'No it's true, it's on records!'

Checker said, 'Blimey mate that's not a funny story, that's history! How about you Cliff, have you got any stories?'

Cliff thought for a moment and then said, 'I will tell you about my father I am sure he would not mind. He told me that at the age of thirteen he left school. His parents were not that well off, they had a small building firm, but in those days the winter time was always cold and so most building work stopped from about December until February. So you had to go inside to work or you did not earn.'

'My father was interested in art so he got a job as a sculptor's improver, then hopeful to gain an apprenticeship. You had to do six months at first, my father really enjoyed his work, he had been there for about four months when the sculptor asked him to take some of the chisels up to the engineers shop for sharpening. When he got to the workshop he gave the chisels to the assistant engineer, a big person well over six feet tall and quite a heavy set man. He was about twenty six and working on a yacht fender, quite large about the size of a boxing punch bag, it was a fender on the boat owned by their employer. Well he asked my father to hold the fender for him. My father did, not knowing that the man was going to hit hard onto the fender. My father being small was not braced against the blow and he was knocked flying across the workshop. He landed on a heap of crowbars, poles and shovels. He hurt my father who did not shirk from a fight no matter how big the opposition. When he got up he went flying at the man, his feet got tangled up with some of the plant, he somehow kicked against a shovel which bounced up and the blade hit the man's shins. So as my father got to him he punched my father to the wall again.'

'When father got up once again he went for the man, as he ran past the bench towards the man who was waiting for him, my father saw his bolster chisel, picked it up and hit him hard cutting his head. The man grabbed hold of my father who was only four feet nothing and about four stone, he walked out of the workshop holding my father high above his head and threw him into a big reservoir tank. They were built all over London to help the fire-fighters, on spare ground mostly, on factory sites during the war in case of during a bombing the main water supply was hit. They were about five hundred feet in circumference and about five feet high.'

'Well after my father got to the side of the tank and climbed out there was quite a few men all around the man who was bleeding. Needless to say my father was sacked. The next employment he had he was also sacked from for fighting with another workmate. He then tried for an apprenticeship at a large garage for a car mechanic, everything was going fine. He was getting on with all the workforce and he was more or less taking over the duties of another lad who was due to sign his indenture agreement which binds him to work for the garage owner for five years. Some of my father's duties were gopher, to go and make the tea and various other work.'

'Then one day they were all sitting around a big old-fashioned pot bellied stove drinking their tea. There was a large brown teapot sitting on top of the stove for anybody who wanted a second cup. Everyone was talking when suddenly there was a noise, my father turned to look, and there was a boy crying, sobbing his heart out. He had his trousers down around his ankles and the whole area around his crutch, the abdomen and the top half of his legs had been painted black. What made the pain worse was that he had been trying to remove it with turps. As he turned and looked some of the men were laughing and some of them were not. Then the workshop foreman leaned towards my father and said, "When you sign your forms you will get the same initiation!" My father replied, "No not me, nobody will touch me!" Then there was a bit of bantering and the foreman made a motion to grab my father saying, "We will do it now!" My father jumped up, grabbed the large teapot and threw the contents and the teapot at the foreman. My father knew he would get fired so he just turned around and left. When he got home he told his father he would like to work for him and train as a draughtsman, which his father agreed to.'

Checker said, 'Blimey mate your old man sounds a bit of a terror, I bet you and your brother had to tread with care!'

Cliff said, 'No he was as soft as anything. My mother, brother and I wanted for nothing. Around us he was an old softie but let anyone outside of the family mess with us and they were in for a slap!'

Then they all looked at T.J., 'Come on T.J. what about you?'

T.J. replied, 'Compared to you I have nothing to tell. I led an ordinary life, school then college, very quiet that's up until I met Checker and you two! Between you, you have shown me more about life and your experiences, more than I have ever known. So you see I know nothing, and have nothing to tell!'

Curly said, 'By the time we have finished with your education, you will have plenty to tell!'

This caused a bit of merriment and on that note they called it a day.

Saturday: T.J. could not wait to tell the others that everything was all right. He met Mr Stutters at his South Croydon offices, exchanged a few legal documents and of course the cheque, and he gave T.J. the keys and deeds to the properties.

T.J. did learn one thing, he said to him, 'There are no estate agents involved.'

'No, there is no need as it was a contract within families.'

T.J. looked at him and said, 'Clifford did not tell me that the seller was a relation of his.'

Mr Stutters replied, 'In a sense he is not! If I were to do a hereditary line of investigation to see who would gain any reward from a will Mr Marchant would not or could not gain from Mr Bashford's estate if he was to die. His wife is a friend of Clifford's mother, who is a twice removed cousin of Mrs Bashford. Clifford's mother went to the same school, together they became close friends and I understand they still remain so.'

Chapter Six

T.J. WAS GETTING ready to go to the match when he heard his mother talking to someone downstairs. He finished getting ready and went downstairs and saw it was Checker.

'Hello, you're early!'

'Well I was a bit footloose, so I came early to ask about the houses and are they ours yet?'

Before he could answer his mother looked at him and said, 'Are you going to tell Stanley or shall I?'

T.J. replied, 'Of course we are the owners, I got the deeds, the keys and the documents to say they are ours.'

Checker gave a yell, shouted great then all of a sudden he realised where he was. He went red in the face and said, 'I'm sorry Mrs Bond, I just felt so pleased and happy!'

Mother replied, 'You shout as much as you like Stanley, for I am happy for you all!'

As they were driving over to Palace, Checker said, 'Let's play the other two, tell them there has been a snag in buying the houses.'

But before Checker could elaborate T.J. said, 'I have a feeling they already know!'

'Did you tell them then?'

'No.' T.J. went on to explain how Cliff would get to know as his mother was close friends with Mrs Bashford.

T.J. parked the car in Wilfred Road. They walked up to the ground discussing the forthcoming game, and what their chances were. When they got into the ground it was almost full, they made their way over to where they normally stood and could see Cliff and Curly already there. As they reached them Cliff said to T.J., 'Everything alright then?'

T.J. nodded, 'Fine, everything is alright, the deal is done and they are all ours.'

There were smiles then Checker said, 'Why did you ask Cliff, you already knew didn't you?'

Cliff looked surprised, then he nodded his head and said, 'Yes, but how do you know?'

Checker replied, 'T.J. told me, the brief told him about the family links.'

Curly laughed, 'I told you Cliff, I told you they would know, solicitors have to talk to each other, that's right T.J?'

'Yes but not on cases where they are held in court!'

Curly changed the subject, 'I doubt there will be any trouble today with all the police about.'

'We didn't see many police, did we T.J.?'

Curly said, 'Christ, you two must walk around with your eyes closed, there was about fifty of them in Whitehorse Road! At least not counting this lot in the ground.'

Checker said, 'They must be in the visitors end, for we came by Tennison and Park Road, we saw a few wooden tops about the average lot we always see didn't we T.J.?'

T.J. nodded and said, 'Yes, not many probably giving the Millwall lot a warning. Mind you there is a lot more than usual in the ground. It all adds to the tension and buzz!'

Around the ground it was exciting, it appeared to be full although there were still more coming in to the ground. The talking, the laughing, some of them shouting out "Eagles". And from the opposition end of the ground, was the cry, a long moaning or mournful cry of "Millwall" over and over.

The Millwall supporters were practically all from around the Dockyards of London. Steavadors or from yards along the Thames, hardworking and hardmen, but seen to be cheerful and easy to get on with. T.J. had been told don't upset them, as they will stick together especially at football matches. The gates were closed, the tension was rising. The noise was getting louder.

T.J. looked towards Checker, he laughed and said, 'This is going to be some game, do you feel the excitement?'

'You know if I had a weak bladder I would have wet myself by now!'

The teams started to come out onto the pitch, the roar of the crowd and the chanting of the team's names was ear shattering. The noise, the crescendo, was unbelievable for the two teams that were lower down, not like Manchester United or Tottenham and the likes of. Today the noise would have matched any of them. When the referee blew his whistle to start the match T.J. felt a shiver of excitement. Palace moved quickly, it looked like they were after an early goal, but Millwall were alert to the game. Palace's little inside right, had collected the ball and ran his movement with the ball similar to the great Stanley Matthews. He was ahead of his team mates, he had nobody to pass to so he carried on. He was within the square, all the supporters were screaming at him, the noise was unbelievable, they were willing him to score, asking him to shoot!

Just as he was about to shoot for goal Millwall's dirty great big centre-half got to him from behind and he kicked him! A hard tackle and not a fair one, Palace's little forward went down hard and the referee blew his whistle for a foul. It was just inside the box so it was a penalty! Palace had a couple of big men in their team and they got up to Millwall's centre-half, you could see they were up for giving him a slap! The Palace supporters were roaring for him to hit him, some of the other players for both sides were squaring up to each other. The referee was blowing hard on his whistle, pushing players apart, shouting at them, somehow restoring order.

The Palace supporters were shouting, 'Off! Off!' over and over again. T.J. looked around the ground, some of the supporters from both sides were fighting. At the Holmesdale Road end the police and security were in amongst the fighting, they were also restoring order, it was very frightening.

In a strange way T.J. was excited, yet tense. He said to Checker, 'Bloody hell!'

'Great, ain't it, where could you go to get all this excitement ah?'

T.J. nodded, 'Yes I suppose that's why we come here.'

'Course it is,' Checker replied.

T.J. looked at the pitch, the referee was talking to their centre-half pointing at him in a threatening manner. It looked like he was letting him stay on but warning him that he was on probation and that one more dirty foul and he would be sent off! The home crowd were still chanting, T.J. looked at their forward, he looked alright, the magic sponge had done it's job. The ref blew his whistle to restart the game.

The Palace centre-forward stepped up, placed the ball on the spot and stepped back about five paces. Then just as he was about to take the kick, the Millwall keeper started jumping about waving his arms making a lot of movement. The referee held up his arm and walked towards the Millwall goalkeeper, wagging his finger and remonstrating that he was not allowed to move before the ball was kicked. The Millwall fans were shouting at the ref, jumping up and down, for the goal area was at the visitor's end where the penalty was to be taken. When the ref walked back to where he could see both the goalkeeper and the centre-forward the Millwall fans were waving their arms, their scarves and some blowing whistles trying to put the centre-forward off. The referee put the whistle to his mouth and blew, there was a deathly hush at the Palace end. The Millwall supporters were still at it, the forward ran forward and kicked the ball, it flew straight into the top right corner, and what a roar from the home crowd!

T.J. was jumping up and down, at that moment he had no control over his excitement. T.J. shouted to Checker, who was cheering and punching the air.

As the players walked back to the centre to restart the excitement amongst the home crowd quietened down. Checker looked at T.J., Cliff and Curly and said, 'It's going to be some game, we need to keep our lead!'

Play had resumed, it was hard, there were fouls galore, Palace were hard pressed but kept Millwall at bay until the whistle blew for half-time.

'I do not know about the players but I am knackered!' Checker said to all of them, 'we need another goal, Millwall are no walk over!'

Checker turned to T.J. and said, 'What do you think mate?'

T.J. replied, 'If this tension keeps up I will need a weeks holiday away from football to wind down!'

'Good, when and where are we going?' Checker laughed with that devil-may-care attitude of his which had T.J. laughing too.

'Checker, I don't know, don't you ever take things seriously?'

'Of course but only when it matters, football is only a game to enjoy, tomorrow you will say what a game and smile if we won, and if we lose you will say there will be other days and it's forgotten about, right?'

T.J. smiled, 'Yes it's only a game but what a game!'

'That's another thing I have taught you!'

The teams started to come out for the second half. T.J. looked to see if there had been any team changes, there had not been. The ref blew his whistle and the game started, this time it was Millwall who were pressing hard for an equaliser. There were fouls, so many, but the ref raised his arms telling the players gesticulating for a free kick to get up and play. He appeared not to take any notice of the sick disease spreading through the game, of players falling over trying to get free kicks or penalties or trying to get the opposition sent off. The ref was playing fair no team was favoured.

At one time there was a scare, Millwall had a corner. As the ball was played into the area there was a lot of pushing and shoving, holding players back, and their centre-half scored with a brilliant header. They groaned, the ref had blown his whistle, they realised he was pointing for a free kick. One of the Millwall players had committed a foul that none of them had seen. The ref had seen it and they were laughing as play resumed. Part of the crowd was singing "for he's a jolly good fellow . . ." which was taken up by all of the Palace supporters. The noise was tremendous, although they could not hear them you could see the Millwall fans were going bananas.

The game ended. Palace had won one goal to nil, there was a lot of unrest.

Curly said, 'Hang about a bit, let a lot of them go and we'll go when it's a bit quieter.'

T.J. was surprised at the rate the crowd diminished. One minute they were in a crowd and the next minute it was just a few stragglers. They walked out of the ground, there were still a lot of police around. They made their way down to their usual café for tea and something to eat and were all talking about the match when Cliff said, 'Hold up! Look who is walking towards us!'

T.J. looked and there was about five or six of the Palace Eagle mob. They were not talking, they just kept coming straight at them!

Checker said, 'It's alright they will be no match for us!'

Curly said, 'Don't kid yourselves have a look behind.'

T.J. looked and there were some of them behind them, it looked very much like they were their target, the friends stopped walking and waited. As the Eagle's mob got close to them they started shouting and threatening. One of them came close and Checker very quickly jumped forward and hit him hard. Curly cried out, he was holding his forehead and there was blood, one of them must have thrown a stone.

It looked as if we was on for a good hiding, when all of a sudden two large police vans came racing up, one from each direction. They stopped and there were about twelve coppers coming out of the vans and they started wading into the Eagle's mob, hitting out with their riot sticks. For one minute it looked as if they were all in trouble and then the next they were watching the police arresting and putting them into their vans. Then a sergeant and one other officer came to them and said, 'Alright lads? We have been watching them!'

The policeman looked at Curly's forehead, got the first aid kit, cleaned the wound and put a dressing on it. The police told Curly to go to the hospital to get a couple of stitches put in it and then left. It all happened so quickly, one minute as Checker put it his April was going and the next it was calm. It had been a close call!

They carried on down to the café for T.J. wanted a cup of tea, Curly would go on to Mayday afterwards. Once seated in the café with their drinks and sandwiches, the talk was about football and then the properties as they had arranged to go there for a couple of hours to look and talk over alterations that Checker had suggested.

That night T.J. spoke up on the point of money, Cliff was about to speak but T.J. held up his hand and carried on, 'We have bought the properties, Checker has designed the proposed layout, now what I am about to propose is that the alterations, electrical, plumbing, decorating, partitions of walls, filling in of doors all takes money. Now I have not mentioned this to Checker or anyone, but Checker could you give us an idea of the cost?'

There was silence, then Checker replied he did not know, he would have to cost it but off the top of his head two to three thousand pounds. For about three minutes nobody said a word. To T.J. it seemed that no-one had very little reserve of cash in hand.

Then T.J. said, 'We could arrange a mortgage on the properties or on one of them.'

The mood seemed to soften a bit then Checker said, 'If Cliff could knock us up some fancy trade cards, you know like builder's cards, electrician, and plumbers that sort of thing. The builder's merchants would then give us discount, you know trade discounts! Course if Cliff puts R.E.G. in one of the corners we would get an even bigger discount! What about it?'

They looked at him and T.J. said, 'You come up with some good ideas mate, but sometimes the way you say it, I have to smile but let's have a vote on it, don't forget we are a company now and we all need to agree or shall we all stand back and think about it?'

'I am glad you have your thinking head on T.J. I for one never gave it a thought. I believed it was just a clean up, a lick of paint and that's it,' Curly said, 'I did envisage some more expense but nothing on that scale.'

T.J. replied, 'I was thinking on the same line as Curly, then I started to think of what Checker had said the other day and I thought it would be about a thousand pounds, but two to three knocked me back a bit.'

They looked at Checker, for once he seemed lost for words.

T.J. said, 'Right, we were all going to look over the houses tonight, let's do it now and Checker can show us. Point out the things that need doing and then let him cost it out and have another meet and decide whether we need to take out a loan or not.'

They did not hang about in the café. As they left T.J. said to Cliff, 'See you there.'

Checker and T.J. made their way to Wilfred Road to collect the car.

Checker said as they were driving to St James Road, 'I would prefer a loan but what do you think T.J.?'

T.J. replied, 'So would I.'

When they got to St James Road both Cliff and Curly were not there.

'Probably still at Mayday!' T.J. said.

Checker replied, 'Yer, you know how long you have to wait at hospitals, hours sometimes!'

'Yes, but come on we have got the keys, we only need to go into one house.'

Checker said, 'Before we do I noticed a newspaper shop up the road. I want to buy some chalk, see if they deliver newspapers, and also see what other things they sell, you never know if you run out of anything!'

You never know!'

They got to the shop, it sold almost everything. As Checker was buying some chalk, he asked the owner if they delivered newspapers and he said that they did.

On the way back to the houses Checker said, 'Don't forget we are going over to Mitcham tomorrow or had you forgotten?'

'No, I remembered.'

The way T.J. said it Checker knew straight away, 'You forgot didn't you?'

T.J. laughed, 'I had!'

'I'll pick you up at 11 o'clock alright?'

T.J. answered, 'Yes okay.'

T.J. got to the houses and there was still no sign of Cliff or Curly. T.J. and Checker went in by the main front door. Checker got out his metal expanding tape measure from his pocket, 'Before you ask I always carry a tape, part of the job.'

Checker then started taking measurements and making chalk marks on the floor. He was able to draw straight lines on the floor and walls without using a straight edge. He was in his element just taking measurements, drawing out diagrams. T.J. just stood there and looked. For someone like him he could see clearly now what Checker had tried to describe.

Checker said, 'Do you want me to tell you?'

'No I can see now I will have to come back here and put it all on paper and send it to the council.'

'Of course, the layout won't bother them, it's soundproofing, fire doors, escape windows, electrics, gas, water, plus rating.'

T.J. exclaimed, 'Bloody hell Checker it's going to cost a bomb!'

Just at that moment Cliff and Curly came in, 'What's going to cost a bomb T.J?'

Before T.J. could answer Checker asked Curly, 'Did it hurt mate, how many stitches?' T.J. looked at the dressings on his head.

'Ay, just two.' Curly replied, 'What's that I heard T.J. say, what's going to cost a bomb?'

Checker told them all that he had said to T.J. plus showed them where the proposed partitions and infill doorways would be.

Cliff asked, 'How much is that going to cost?'

Checker said, 'I do not know until I bill it all out.

There was quietness for about three minutes.

Cliff turned to Curly and said, 'It's got to be a mortgage mate.' He continued to Checker and T.J., 'Curly and I were hoping not to have to borrow any money, but now that Checker has laid it on the line what do you two think?'

They both replied, 'A mortgage!'

Then Cliff said, 'Well it's up to you T.J. it's no use saying get us the best and the best rates.'

T.J. replied, 'Don't forget Cliff, it's going to cost me as well you know! Meanwhile it's down to Checker with the drawings and costings.'

Cliff replied, 'Sorry mate I was out of order.'

Checker said, 'That's alright, I want to get off now, I'm meeting Jean tonight and I don't want to be late.'

'Me too!' T.J. said.

Curly said, 'You meeting Jean as well then?'

It caused a ripple of laughs as Checker play-acting said, 'Oy you keep away from my girl!'

'Oh by the way Cliff, can you do those trade cards that Checker suggested, you know trade cards?' T.J. asked.

With that Checker said, 'I might not be here next week so I will leave a list of materials we will require. I suggest that builder's merchants just up the road over the bridge on the right might be ideal as there will be no transport charges.'

Cliff asked, 'Do you think those trade cards will do any good?'

Checker replied, 'Of course they will, builder's merchants easily add about fifty to sixty percent onto the cost so they can give a little part, say twenty to thirty percent, to their customers that are in the trade, and the general public have to pay the full cost.'

'That much?' T.J. said.

Checker answered, 'Yes it covers breakages, pilfering by persons unknown or by cowboy builders who will take anything if the yard man is not looking. Ask Curly if he gets a big discount on all materials?'

They looked at Curly, he replied, 'I do get a little, well a man's got to make a living, look at the overheads I have!' As nobody answered he said, 'Alright I'll give you all a discount.'

T.J. turned to Checker and asked, 'What do you mean you are not going to be here next week?'

'Jean's parents had booked and paid for a hire boat from a well known boatyard on the Norfolk Broads. Jean's father likes to go coarse fishing and they normally book a boat in October or November on the Broads every year. Well they have booked it and Jean's father is waiting to go into hospital for an operation, and if he does go in next week he is letting me and Jean take their places and go. Jean's mother has already bought all the food so it's a freebie holiday!'

'You lucky devil, how many berths has it?'

Checker said, 'Before you ask, no way am I sharing. I don't want anyone watching me and Jean, anyway I might want to try every bed!'

'Come on, we are mates!'

Curly said, 'And us you know!'

Checker laughed, 'There are mates and there are mates, but I am only taking one mate and that is Jean!'

There was a little bit of ribaldry, 'Hope the old man don't go into hospital and hope it rains all week!' But it was all said in fun.

As they called it a day T.J. got a set of keys from the car and gave them to Cliff. When he dropped Checker off at his house he said, 'Don't forget I'll pick you up at eleven o'clock tomorrow to go over to Ruby's.'

'Alright, I'll be ready.'

Sunday: right on time Checker arrived at eleven o'clock. Just as he got to the front door T.J. opened it and said, 'Come on in!' as they could not go without mother seeing Checker, she seemed to have taken a liking to him.

Maybe it was his cockney sayings he said now and again or his nonchalant laid back attitude. Mother as usual made Checker welcome and asked after his parents and did he want a cup of tea? He surprised T.J. by saying, 'Yes please Mrs B, as I want to explain a few things to Terry before we go.'

He then turned to T.J. and said that he would be going to Norfolk as Jean's father had got a letter on Saturday morning to say he goes in to hospital on Tuesday morning.

'You lucky devil!'

'I know, so I stayed up late last night and I have done the drawings and what we propose to do to turn the houses into four flats. I want you to send them to the planning department at the council. Also here is a list of the materials we require and my own belief is that you ought to apply for a three thousand pound mortgage.'

Mother, who had been listening said, 'Stanley you have worked all this out yourself? What are the others doing?'

Checker laughed and replied, 'It's no problem Mrs B, they are all going to be my labourers, they'll do their bit!'

Mother asked, 'More tea Stanley?'

'No thanks, got to be going, come on Terry. I'll get him back by one o'clock Mrs B.'

Mother replied, 'Mind how you go now!'

As they got in the car T.J. said to Checker, 'You jammy sod!'

'Yes, normally Jean goes to Norfolk with her mum and dad but this time she is going with me!'

As they drove to Mitcham T.J. asked Checker if he knew what Ruby wanted. He said all he knew was that they had got a letter and they wanted them to open it.

T.J. asked, 'Don't they open their own letters then?'

'Gypsies don't write, very few of them do, only the youngsters that have been to school. And very few of them can read. Manty can as he went to school, but almost all gypsies work and deal by speaking. You know a gypsy after talking and looking at you can tell whether they can trust you or not.'

T.J. said, 'If Manty can read and write why don't they let him deal with it all?'

'Small things yes, but dealing with the nobs, no! You see they don't trust them, it goes right back to the dark ages when they were persecuted by the gentry i.e. the nobs. So if they know somebody who they trust and speaks for them they ask them and that is us!'

As Checker drove into the yard Manty was there with two of the young boys, they were grooming a big shire horse.

'That's a big horse,' T.J. said to Checker, 'A shire horse, I didn't know they had that type of horse.'

'It's the smaller type. I'm not quite sure there are so many different types, the only name I know is a Suffolk Punch. Anyway let's see Ruby.'

They got out of the car. As they walked to the caravan Manty came over, gave Checker a sort of hug and at the same time said, 'Thanks for coming mate, and you T.J. Ruby is waiting to see you.'

They went into the caravan. For it's size it looked like one of those chalets, but this one had wheels. Once again the whole family was present. After the greetings and handshakes Ruby motioned to Manty to get the letter, who in turn passed it to Checker. He opened and read it for a while then he looked at Ruby and his family and said, 'The council have refused permission to build stating it would increase the volume of transport on an already heavily used highway, which in turn would cause a congestion of traffic.'

Ruby and his family looked on waiting for Checker to say more.

Checker said, 'Great, you've got an open and shut case. Whoever wrote this letter thought he was dealing with a lot of uneducated ignorant gypsies, he has shot himself in the foot! If Ruby and his family cannot develop it because of the increase in traffic neither can they! All you have to do is write to them thanking them for their correspondence, saying you can understand their reason for denial but find them very weak. Your client will be resubmitting their application in the future.'

T.J. said to Checker, 'You seem to have it all there, why don't you write to them?'

'Don't be daft, you write with better words and that fancy headed note paper. When they see your governor's name on top, that bloke will turn summersaults.'

Checker laughed and said to Ruby, 'Don't worry, T.J. is going to write to them on his governor's headed note paper, right T.J.?'

T.J. said, 'Yes, but Ruby has to understand that involving my governor's firm, as you put it, will cost money.'

Before Checker could say anything T.J. saw Ruby motion to an elderly man beside him. T.J. believed it was one of his sons. He got up and came over to T.J. and pulled out of his pocket a whole load of money. There were fifty pound notes, twenties, T.J. looked at him and then to Checker for help.

Checker laughed and said to Ruby, 'Not now, later, much later.'

Checker then said to Ruby that he was going on holiday next week to Norfolk, so he would get in touch when he got back. He then turned to T.J. and said, 'Come on T.J., I promised your mum I would get you back home by one o'clock.

As they were driving home T.J. said to Checker, 'Did you see that pile of money? There must have been two to three thousand pounds there.'

Checker laughed and said, 'Yes and if you asked them to empty their pockets there would have been a whole lot more. You see they all wheel and deal, and cash is the only currency they understand, and it would have to be a very good conman to have them over, more like the other way around. Before I forget, I phoned Cliff and told him not to print the cards in our company name. I told him to print them as T.J. Bond and Sons Builders.'

T.J. looked at Checker and said, 'Why my name, what about you, Cliff and Curly? Why me?'

He replied, 'It looks better being a family and you have charge of all of the money when you get the mortgage. You can keep a check on things.'

'Thanks a lot, what about the others?'

'Oh they have agreed, alright?'

T.J. answered, 'Well it looks like I have no option.'

As they drove up to T.J.'s house he said, 'Have a nice holiday governor! Don't forget to send us a postcard, and I will try not to forget all the jobs you have given me to be done before you get back.'

He looked at T.J. and laughed, 'If you don't I will have you sacked!'

'Oh good, what about now?'

They both laughed. T.J. said, 'Enjoy yourself and don't forget the card!'

Chapter Seven

CHECKER AND JEAN drove away from her home saying their goodbyes, with Jean's mum telling her to write. Checker said to Jean, 'This is going to be one of the best holidays I have ever taken, a freebie!'

Jean said, 'It might be a freebie, but what if it rains all week?'

'Good we can stay in bed all week!'

'No we won't. I thought you might say that so I packed dad's big raincoat that he wears when we go to the Broads. I am going to enjoy this holiday and it won't be on my back looking at the ceiling all the time! I shall be with you, not my mum and dad doing what they want to do, but what I want to do. There will be plenty of time for the you know what as well! But I want to do things alright Stanley?'

'This week we will do all the things you want to do Duchess, and mine!' Checker said with a laugh.

When they got to the boatyard Checker was surprised at the look of the boat. Also the parking of the car could not have been safer, it was within a large building in the boatyard. The boat was shaped like those old torpedo boats that you see in the war films at the flicks. It was much smaller of course, it was a six berth boat. The boatyard owner recognised Jean and asked where her mum and dad were then when Jean told him he hoped her father would make a speedy recovery and looked forward to seeing them both in the springtime, just after Easter as usual.

Once the luggage was on board the boat the owner showed Checker the controls and went up the river about half a mile then back to the boatyard. He got off and let them go on by themselves. Jean turned to Checker and said, 'Shall I operate the boat?'

'No I shall drive.'

Jean laughed and said, 'You mean steer Stanley, it's not a car!'

He replied, 'Car, boat, it's all the same to me, easy!'

'I have been coming with my parents for the last ten years and my father has taught me all about boats and how to handle them. I have been at the wheel longer than I have known you!'

'Alright Duchess I will let you have a go, but at the moment it's a man's job.'

Jean's retort was sharp, 'Right Captain Bligh, I am going to the galley, kitchen to you, to make myself a cup of tea!'

She stormed into the galley at the bow of the boat which was just below the wheelhouse. Jean filled the kettle with water and lit the Calor gas ring. She put the kettle on it and sat fuming about Stanley saying it was a man's job. Then her thoughts were abruptly cut short by a large bang, and she was enveloped with hot air. Jean shouted out to Stanley, who also felt the hot air pass him. He left the steering wheel, quickly pushed past Jean and went to under the open units where there were three gas cylinders. He quickly turned all the gas cylinders off and made sure everything was safe. He then went up to the wheelhouse where Jean was sitting, looking a bit aback as he was asking if she was alright, he was interrupted by a clarion of sirens, hooters and other noises. He looked out of the window and realised that their boat was going down the river sideways. In his rush to help Jean he must have turned the engine off! Down river there were boats taking evasive actions, some going into reverse, others steering aside.

Checker got the engine started and then turned the wheel. Because it takes a bit longer to turn, not like driving a car, Checker started to turn the wheel even harder over. When the rudder responded the boat started to turn in a circle. By then Checker was in a bit of a panic and he started turning the wheel hard in the opposite direction. All the while the people in the other boats were still sounding off the boat sirens, Checker started shouting at them.

Jean, by then had recovered from her scare, calmly said, 'Let me do it, slow down Stanley!'

She cut the throttle down, neatly reversed the boat towards the bank. She shouted to Checker, 'We will stop here, there's a post there, jump off and tie the boat up then I'll stop the engine.'

As Checker secured the rope Jean stopped the engine and went forward to cast the rope to Checker to tie up. When he got back on board they started to discuss and analyse what had happened to cause the bang and blast of hot air. Checker went into the galley to check all the gas pipework to the cylinders. He found the gas water pilot tap was turned on and that the leakage had been from there. Checker turned the gas supply to the water heater off then turned the gas supply back on to see if there were any other leaks. Everything appeared to be fine, he then lit the stove and put the kettle on for hot water and lit the gas water heater pilot.

Checker and Jean sat outside on the main deck drinking tea and just talking about the possibility of what could have happened. They were thankful it had not, but Checker would be having words with the boats owner.

After a while they decided to move on. Checker turned to Jean, 'Right you, untie the mooring ropes, I'll start the engine and drive.'

Jean retorted, 'Are you sure? After the balls up you made last time! Don't forget it was me who took over and steered the boat here whilst you pratted about shouting at everybody.'

Checker answered back, 'Who caused the bloody trouble ay? I'll drive and you will see there will not be any more cock-ups!'

Jean, fuming, retorted, 'We will see Captain Bligh, you can be assured there will be no cock-ups for you!'

She turned and jumped off the boat, untied the mooring ropes and was just about to jump back on board, when Checker, who had started the engine, put it in gear and the boat started drifting away from the river bank.

Checker called out, 'Jump!' The side of the boat was a good yard from the bank and was going forward as Jean ran alongside the boat shouting, 'Bring that boat here and I am not going to jump!'

Checker laughed and shouted out, 'No you had better not jump or you may split your kipper!' But whilst he was laughing about the remark he was trying to get the boat to the side of the bank.

He stopped the engine but it was no good as the current of the river was taking him further away from the river bank. Jean, still running alongside, started to tell him what to do, 'Stanley slow the engine down, put the gear into reverse and do a quarter turn of the wheel to the right.'

Checker realised that Jean was right. As the boat slowed down the stern started to go into the bank. Then Jean told him to turn the steering wheel back to the left a quarter of a turn. The boat straightened up and slowly edged along the side of the bank.

Checker shouted, 'Quick jump!' Jean hesitated, he shouted again, 'Jump you silly cow. Jump!'

Jean jumped on board, went up to Checker and said, 'Who do you think you are calling me a silly cow? You are an idiot, you got into that mess, you don't know how to steer a boat! What did you say Captain Bligh, driving a car or a boat it's easy, well let's see what kind of mess you are going to get us into next?'

With that she went down to the day cabin leaving him in the wheelhouse. Checker left to himself started to think how did he get himself into this mess. All of a sudden the romance of driving a boat was gone, he felt miserable, thinking once again he had jumped in with both feet not thinking. He should have let Jean drive the boat and teach him how to drive a boat properly, and who the hell is this geezer Captain Bligh? He thought he may be a famous war hero or a bloody idiot like Jean kept calling him. Still it doesn't hurt to eat a bit of humble pie, so he called out to Jean. No answer, so he called again.

Jean came out on deck, 'What do you want now Captain?'

'Sorry, I am very sorry, I should have listened to you and let you show me how to drive this boat.'

Jean gave a little hint of a smile and said, 'You are always the same Stanley ,you never think, you believe men, well you know it all and girls are bimbos, well this one's not! Now move aside and let me show you how to steer the boat and what to do in an emergency. How to slow down and how to berth the boat along-side and tie up and after you have mastered that you can steer, or drive as you put it, all day and all night if you wish! Until then we will stay on this side of the Broads alright?'

'Sorry Duchess! It's just it was the first experience on a boat let alone driving it, I was like a kid with a new toy, you know what I mean ay?'

Jean laughed, 'Alright then I will teach you, if I don't you will sink all the bloody boats including ours on the Broads!'

As Jean was teaching and showing him how to handle the controls Checker was getting closer to Jean who stopped talking, turned and said to Checker, 'Concentrate! Keep you hands to yourself, you are not out of the fire yet! Now do you think you can handle the boat controls now?'

Checker replied, 'Yes,' and as an afterthought said, 'If I behave and have no problems will I be out of the fire then?'

Jean answered, 'Maybe. Now I am going to make a cup of tea.'

Checker replied, 'Cushty' as Jean made her way to the galley. Checker's thoughts were keep it straight and slow and we could be on for a winner tonight Checker my boy! Get my card stamped, triffick!

Jean came up to the wheelhouse with a cup of tea and a piece of fruit cake. Checker thanked her and told her he saw a sign just back there saying a village next left. Jean said she didn't know as they always went the other side. Just as she said that there was a smaller waterway to the left.

Checker said, 'Well, shall we take a look?'

Jean hesitated, 'Alright Captain, go on then, but be it on your head if we get stuck. You ought to know it is tidal waters from Great Yarmouth.'

'Is it?' Checker said, 'Great, is that what you mean about the other side, you mean it's better than where we are now?'

'My father always thought so, but we have to cross a wide anchorage for large ships and we are not going until you behave sensibly and treat this boat as a boat and not a car.'

'I will. I guarantee there will be no more problems, no more cock-ups! I will drive this boat and you will think you are on a cruise liner.'

Jean laughed, 'We will see. We have not been on this boat half a day yet and apart from trying to sink other boats, leaving me stranded on the bank, now you are promising me a trip on a cruise liner! Well don't forget Stanley, on cruise ships the passengers don't cook their own meals Captain!'

'That's alright Duchess, we will be alright, trust me!'

'If I did that you would have sunk the boat by now!' With that retort Jean went down to the day cabin to look at the Broads map to see whereabouts they were and where the tributary went to.

Before Jean could see the map she heard Checker calling her to go up on deck. As she joined him she could see that the waterway came to a dead end. There were some posts on the bank for tying up to. Checker said, 'Shall we stop here then?'

'There is a path. It must lead to the village which was signpost-ed, you know Stanley you said you saw it signposted, you are playing Captain today so you decide.'

'Right,' Checker answered, 'let's go then.'

With that he brought the boat alongside of the bank, stopped the engine and as the boat was in still waters it was easy for Checker to throw the mooring ropes onto the bank. He jumped onto the bank and tied up. Jean smiled to herself, he had berthed the boat properly but he was in still water.

Checker interrupted her thoughts shouting, 'Come on then, gimme your hand, I'll help you up.'

As her pulled her off the boat he said to Jean, 'Not bad ay? I handled it perfectly didn't I?'

Without waiting for an answer he said, 'Come on let's go.'

Jean said, 'Hold on Captain aren't you forgetting something?'

'What?' asked Checker.

Jean pointed at the boat and said, 'You have left all the cabin doors unlocked and the keys are still in the ignition.'

'Bloody hell Jean, you could have locked up!'

'No, you are the Captain Stanley.'

He mumbled something, jumped down onto the boat and made an over-the-top show of locking the doors and also removing the keys from the ignition. He jumped back onto the bank and said, 'Come on!'

Jean laughed and said, 'Who's got the grumps now little boy?'

'Alright, you win cheeky cow, my day will come!'

With that they both walked along the path holding hands. Checker said, 'What a day. If it carries on like this I will be knackered when the holiday is over.'

Jean said, 'The day is not over yet!'

Checker said, 'Nothing more can go wrong. I've learnt how to drive a boat, to berth it, to tie it up, there's nothing else is there?'

'We will see. We have another six days yet, who knows Captain?' Jean replied. 'I mean you have tried to sink it once, who knows you might succeed, who knows?' She burst out laughing and ran off along the path with Checker chasing.

When Checker caught up with her he laughingly said, 'You'd better behave yourself. The last crew I had on board my boat were made to walk the plank for far less!'

'Promises, promises!'

As they came into the little village, they saw a grocer's shop, a couple of cafés, a paper shop and of course a pub. They could see about twenty to thirty cottages but there were possibly more.

'Cor I could live here, it's smashing, look at it Jean, it's beautiful, what a place, no noise or nosey parkers.'

Jean answered, 'Yes, it is beautiful but I bet the houses cost a small fortune and where would you find work?'

'Yes, I suppose Yarmouth is a long way off. Never mind it is a nice dream as they say. Come on let's have a look at the menus and see what they offer.'

The pub had on their board outside mainly salads, ploughmans and sandwiches. One café was closed and the other one offered homemade steak and kidney pie and veg, so they settled for that.

They went into the café, there was only one other couple having lunch. They sat at one of the tables and a homely looking woman came up to them and asked if they wanted a meal or just tea. Jean answered and ordered steak and kidney pies for both of them and a pot of tea.

As the woman went back into the kitchen Checker looked about and said to Jean, 'I hope the food is alright they don't seem to be busy.'

Jean said, 'You forget Stanley we are on holiday out of season. I bet if you came here in the summer you would be moaning because it is too crowded.'

'Yes I suppose so.'

'Come on Captain brighten up, soon after we have eaten our meal you will be able to get back to your little boat and sail the high seas again', said Jean with a little smile.

Checker laughed and said, 'I will set sail without you if there's any more sauce from you first mate, and you will walk the plank, twice over!'

Once again Jean replied, 'Promises, promises,' just as the lady of the café came to the table with their food. She laughed, 'If he is anything like my old man that's all you get love, promises promises!'

This caused all three of them to laugh and Jean said, 'Too true, too true!'

As they started eating their meal Checker said, 'This is good, it's tasty.'

'Yes it's very good' Jean replied.

No more was said as they both tucked into their meals. They cleared their plates and Checker leaned back and patted his stomach, 'That was very tasty and just hit the spot.'

Just at that moment the lady came to the table to collect the plates. 'That's what I like to see, empty plates, it shows I can still cook.'

Checker replied, 'That meal was beautiful and a credit to you.'

'Thank you, it was nice of you to say so.'

After they had finished their tea paid, the bill, then went out Jean said, 'We must go to the grocer's shop as we want some fresh milk.'

As they got to the shop Checker said, ''Ere did your old man pack any wine or beer in the goodies?'

Jean replied, 'If you mean my father, the answer is no. We generally stop at hotels located near the Broads when my parents want a drink, yes, so you will be able to have a drink.'

Checker said, 'We had better get a four pack of lager just in case.'

'If you insist Captain, after all you are paying!'

After they had got their shopping they made their way back to the boat. When they got there Jean started laughing whereas Checker said, 'Bloody hell what do we do now?'

They looked at the boat which was high and dry on a mud bank, still moored to the bank. There was water in the middle of the river but the mooring ropes had held the boat tight to the bank. Checker turned and said, 'What are you laughing at we are stuck here now!'

Jean said, 'It's alright Captain, don't get your knickers in a twist, I told you the river is tidal. We will just have to wait until the water returns. You were the one who insisted we came here so now we wait. You know I am beginning to have reservations about you being the Captain? Have you ever heard of the word Jonah, it is about a man who is a jinx on whatever boat he sails on.'

Checker laughed, 'This is not a sail boat and it could be you who is the jinx. Don't forget it all started with you trying to blow the boat up.'

'Touché,' Jean replied and laughed.

Checker looked at her and with a smile said, 'Alright I know that my grammar is not as good as yours, but what does that mean, touché?'

'It means Stanley you have won that point!'

'Good,' he replied, 'let's get on board, I can think of other things to do than standing here waiting for the tide to come in.'

Jean coyly asked, 'Whatever do you mean Captain?'

Come on and I'll show you, and by the way I know a rhyme about a Captain of a Lugger who was a dirty bugger, I will not copy him but come on and get your knickers off, I have got to know if my first mate responds to all my orders!'

'If you insist sir, but please close the curtains.'

'Wait a minute I haven't got my jeans off yet!'

136

Jean replied, 'Oh well shall I get dressed again then?'

Checker said, 'You stay put,' as he struggled to get his foot out of his jeans, then he got onto the bed.

Jean said, 'About time!'

Checker and Jean consumed and sexually satisfied each others needs and both fell asleep.

They were slowly but gently awakened by the movements of the boat and the sound of water splashing up against the side of the boat. Jean got up and went up on deck, the tide had come in and they were in deep water. She went back into the cabin. Stanley was still laying on the bed, he beckoned her to join him.

Jean said, 'Come on, plenty of time for that. Let's get the boat in deeper waters, I don't want to be stranded on a mud bank all of the time. If you want to go to the other side of the Broads you will have to allow for the tides for this has a deeper keel than most boats. Also the owner does not like this boat to go across the River Yare to the other side because of the low bridge. Come on, we have got to be in position by morning to cross, come on!'

Checker got off the bed, dressed and as he went to start the motor Jean was already there. He noticed that she had already untied the mooring ropes and pulled them on board. She had put it into reverse gear and was slowly steering the boat back up stream. When they got to a wider part of the river she slowly manoeuvred the boat around to face up stream.

Checker said, 'I see you have done that before! Do you want to carry on and I'll go and make a cuppa alright?'

'Alright and I'll have some biscuits too please!'

When they got to the mouth of the inlet Jean turned the boat right into the main river heading back from where they had come from. It was getting to five o'clock when Jean said, 'Ha, there it is', and she pointed over to the left. 'We will moor up here tonight as it is nearly dark and just up that lane there is a pub/hotel.'

Checker said, 'Great, what's it like?'

'They often moored up there but mother and me used to stay on the boat as mother did not hold with going into pubs. So father would go there on his own.'

'Well you can stay on the boat if you want whilst I go and have a look!'

Jean answered, 'That's alright, if you want? But the boat won't be here when you come back, how does that grab you?'

137

They both had a little laugh and Checker said, 'I wonder if they do food?'

'There's only one way to find out Stanley, we will get washed and tidy ourselves and go on up there.'

'Come on then, last one ready walks the plank!'

As they walked up the lane towards the pub Checker said, 'Your father always came to the pub, yet you say you all used to go to the other side of the Broads?'

'That's right,' Jean replied, 'like us we always got to the boatyard between ten or eleven o'clock so we always stayed on this side the first day. Then we would go over the next morning bright and early alright?'

'Sorry Duchess, I didn't mean anything honest!'

'That's alright Sherlock!' Jean replied.

Checker laughed, 'I wonder how many names you are going to call me on this holiday? So far I am an idiot, some geezer called Captain Bligh, and now Sherlock!'

Jean retorted, 'Don't worry love, there will be plenty more.'

'There you go again, that's another one.' They both looked at each other and laughed as they got to the entrance of the pub. It looked like a village pub but the swinging sign said the Captains Hotel.

They went in, it felt warm and cosy. The door on the right said 'restaurant' and on the left one it said 'saloon and lounge'.

Jean said, 'The lounge, we could ask for the menu and have a look at it whilst we have a drink.'

Checker agreed, in the lounge there were no other people. The barman asked what drinks they would like, Checker ordered and also enquired if the restaurant was open and what meals were on the menu. The barman came over with their drinks and also the menu card. He recommended the steak and said, 'The roast beef and fish are not on tonight as we are only open for our regulars. We don't get no call for holiday people out of season like, but the wife is a good cook, she does a luverly steak, chips and peas, rump steak that is sir.'

Both Checker and Jean looked at each other and at the same time said, 'Yes please!'

'Right me hearty's, I'll get my woman away from the tele.' He laughed and walked off.

Checker said, 'He talks with an accent, wonder where he comes from, up north I suppose?'

'No they all talk with that burr like brogue, it might sound like up north to you but it's softer, rounder and they drop a few vowels. I like it, who are we to speak, cockney language! Bloody hell, even I can't understand them half of the time, especially in the East End!'

'There's nothing wrong with how we speak is there?'

Jean replied, 'No Stanley, it's just different parts of the country have their own way of pronunciation of the English language, leave it at that now alright?'

Just at that moment the owner of the pub came over to them and asked if they wished to eat their meals where they were sat or go into the dining room. Jean answered, 'Here would be alright thank you.'

With that the man proceeded to collect the cutlery and condiments from behind the bar to lay out on the table. As he put the cutlery on the table he asked, 'Have you come from far sir?'

But Jean answered, 'From Norbury, just south of London.'

He replied, 'Norbury, we normally have a gentleman in from around there, he comes about twice a year do you know of him, luverly man he is, a right gent. I always look forward to him coming, he talks all posh like, but he is a right old gent. He once told me he leaves the wife on the boat, best place for her he said. She don't hold with pubs, only hotels for her. I told him this is a hotel. He said I know but she doesn't, we both had a good laugh.'

Jean laughed and said, 'He sounds a good man.'

He answered, 'Yes he is that. I always look forward to seeing him. He tells some right jokes.'

Just at that moment his wife came out to them carrying their meals. She said to the landlord, 'There you are gossiping as usual. Let these young couple be, let them eat in peace, go and play with those pots and pans, they need washing up', she said with a smile.

He answered her back, 'Who is going to tend the bar then, if you do you'll miss your tele!' And off he went out through the kitchen.

His wife turned to Jean and said, 'He's a good old stick, I would not change him mind you', she said with a smile, left and went into another part of the pub.

As they started to eat Jean said, 'Two dinners in a day, carry on like this and we will be a couple of fatties by the time we go home!'

'No, we will soon knock that off. They say plenty of the other keeps you slim and I'm going to make sure we keep slim!'

Jean laughed and said, 'Don't forget, ladies get plenty of headaches!'

'Good thing you're not a lady then!'

They finished their meals and Jean said, 'I would like a nice cup of tea now,' so when the landlady came back to clear the plates away Jean ordered a cup of tea for herself, looked at Checker who said, 'I'll have a coffee please.'

As they were walking back to their boat the night was fairly light as there was a full moon. Then all of a sudden a bat went flying past, then another and another! Jean screamed out, 'Stanley do something!'

He said, 'They won't hurt you!'

'Yes they will,' Jean replied, 'I read somewhere that a woman had one caught in her hair and they had to cut away her hair to get it out.'

By now Checker was getting nervous, there seemed to be a lot of them, possibly because of the tall trees either side of the lane. They were just flying between them, Jean shouted out, 'Give me your jacket Stanley, come on! Hurry up I want to put your jacket over my head, come give it to me.'

Checker took off his coat and gave it to Jean saying, 'Come on let's run!' In his own mind, he was telling himself that the bats have some sort of radar which stops them hitting objects but thinking but have they?

By the time they got to the end of the lane they were glad yet a bit frightened, although Checker was telling Jean everything was alright and there was nothing to be frightened about!

'I told you' he said.

Jean replied, 'Oh yer, why did you want to run then?'

They got to the boat and got on board. As they went inside Jean said, 'I never want to experience that ever again, I was really frightened.'

'Come on sit down and I'll make you a nice cup of tea, you'll be alright after that.'

'Thanks Stanley, that will be nice, it was such a lovely evening and then that happened, still maybe tomorrow we might laugh about it, but the thought of it at the moment makes me shiver.'

Checker said, 'That's the spirit love, here's your tea.'

They both sat drinking their tea in silence. When they had finished Checker said, 'I'll wash the cups up, you get yourself into bed. We have a long day tomorrow so you have told me, up early to go across to the other side.'

As Checker joined Jean in bed she cuddled close to him, he started to respond sexually but Jean said, 'No not tonight, just hold me, I just don't feel right. Those bloody bats have put me on the edge.'

'That's alright Duchess,' he said, 'I understand they worried me a bit' and they both fell into a deep sleep.

It must have been about four in the morning when Checker was woken up quite roughly. He woke with a start to say loudly, 'What's up?'

But Jean uttered with a 'sssh' and told Checker someone was on the boat. She could hear them moving about on the deck outside. They both sat up in bed keeping very quiet, listening. Now and then they heard a noise like somebody creeping about.

Checker whispered to Jean, 'I'm going out there, it could be a peeping tom or someone trying to nick something. But whoever it is when I get my hands on him he is going in for a swim!'

Jean said, 'Don't go, you might get hurt and I don't want that.'

He laughed quietly and said, 'No, that won't happen the only people creeping around this time of night are tea leaves or peepers. They've got no bottle, they just leg it off quickly in case they get nicked. Anyway if they look kinda handy I'll come back fast alright?'

Jean answered, 'Promise?'

He laughed, 'Alright I promise.'

Checker got his jeans on and crept slowly to the day cabin which led to the door to the deck. But just as he was about to unlock the door he suddenly thought, if it is a peeper he could get Jean to try to distract the peeper allowing him to catch the bastard before he did a runner. Checker returned to Jean and told her to make her way to the shower cubicle to have a shower before coming back to bed.

Jean made her way to the shower, and called out as planned. Checker answered 'okay' and once more crept slowly to the door. He stood by the door, slowly unlocked it, then inched it open, trying very hard not to make a sound. With the door open he made his way up on deck, keeping very low, a trick his father had taught him. By keeping as low to the ground, in this case to the deck, he would be able to see any movement against the skyline. There was still enough light, although the full moon by this time was low down, then he saw a movement up near the front of the boat. He could not clearly make out what or who it was.

Checker slowly crept forward. He felt a feeling of nervousness, like a shiver of fear or excitement, whatever, but he felt his old April going! He told himself, right no matter what, get in first, don't ask questions, just hit first, it's the only way, the sure way to win. He slowly crept forward keeping low and straining his ears and eyes to try to see or hear anything. Then he stepped forward and stubbed his toe against something that hard that he let out a curse and fell forward catching his shoulder against the side of the boat.

'That hurt!' he swore out loud. As he was getting up he heard something or someone running along the footpath alongside the canal away from the boat.

He shouted out, 'You bastard!'

The he heard Jean calling to him, 'Stanley, are you alright? Stanley, where are you? Stanley, answer me, where are you?'

He called out, 'It's alright.' He stood up and limped his way back to where Jean was standing by the doorway.

'You alright?'

'Yes I'm alright,' Checker answered.

'Did you see who it was? Did they hurt you? I told you not to go out in case you got hurt, it's your own fault. Come on, let's get inside, let's see the damage you bloody idiot!'

'Don't call me an idiot!' Checker replied, 'I am not an idiot and never was or will be ever. If I was I would not have got my dipp!'

'I'm sorry Stanley, I know you are not, it's just I care for you so much that when you put yourself in a hazardous situation, just like now, I get frightened.'

Checker thought for a moment then said, 'Sorry Duchess, I spose I acted a bit stupid but most men with balls would have done the same. It's like looking out for your woman, anyway you know me, I never back down, sorry luv!'

'I know,' Jean said, 'Come on let's get inside and look at the damage.'

'It's alright, no harm done!'

As they got into the day cabin Jean said, 'Come on show me, where does it hurt?'

Checker sheepishly said, 'I stubbed my toes on something hard on the deck, it caused me to fall over and I knocked my shoulder against the side of the boat, and that hurt! I swore out loud and whoever it was scarpered off along the bank.'

Jean looked at his feet and realised that he was not wearing any shoes. 'You went out there with no shoes on?' Checker nodded his head, Jean looked at him and started to say, 'You, you, you fool Stanley!'

'I know, I know, but I was just trying to be as quiet as a mouse, if I had not hurt my toes I would have got them.'

'Oh yer Stanley and what would you have done if they had stamped on your toes, ah?' Jean started laughing and hopping about singing, 'I'm Jake the peg with a wooden leg.'

Checker made a grab for her and said, 'Come here you saucy cow, you are going to pay a penance for that, and I won't accept any excuse of a headache!'

'Well come on then,' Jean replied, 'but turn off the lights, we don't want to give that peeper a show!'

Next day, seven o'clock in the morning, Jean woke Checker up with a cup of tea saying, 'Come on Jake, shake a leg or peg.' She stood there with a little smile. Checker opened one eye saying, 'What time is it, it's still dark?'

'It's nearly seven o'clock,' Jean replied, 'Come on, when you have drunk your tea go and get a shave whilst I cook the breakfast, bacon, eggs with two slices of toast, will that do you?'

'Cushty. Cor, this is the life! Freebie holiday, cruise, breakfast in bed and a willing waitress, what more could a man want?'

'Enjoy it while you can for tomorrow it's your turn to play early call and cook.'

'I can't do that I'm a man!' replied Checker, 'Cooking is a woman's job!'

'Would you like breakfast this morning cooked by me, or watch me eat mine, then afterwards I will show you where the cooker is?'

Checker grabbed hold of a pillow and threw it at Jean saying, 'You saucy mare, when I have drunk my tea beware!'

Jean laughed and left to go to the galley calling out, 'Promises, promises.' As Checker got out of bed he felt a sharp pain in his right foot. He looked at it and saw that his big toe was a bit bruised, he thought bloody hell I hope it is not broken!

He called out to Jean who replied, 'I'm not playing games yet, I am preparing breakfast.'

'It is not a joke, it's real honest, you come and have a look, I think I have broken my toe.'

Jean called, 'Alright, I'll come, but if you are playing games to get me into bed I will break it for you! Then you really will be Jake the peg.'

She walked into the bedroom and saw Checker looking at his big toe which looked a bit blue and bruised. He looked up and said, 'See I told you I was not playing about.'

Jean looked at it and told him to wriggle his toes, Checker complied.

'Well,' Jean asked, 'does it hurt?'

'A little bit, it hurt when I knocked it when I was getting out of the bed.'

Jean said, 'It's not broken, come on get a shower and after breakfast I will put a cold compress on it, that will help take the bruising out. Come on Captain Ahab! You will be alright, you won't loose your leg!'

'Who is bloody Captain Ahab, how many more Captains do you know?'

'Ho, don't be silly Stanley, you must remember that Captain, we both saw the film together, you know Moby Dick, the giant white whale.'

'Ho yer, I remember, didn't he die tied to the whale?'

'Yes that's right Stanley. Don't worry, I won't tie you to a small fish, I will just throw you overboard!' She laughed as she ducked a flying pillow. As she returned to the galley she called out, 'Breakfast's ready in fifteen minutes, get your one skate on!'

After breakfast Jean put a cold compress onto Stanley's foot. 'Now you stay put, I will take the boat up river and I'll call you when we cross the river, alright? It's a nice view, it will be about thirty minutes. I'll just untie the ropes and get going.'

Jean left Checker sitting in the day cabin, he called out, 'Do you want me to drive?'

She replied, 'No that's alright. I must not tire the old invalid out, you have got to have your rest. I don't want to extract too much energy from you, I might call on you for extra duties tonight!'

Checker shouted out, 'Is that a promise?' 'Maybe' was the reply.

144

He thought, this holiday has a lot of benefits, getting my card stamped every day, that's a winner. My old man has got his work cut out and if it keeps up I will be bloody knackered when we get home, nice thought though. We have got to do this lark more often, cushty!

Checker heard Jean calling him to come to the wheelhouse, he must have dozed off because Jean shouted out, 'I'm not going to call any more!'

He hobbled out and up to where Jean was. 'It's about time I bet you was asleep, you lazy toad.'

'Just getting my energies up in case I'm called for extra duties!'

'Oh well that's alright then, you can go back to bed again if you want.'

Checker replied, 'No that's okay, I'm ready for any action now.'

'No, not now Rover, calm down. I only called you for as you can see we are entering the wide River Yare. Look over there, do you see those big boats?'

'Yes, is that a big harbour over there then? Are we, can we go over there? It only looks a couple of miles away, maybe less. Come on lets go over.'

Jean said, 'No, I am not sure if we are allowed and I have been coming here for ten years with my parents and not once has my father taken us over there.'

'Well stop the engine then and we can take a longer look. I wish we had brought some bins with us, you sure we can't go over there?'

'No, I am not sure but we are not going over there. No, we will carry on and you can enjoy the scenery. When we get to the other part of the Broads you will like it for it's much bigger and has a lot more going for it.'

Checker replied, 'Right Captain I'll take your word for it, carry on sir, I mean madam!'

'You are not doing yourself any good, more of that kind of remark and you will lose your extra duties!'

Checker tried to imitate an old seaman of long past years, pretending to doff his hat, slightly bowing with his hand to his head saying, 'I beg your pardon sor!' As he backed away, 'I beg your pardon.'

Jean started to smile, then Checker's legs hit the bench seat causing him to lose his balance and he fell backwards onto the seat which had Jean laughing. Checker had to join in with Jean's laughter at the same time saying, 'My day will come you saucy mare!'

Checker stayed where he was seated, looking across the river as Jean had said. It was a beautiful scene, the boats alongside the harbour with the background of white fronted buildings, although it was some distance, with the water in the foreground it looked idyllic. He said, 'Slow the boat down I must get my camera to take a couple of photos, it looks fantastic!'

Jean put the gears to neutral, 'I'll get the camera Hoppy, it won't take a minute.'

As she made her way down to the day cabin she heard Checker saying, 'Cheeky mare!' This brought a smile to her face. Upon returning to the deck she gave Checker the camera telling him that she had heard what he called her.

Checker replied, 'Tooche, I think that's how they say it, I was getting my own back for calling me Hoppy.'

'It's pronounced touché and yes, you were right.'

Jean returned to the steering wheel telling Checker to take his photos then they could carry on. Then she said, 'You have not taken one of me yet, come on take one of me at the wheel. Then I will take one of you sitting on the bench seat with your gammy foot Hoppy!'

'Alright, I'll get my own back you saucy mare, just you see!'

Jean replied, 'Ha, has my little man gone all grumpy again?'

'Come on, let's get these pictures taken then we can be on our way again, but beware, young Stanley Wolf will have his revenge!'

Jean laughed and said, 'When tonight?'

As they reached the tributary they turned left and continued for about ten minutes, they then came to a bend in the river and Checker saw the low bridge that Jean had told him about. As their boat approached he thought that they would not be able to pass through, but Jean had told him they would be able to, but she advised him that the headroom would be about ten inches of clearance.

As the bow started to go under the bridge Checker unconsciously started to duck down. He heard Jean laughing and calling out, 'Scaredy cat!' He answered back, 'I am taller than you and I am not taking any chances.'

As Jean had said they passed under with about a foot to spare. He asked Jean why they had not waited for the tide to go out a bit more, as then they would have had more clearance? She replied, 'As I have said before this boat has a deeper keel, so it is not about headroom but about deeper water and now that we are through I will pull over to that mooring place, tie up and make a cup of tea for us.'

As Jean made her way to the galley Checker asked, 'How about a sandwich then, bacon if you are cooking?'

'You have not long had breakfast.'

He laughed and said, 'I have got to keep my stamina up for extra duties for when I am called upon!'

'You are a dustbin Stanley, you never stop eating!'

After about ten minutes Jean returned with two mugs of tea and the tin of biscuits.

'What no sarnies?'

Jean replied, 'If you want bacon sandwiches Stanley you know where the galley is, and if you want me to be cooking all the time you will have to do your share when I am at the wheel, it's my holiday as well you know!'

'That's alright Duchess I was only joking. This is a fifty-fifty party, I can cook when it's my turn.'

'Good,' Jean replied, 'You can cook lunch today then.'

Checker laughed and said, 'Are you forgetting I am on light duties from being wounded in battle defending your honour!'

Jean laughed, 'I don't know Stanley you can sure come up with the porkies! Anyway after this cuppa you can take over the steering wheel and as for lunch I know of a nice little café further up river that mum and dad used, and from what I can remember the food and the cooking will be far better than yours.'

'Ah, now that's an idea I like. You know I believe this will be one of the best holidays I've had, wait until I tell the boys!' He paused and then said, 'I hope T.J. wrote that letter to the council for Ruby and got the mortgage for our props.'

Jean said, 'Ah, we are on holiday not work so forget it. Look around, it's beautiful, what more do you want?'

'Well, you in bed. Come on drink up, you have got a date with me down below deck!'

She laughed and said, 'Oh you are awful!'

Later, as they were going up river with Checker at the helm, Jean who was sitting forward, turned and looked at Checker. She could see he was in his element, he was probably thinking he was at the helm of a large ship sailing the seven seas. He was quiet and had a slight smile on his face, she thought, if that shop is open next to the café I will buy him one of those captain hats, the one like her father had got. Then she thought about the operation and she hoped it was going alright, she must get some cards and post them. Then she looked over to the river ahead and she saw the small quay over to the right about half a mile ahead. She turned and called to Checker pointing to the quay, 'We will moor up there alright?' He nodded and started to slow the engines down allowing the tide to take them in.

When they had berthed the boat and secured the mooring ropes they made their way to a small esplanade with a few shops and a café. It was open and Jean and Checker studied the menu board outside the café. The main course appeared to be fish.

Checker said, 'I think I will have cod and chips. They say fish helps put lead in your pencil!' He laughed and said, 'I don't know about you though.'

Jean replied, 'Many times I have heard you say that and about other food and drink, do you really believe that?'

'No, but it's a good saying. Come on, let's go in and get some food inside us.'

Jean said, 'Don't forget we need to get some milk, bread and bacon from the grocer's shop on the way back.'

On their way back to the boat they called into the grocer's shop who not only sold food but also items of clothing. Jean said she had not noticed but was rather taken by the hats on sale, most of them in the line of naval type, some with a peak with the word 'Captain' on them. Jean chose one for herself. Checker said, 'Hold on, I will have the one with 'Captain' written on it, after all I am doing most of the driving. You can have the one over there, the one that has 'Bosun', or that one there that says 'H.M.S. Duck'.'

Jean smiled not letting on that she already had the 'Bosun' hat at home which she had purchased with her parents the year before. When they got back to the boat Checker looked around the area and he saw a sign saying hotel one mile further on. He said to Jean, 'How about mooring up here and walking up to that hotel?'

'No need,' replied Jean, 'They have their own moorings at the hotel about fifty yards away, as my father says if you are slightly intoxicated it's not far to fall into bed, not that mother would allow it!'

'The poor sod, he ought to come out with me,' Checker said.

'Oh don't worry about my father, he has his moments but mind you he does get the silent mood from mum. He doesn't worry, we have a talk and that seems to break the ice.'

Checker said, 'Come on let's go!'

As they made their way up the river Checker noticed an inlet to what appeared to be a small lake on the left. He slowed the engine down and steered towards it.

Jean asked, 'What are you doing?'

'I'm only going to have a look at it.'

Jean reminded him that the boat had a deep keel and they didn't know how deep that lake was. Checker said, 'I will only go a little way, don't worry!'

They had only gone about fifty yards when they heard a big bang, then the prop shaft or propeller started shaking the boat.

Jean shouted to Checker, 'You bloody fool, now look what you have done!'

Meanwhile Checker had stopped the engine, he was at a loss for words. All he could say was, 'Don't worry, don't worry!'

Jean just sat there shaking her head and looking at Checker. She could see that he was worried but tried not to show it. He put the boat in reverse, the noise coming from underneath the boat was a loud vibrating, but the boat did slowly reverse into the main canal once again. He put the boat into forward, then once the boat gained motion he put it into neutral letting the flow of the river take them to a mooring.

He called to Jean, 'How far is that hotel?'

Jean said, 'You will see it in a minute, it is just around the bend.'

After Checker had moored the boat he turned to Jean who apart from telling him where the hotel was had said nothing. She looked at him shaking her head and said, 'You have done it once again! You don't think, you just go in saying don't worry. So now what Stanley, have you got an answer?'

He muttered, 'Sorry luv, I thought it would be alright.'

'Well, what are we going to do then?'

He said, 'When the hotel opens I will nip up there to see if they can help us out.'

Jean's reply was, 'Forget it, now wait a minute.' She went down below and got the river maps from the draw and a small book which had the boat owners name and telephone number in it. She went back on deck and gave Checker the telephone number. 'Right, if you go up to the front of the hotel you will see a telephone booth. That is the boatyards number, you can telephone them and tell them where we are and what's happened to their boat. I am going to make myself a cup of tea!'

Jean sat in the day cabin drinking her tea but fuming, wondering if the holiday was now over. Her thoughts stopped as Checker returned to the boat. He appeared to be more relaxed and he had a smile on his face. He said, 'Everything is cushty, the boat owner said they will be out at nine o'clock tomorrow morning. I told him we were just going along and something must have hit the propeller. He did say he could not understand it as the dredger only went through the canal last week!'

Jean's words were, 'I don't think he believed you Stanley. As I told you before, we have a deeper keel so we would have pushed any floating object aside. But our holiday is still on I hope as I have been coming here with my parents and we have never had all the mishaps that we have had. You must be a jinx with boats Stanley! Of all the holidays I have spent on the Broads I believe I will only remember this one. If the man from the boatyard can fix it I will insist that the last two days we spend on the main canals and there will be no more let's try a tributary, pond or lake. We will just relax and enjoy a quiet boating holiday like other people do.'

Checker smiled, 'Come on Jean, where's your spirit of adventure?' But one look at Jean's face made him say as an afterthought, 'Only joking, of course we will stay on the straight and narrow and have a nice quiet holiday, promise!'

'You had better Stanley or you will be sleeping in the single berth!'

'I'll tell you what Duchess, I will make a nice cuppa and a slice of that fruit cake, you just relax and then tonight we will go up to that hotel and I will treat you to a nice slap up meal, alright?'

'Yes that would be nice, but it's a bit pricey. Have you got enough money?'

'Naw that's alright, I have got about a ton. Blimey at Brian's nightclub with entertainment and a meal for two, as you know, only came to forty-five pounds and that's in London! Bloody hell they can't be dear in the sticks!'

Jean said, 'You've got all that money, I only thought you had about twenty pounds. You didn't tell me and here's me going fifty-fifty with all the shopping, you crafty sod!'

Checker laughed, 'You didn't ask me, I would have told you if you had asked just like now!'

'Right Stanley Wolf, tonight I am going to have steak with all the trimmings as well, a nice glass of red wine followed by coffee.' Jean said looking at Checker with a question like look.

'For you Duchess that's no problem and I'll go and make that tea now, alright?'

With that he made his way to the galley with Jean calling after him, 'Stanley you are a villain!'

That night at the hotel they went to a small bar for a drink before their meal. The table had been booked, Jean had a coffee and Checker had a small lager. Checker looked around the bar and remarked that it looked a nice place and as Jean had called it 'expensive'.

Checker turned to Jean, 'Have you had meals here before then?'

'Yes and it was very good. Mother likes this place very much but dad says it is too pricey!'

At that moment a waiter came over to them to let them know their table was ready, but then the waiter said, 'Miss Jean how are you, long time no see! Your mother and father are here too?'

Jean replied, 'No, I am here with my fiancé,' as she looked towards Checker she noticed that he was not smiling, just looking at the waiter, who looked in his late twenties, good-looking. She guessed that Checker was asking himself a few questions like, who is he and was he more than just a friend? Jean was tempted to tease Checker a bit but decided not to, knowing at times he could be a bit volatile.

She turned to the waiter and said, 'Hello Eric, how is your lovely wife and of course your baby daughter, she must be two now.'

Eric replied, 'We are all well thank you and our beautiful little girl is three now. You will see my wife Sally as she is in charge of the restaurant and kitchens and I am in charge of the bars and guests. We are in charge as my parents are away on holiday abroad, they will return after Christmas, then my beautiful wife and daughter will go abroad for a holiday.'

'Where do you go then Eric?' Checker asked as he suddenly brightened up.

'Oh we go to my parent's flat in Spain. We always go there on holiday, it's in mainland a place called Alicante on the coast, the Mediterranean side do you know it?'

Checker paused and then said, 'No I can't say I do, I have heard of it. I am an island man me self, there is always a lot going on there.'

Eric replied, 'We like the quieter life, any how your table is ready, shall we go?'

After Eric left their table Checker was reading the menu when Jean spoke quietly to him saying, 'I'm an island man myself! Ho yes and what one did you go to? You might have been asked.'

Checker replied, 'Well if mummy and daddy didn't have a flat there I doubt he would know, anyway it's dear going abroad!'

Jean laughed, 'Do you realise Stanley, that hundred pounds you have in your pocket would be enough to pay for two separate holidays for two people!'

'Don't be daft, what about air fare ay?'

Jean answered, 'Yes and the air fare is included and if you did not go around trying to buy everything you see you would have some money over.'

Checker looked at Jean, then with a smile he said, 'Alright when we get home you prove it to me and if you are right we will go, mind you I will have to get a passport first.'

Jean answered, 'Right, you are on. But whilst you are waiting for your main passport you can get a temporary one at the post office. You won't be able to back out of this one Stanley! Oh and by the way, what island did you go on your last holiday?' Jean couldn't resist that one just to see Checker's face.

He leaned across the table, 'Tonight you will be keelhauled and walk the plank! But that will be after I have had my evil way with you!'

Jean laughed and said, 'Oh goody!' They both laughed.

Checker said, 'Have you made your mind up what you are going to eat yet?'

'Yes I told you, I am going to have fillet steak and all the trimmings, chips, mushrooms, peas and tomatoes. What are you having?'

'I'll have the same.'

Just as Checker was about to call a waiter, a smart good-looking girl came over but before he could say anything she started talking to Jean. Like old friends he thought to himself, she must be Eric's wife, and he thought how could a bloke like Eric pull a bird like her. He thought, I wouldn't kick that out of bed, blimey you wouldn't think she had a kid, with a body like that. I mean Jean's got a great body and looks but she has not had a kid. But that birds still got everything and she has had a kid.

Jean broke into his thoughts by saying, 'I would like you to meet Sally, Eric's wife, Stanley.'

Checker said, 'Hello, pleased to meet you.'

Sally smiled and said, 'Likewise Stanley, I hope you will like our hotel and visit us more. Now I will go and get your order placed, enjoy!'

She walked off and Checker watched her go, then Jean laughed, 'She's got two legs, a nice bum and a good body, and down Rover because she is married!'

'Sorry love, I was thinking how could a bloke like Eric pull her?

'Well I wouldn't call Eric ugly. Anyway Stanley, I have been thinking about the flat in St James, what are you going to do with it? Are you going to live in it and am I involved in any way? You see I have always thought of us as an item, I hope you do not think I am being presumptuous, but I do have to know.'

'Blimey girl you do know how to knock me back. Firstly, the flat is a stepping stone and an investment. Whether we live in it or not I don't know. Yes, we are an item as you put it and yes, you are and will be involved in everything I do. But, until I have enough money and feel safe my plans are to have a house, detached, four bedrooms with no worries. Is that answer good enough?'

'That's all I wanted to know, to feel safe and no worries as you put it.'

Checker said, 'Right let's forget the soppy talk and enjoy as your mate Sally said.'

The meals were served and while they were eating Sally came over with a bottle of red wine that Checker had ordered. Checker pulled the cork, Sally poured the wine and asked if the meal was alright. Both of them acknowledged that it was good and Sally left. No more was said until the meal was finished and the wine consumed followed by coffee.

As they left the hotel they said goodnight to both Eric and Sally. As they walked back to the boat Jean said, 'Thank you Stanley for a lovely night.'

'Good but I don't want you to go all soppy on me, after what we said. We are still happy-go-lucky with a few laughs and jokes eh?'

Jean laughed and said, 'Yes I wouldn't have it any other way but thank you.'

'Daft.' was Checker's reply.

Next morning, six thirty, Jean woke Checker up saying, 'Come on here's a cup of tea.'

Checker noted that the curtains were still drawn, he looked at his watch, saw what the time was and said, 'Bloody hell Jean, that bloke doesn't come until nine o'clock!'

'What if he comes earlier?' Jean replied.

'He won't!'

'He is not like you Stanley, a nine to five. People that have their own businesses get up early and go to work. I am now going to have a shower and then cook breakfast, course if you want me to come back to bed, and I don't mean for quickie. To laze about in bed and if the man comes early he will no doubt see me in my birthday clothes. Which of course you wouldn't mind?'

Before she could say any more Checker laughed, threw a pillow at her and said, 'Get yourself gone you cheeky hussy, I am the only one to ogle at your beauty!'

'Ho thank you kind sir,' laughing, Jean went to the shower cubicle.

After breakfast they had only just cleared away and washed up when they heard the man come aboard. Jean looked towards Checker then at her wristwatch. The time was twenty past eight. She held both hands out in front of her and smiled. Checker did not need telling, he knew what she was implying. There was a loud knock on the door, as it started to open the man shouted out, 'Is it alright to come in?'

Checker opened the door wider and said, 'Come in, we are sorry to cause you inconvenience, but it was something out of our control. I do hope it is something that is repairable.'

The man said, 'We will soon see, as soon as I get the floorboards up and look at the prop shaft.'

Jean asked, 'Can I get you a cup of tea or coffee?'

The man replied, 'Yes please, a coffee, white with two sugars.'

While Jean was making the coffee he went to the back of the boat, unlocked the padlock and then what looked like a mortice lock. In a small cupboard was a toolbox. He carried it back inside, looked at Checker and said, 'Best keep tools secure, there's a lot of pilfering on the boats especially when holidaymakers like yourselves go off the boat for some shopping or a meal.'

Jean came back with his coffee just as the man had taken up the floorboards. He was looking at the prop shaft and he took the coffee from Jean. Checker said, 'I wonder if that's what happened the other night?'

The man said, 'What's that then?'

Checker then relayed what had happened on their first night. The man smiled and asked where it had happened. Jean then came into the conversation by telling him where. He turned to Checker and asked, 'What happened when you fell down against the boat, what was the noise like, did it sound like two people running?'

Checker replied, 'Yes.'

'Well,' the man said, 'it could have been two people but we do have some nice animals here that live on the Broads. They won't hurt you, they would run away as soon as they saw or heard you.' But the little smile on his face made Jean believe he was, as they say, pulling their legs. The man returned to work on the prop shaft, 'This won't take long, it appears that the mounting on the bearing has come loose.'

Within half an hour they were thanking the man as he said goodbye and that he would see them both in a couple of days. As agreed the last two days they stayed on the main canals. It was quiet and beautiful and Jean joked that both of them would have to wear dark glasses as they spent more time in bed.

Checker laughed and said, 'I will have to phone work up and report sick, it will take me a week to recover!'

155

They returned the boat to the owners and were driving home. Jean asked Checker if he had enjoyed the holiday?

He replied, 'Fantastic, loads of sex and all the problems we had sort of made the holiday didn't it?'

'Well just a bit.' Jean replied.

When they got to Jean's home both parents were there to greet them. Everyone was happy. Checker thanked Jean's parents for the holiday and afterwards Jean relayed all the things that had happened with Checker's driving skills. 'But on the whole it was a lovely holiday!' Jean's father's operation had been a success.

After he had left Jean at her parent's house, driving home he could not get over what a nice holiday they had had. In fact his first holiday had been camping with the scouts when he was a kid but this was his first holiday ever! He had to smile as he thought of a freebie holiday and Jean's parents allowing her to go unchaperoned with a raunchy git like himself. Still he believed that her parents were quite aware, as Jean put it, that they were an item. When he thought of it it gave him a good feeling.

Chapter Eight

SUNDAY MORNING, CHECKER went round to T.J.'s house to see if everything went to plan; the mortgage, the materials for the alterations and of course Ruby's letter to the council. As he was about to knock on the front door it opened. T.J.'s mother was there, she smiled and said, 'Welcome back Stanley!'

As she led him into the lounge she asked him if he had had a nice holiday.

'Fantastic Mrs B I can honestly say the best holiday I have ever had, can't wait to tell Terry.' He said with an enquiring look. T.J.'s mother looked at her watch and said, 'He and his father will most likely have almost finished their round of golf by now, I would venture to say they will be home in about half an hour. Would you like a cup of tea whilst you wait? I was about to make myself one.'

'If it's no trouble Mrs B.' he answered.

She replied, 'No trouble,' and she left to go to the kitchen.

He started to look around the room. He noticed a photograph of T.J. in a gown and mortarboard cap with his parents on a table, well it looked like one of them antique small card tables. It must be worth a few bob. Then looking around the room in general he said to himself, 'Blimey there must be a fortune in gear here, the pictures and the silverware.'

He mentally calculated how much when Mrs B returned and placed a tray on a small coffee table. At the same time she said to Checker, 'You look deep in thought, nothing serious?'

Checker, flustered, answered, 'No, no Mrs B, I was deep in thought about the properties and hoping that everything is okay.'

'I am sure they are, now how was your holiday Stanley? Terry tells me it was a boating one on the Broads.'

As she poured the tea Checker started to tell her about the holiday, how he thought driving a boat was like driving a car and how he had made a few mistakes. He told her about all of the problems which had them both laughing quite loudly. Mrs B was wiping a tear from her eyes and said, 'I don't know Stanley, that's one of the best laughs I've had for years.'

Checker laughed and said, 'That's nothing Mrs B you want to be with us when we really get going.'

She replied, 'No wonder Terry likes you, he seems to be happier and not so studious. Rita is good for him as well, she has a few laughs!'

Just as she said that they heard the car drive up to the garage. She stood up and said 'I think I had better make some more tea,' and she left Checker in the lounge and went to the front door to greet her husband and Terry.

Checker heard Terry say, 'Is Checker here?'

Terry's mother replied, 'He is in the lounge.'

'Hello mate, nice holiday? Got your card, thanks.'

Checker answered, 'Slow down, one question at a time, I had a fantastic time. Jean and I are going again, but it was great once I got used to driving the boat, but before that I did make a few mistakes!'

He went on to relay all of the story of his mishaps which had Terry laughing. Terry's mother and father came into the lounge carrying another tray of tea and cakes. Terry's mother told Checker that she had told father all about the holiday and sequence of events, it was hilarious.

They looked at Terry's father and for once there was not the usual hump, he had a smile on his face, then he said, 'What mother had told me reminded me of myself when I took a motorboat on the water and the same thing had happened to me.' He had tried to drive it like a car.

Terry looked at his father and said, 'Well what happened then?'

He replied, 'Ha, that's another tale!'

Terry's mother said, 'Don't worry Terry, I shall winkle it out of him and I will tell you,' she said with a smile looking at father, who smiled and gave his usual humped look which had everyone laughing.

After tea Terry's parents left them to talk about the properties. Firstly Checker enquired if they had got the mortgage? Did they get the materials? And lastly did T.J. write to the council about Ruby's planning appeal? T.J. answered with a quick, 'Answer is yes to all three. I have a very good repayment mortgage over twenty years, all the materials have been delivered; paint, timber, plasterboard, screws and nails, everything you ordered.'

Checker replied, 'Good, and Ruby's letter?'

Terry gave him a letter which he had sent to the council. Basically it had thanked the council for their reply to the planning application, but his client was saddened by the council's refusal and asked if the council could inform this office of Mr T J Bond of Bowen, Bowen & Bowen to clarify the reasons for refusal. Checker looked at T.J. and said, 'What about in their letter where it said about the road and vehicular access?'

'It's in the file there. I just wanted to give them a little bit more leeway to, as you put it, shoot themselves in the foot.'

'You crafty sod!' Checker answered, 'Anyway, what else have you been doing? I know, alright clever clogs, come on tell me.' Checker smiled, 'You have been cleaning your flat up and doing some painting haven't you?'

T.J. looked at Checker, 'Alright, who told you? Did my mother tell you?'

Checker laughed and pointed to his hair, 'Or is that highlights you are wearing?'

T.J. got up from his chair and went over to the large mirror looking at his hair saying, 'I cannot see any paint.'

'Just checking to see if you have been painting.'

T.J. laughed, 'Well Rita and I have nearly finished one room, Cliff has done one room in his flat and Curly, well he's almost finished two rooms in his flat!'

At that moment Mrs Bond came into the lounge to ask Checker if he was staying for dinner. He replied, 'I'm sorry Mrs B but I have promised mum I will be home for dinner as she has also invited Jean, as much as I would like to stay.' Checker spread his hands.

T.J.'s mother said, 'That's aright Stanley, don't worry but you are welcome anytime.'

'Thank you Mrs B that's great, I'll take you up on that some-time.' Then he turned to T.J. 'Are you going to the flats this afternoon?'

T.J. nodded, 'Yes, Rita is coming over for dinner and then after we will go over.'

'Good. I have a suggestion to make to all.'

'What's that?'

Checker replied, 'I'll see you there this afternoon.'

When T.J. and Rita arrived at St James they could see by the cars parked down the side of the road that everyone was there. As they walked around to the front Checker was on the top step by the front door. He beckoned them in. As they walked inside T.J. could see that Cliff and Curly were there. Checker said, 'Right,' as they went into the front room, 'I have a suggestion to all,' having got their attention he said, 'We are all mates yes?'

Looking at them they all agreed, 'Right I suggest that we all work together in one flat at a time, that way they will all be done quicker. But if we carry on as we are now it will take longer. Also you seem to have forgotten the rewiring, plumbing, gas works and the other things that will possibly mess up some of the work you have already done.'

Cliff said, 'Right, I agree,' the others answered yes to the idea.

Checker said, 'Right, Curly appears to have got the most done so we will start there. Now I know of an electrician, his name is Reg. He is good and I believe we can get him cheap as long as we let him live in one of the flats whilst he is working. Don't forget it is a complete rewire of four separate flats with their own fuseboards.'

'What is he then an old dosser?' asked Curly.

'No, he is a person who has had a problem, he appears to have got over it, I don't know for sure alright?'

'Then what's his problem, we have a right to know?' Cliff said.

'Right, I will tell you but I must have your promise that you will not mention it to him, of course that's if I can get him. If I do he will half the cost. I first met Reggie when I was in the early start of my apprenticeship. As you know my parents were not well off so at weekends and on odd days and holidays I used to work for a builder to earn extra money so that I did not and was not a drain on my parent's purse. Well we used to do a lot of work for a property developer, he owned half of Thornton Heath, some places in Mayfair, Lewisham, Norwood and more and so Les and his firm were always working. That is where I first met him. He used to do all the electrical work for the property owner and some for Les. I found out he always kipped down in the houses he was working in, then Les told me why. He said that Reg was always a happy man, married with two children, a daughter and a son. He owned his own house as well, paying the mortgage off.'

'Well one day he went to work and forgot to take something with him so he drove back home and he caught his wife in bed with the milkman. The long and short of it all is that his wife told him that she did not want him and he agreed to let them live in his house for the sake of the children, so he still pays the mortgage.'

Cliff said, 'Bloody hell, I would have kicked their arses out of it!'

Mary said, 'What about the children then?'

It went a bit quiet for a moment and then T.J. said, 'He can kip down in my flat and there is a cooker and a kitchen, he can use that.'

Jean said, 'Well put T.J. I think dad's got an old camp bed in the garage, I will get that.'

Curly said, 'If he likes it he will move in. What do you say to that T.J.?'

Checker said, 'He won't do that. Once work is done he will move on.'

'I'd better warn you another thing about Reg.'

Curly moaned, 'Oh don't tell us he is a person that likes boyfriends!'

Checker answered, 'Your mind Curly. First he is going to move in and then have boyfriends. No, what I was going to say was he likes a laugh but unfortunately his laugh goes like hee hee hee. The first time I heard it I was in a café with Les and Reg. Well Les is always one for jokes and he gets Reg laughing. It's not long before everybody in the café is laughing at him as well. He has a very high pitched laugh like a soprano, in fact he could sing. I went to a working man's club with him and his wife, we were there about an hour just sitting at one of the tables having a quiet drink. The compère on the stage introducing various acts said to the people in the club "how about a bit of our Gracey then?" Just as the compère said "come on Les" his wife leaned across the table and told him to stay where he was as she didn't want him showing her up. Les said "it's alright" and got up to go to the stage. His wife went to a different part of the club. I just sat there and listened, the band started to play and Les started to sing.'

'The song was Sally and if you closed your eyes and listened you would have sworn that it was being sung by Gracey Fields. When he had finished the crowd clapped asking for more, but he said "later" and got off the stage and came over to me. I told him his wife went to the other part of the club and he said "she will be back". I then asked him how he could sing like that and he told me that when he was very young he sang in the Roman Catholic church choir and he had been the boy soprano, that was when he found out he could impersonate Gracey Fields. Anyway back to now. I will try and get Reggie, all agreed?'

Everyone agreed.

'Well the plumbing, I think me and Curly can do that,' said Checker looking at Curly.

Curly said, 'Piece of cake.'

'Now the cleaning and painting is down to the girls. T.J. and Cliff, tomorrow I will get in touch with the gas board for their input. So let's get started!'

Everybody looked at each other and it appeared that they had accepted that Checker had taken charge and they all started work at their allotted jobs.

He was right, the work went well. It had only been a week. Nights, Saturday mornings when Palace were at home and Sundays. They had finished Curly's flat, staying in the same house they were starting on Cliff's. Checker and Curly had finished what plumbing work had to be done in his flat and were halfway with the studding dividing the two flats. Next week Reg the electrician was going to start. Everyone was looking forward to him starting and meeting him. By now the girls were working together and had become closer. There had been a few laughs, such as one person had left the room and they had painted the underside of that person's paintbrush handle. There were a lot of other jokes played on each other but nobody took offence. If anyone had picked an argument with them there would have been war but somehow the girls took it upon themselves to make Reggie feel most welcome. They bought him cups, plates, cutlery and other pots and pans, a few tins of food. Curly and Cliff did make a few comments but the girls soon put them right. The biggest laugh had been when T.J. worked and walked around all day with an 'L' sticker stuck on his back.

Rita and Jean had planned that Rita would ask T.J. for a hug as she felt a bit tired. As T.J. Responded, Jean walked up to them and patted T.J. on the back saying "come on, there's plenty of time for that". Later there were comments from the others but he did not twig a thing.

162

Monday night, five o'clock everyone had turned up. About half past there was a knock at the door and someone was calling. Almost everybody went to the door but the girls got there first. There was quite a bit of chatter and laughing, then the girls returned to where everybody was. They had in their company a man who was about five foot six in height, rather stout, grey hair with a big smile on his face.

Checker stepped forward, held out his hand and said, 'Thanks for coming mate, it looks like you have met the girls.' He gave a big smile and said, 'Yes and they are lovely!'

Checker started to introduce everyone then Curly could not resist making a joke as he shook hands with Reg. 'Here's the man that will put a bit of spark into the house!'

He looked around to see if anyone was laughing but he was met with silence. Mary looked coldly at him, turned to Reg and took his hand and said, 'Come on Reg, me and the girls have got a bit of a surprise for you.'

Off they went leaving them looking at Curly who told them it was only meant as a joke. Checker laughed, 'I would not like to be in your shoes tonight mate!'

About twenty minutes later they all returned, Reg was beside himself. He said thank you to everyone and more so to Checker who replied, 'It's all the girls doing!'

Reg said, 'Did you know that I will only be doing the work at nights and weekends? I will still be doing my main work during the day time.'

'That suits us,' Checker replied, 'but how do you like your digs?'

Reg answered, 'It's lovely, thank you.'

'Don't thank me, it's T.J. and Rita who said "it has two benefits". Reg, you will be looking after our flat as well so you are welcome.'

Checker said, 'Alright mates, let's get started and I will tell Reg what we want.'

Everybody started to carry on where they left off the night before, whilst Checker went off with Reg describing in detail separate consumer units for each flat and the mains fuse from the electricity company. Two power points to each room except the kitchens where there would be four double power points. Reg asked, 'You want me to supply materials then?'

Checker answered, 'Yes please Reg. You will know what is required and we won't so it will be easier for you.'

'Right. I will take some measurements and work out what materials I need.'

Checker answered, 'Well I will leave you to it, but keep your ears pinned back as we will be having a cup of tea soon, I will give you a shout.'

Half an hour later they called 'tea's ready' and by the time Reg walked into the room almost everybody was sitting on the floor with their tea and a piece of cake. As Rita gave Reg his tea Sue opened a tin and gave it to Reg. There were some ham sandwiches and cake saying, 'I hope you like ham,' but before she could say anymore Reg answered, 'Yes, that's kind of you, thank you.'

Cliff interrupted by saying, 'Where's my sandwiches?'

Sue turned to Cliff, 'You will be getting supper when you get home tonight and Reg won't unless you want to nip up to the chippy.'

She turned to Reg and said, 'Take no notice of him he is only joking!'

Everybody started to laugh at Cliff who said, 'She's right, I was only joking'

Sue replied, 'You better had or it could be cold tonight!'

The rest of them went, 'whoo!' then started laughing which caused Reg to join in his laughing as Checker had already told them was true which had everyone in fits.

After about five minutes they had stopped. Rita said, 'Bloody hell Checker I nearly wet myself!'

Jean said, 'Me too!'

Cliff turned to Reg and said, 'Put those sandwiches down for later, I'm going up to the chippy. Will cod, chips and peas do you mate?'

Reg stuttered, 'Yes please.'

Cliff turned saying, 'Won't be long,' and off he went.

Reg closed the tin box and looked around at everybody. His looks were more or less questioning is it alright Checker? Checker laughed and spoke, 'Looks like you have struck gold there me old mate, getting Cliff to put his hand in his pocket.'

As he turned to look at the others he winked at them to say that's alright ain't it mates? They all answered yes. Sue said, 'I have to take his temperature when he gets back, I hope he is alright,' which caused a lot of laughing.

With Reg working on the properties, the gas board supervisor had been to take some measurements and had promised a quick response. The work had been getting finished fast with the continuity and repetitive of the cleaning and painting. The girls joked about starting and forming a decorating company.

Well, come Saturday Palace would be playing Southampton at home. It should be a walkover they all thought but it would make a break from the properties. The girls were going shopping, Reg would be the only one there but whether he would be working or not only he knew.

Cliff brought an old T.V. from the second-hand shop in Cheery Orchard Road. The owner repaired them and it only cost him fifteen nicker and it worked well so Reg watched that now and again, probably at night when he finished work. But who cared, the work was really progressing fast. They had just started in the next house and Reg reckoned he would join them in the next day or two. That night they all left telling Reg they would see him on Monday as they were having the weekend off.

As T.J. drove home after dropping Rita off he thought, or mused as some would say, about how in roughly three months he had become a property developer. The properties were worth a considerable amount more than they had paid for them, all down to Cliff's mother who was a very good friend of Mr and Mrs Bashford. And they just wanted to give Cliff a good start in life and as luck would have it the rest of them as well. With Checker's knowledge of the construction trade and his contacts, such as Reg, then getting trade discounts by pretending to be a building company. They borrowed three thousand pounds via a mortgage and so far they had spent two hundred and eighty-five pounds, but they still had to pay Reg, the gas company and S.E.E. Board.

Saturday: Checker called round at one o'clock to collect T.J., then as they were driving to Thornton Heath he said that Reg would like some money to cover the cost of the materials. 'He asked me to tell you what he wants but said it has to be cash T.J.'

'Just let me know how much and I will get it for him, but at the moment I just hope this match is going to be good, Southampton are not a bad team and you just never know.'

Checker laughed, 'What are you trying to do put a jinx on the game? We will skate it!'

They parked the car in Wilfred Road and as they walked towards the ground that old feeling started to course through T.J. in anticipation; the adrenalin pumping away. Checker must have had the same feeling. T.J. found that the both of them were walking quite fast. When they got to the grounds Cliff and Curly were already there in the usual place.

There was the usual buzz of noise around the ground, mostly talking, a few shouts of Eagles, then Checker said, 'Hello! I don't see Hookey. There's a lot of his mob and also a few older ones but I wonder what has happened to him?'

Cliff turned to T.J., 'Haven't you told him then?'

Checker looked at T.J., 'Alright, what haven't you told me then, aye?'

'Oh I thought you knew, it was in the papers.'

'No, I don't know. What was in the papers?'

T.J. then started to explain why Hookey was not at the match. 'You remember that fracas at the Norbury Hotel? Course you remember.'

'Course I remember. I was there wasn't I?'

'Give him a chance Checker!'

Cliff said, 'Yes alright, what happened then?'

T.J. started again, 'Well the police arrested him and when they got him to the police station they also found out he was on probation for the same action of disturbing the peace. So when he went to court the judge gave him three months so there you have it right.'

Checker answered, 'Cor that's a turn up, when did he go down then?'

'Two weeks ago.'

'Did your firm have anything to do with it then?' Checker enquired.

'No!' T.J. Said. 'Now we can get on talking about football and hopefully watch some.'

Checker laughed and said, 'You know T.J., getting you to talk is like drawing teeth sometimes, especially when it's about the law. Loosen up mate, it's no big deal, enjoy yourself! I know what it is, the painting and the other work is getting to you isn't it?'

T.J. answered, 'Sorry mate I suppose it is. I am finding I am not able to concentrate at work as much and it is a bit worrying.'

'Why don't you go and see the quack and he will give you something to unwind, won't he?' Checker said looking at Cliff.

'Don't worry T.J., relax, you don't have to do painting and cleaning every night straight from work. Take a night off and take Rita out for a meal and a bit of the other, that always works for me,' Checker said which had everyone laughing.'

'T.J., I don't have to pay for a meal for it, there you go, see, relax!' Cliff answered.

The subject changed as the teams started to run out onto the pitch. As the roar went up so that old tingle started to cause that sensuous feeling of anticipation, of expectancy of a match of football. T.J. had forgotten his problems, he realised why he was getting a bit up tight. This was the first football march for nearly three weeks plus working in the houses with Rita, neither of them had any knowledge of what they were doing, it was like the blind leading the blind. They were working hard but getting nowhere. It was easy for Cliff and Curly, they had a certain amount of knowledge on decorating but T.J. had not realised how he had come to so reliant on Checker on things outside of the life he had chosen. Coming into the real world as Checker would say.

T.J. was taken away from his thoughts with Checker saying, 'Come on T.J., you are not still moping are you. Bloody hell this is a football match. You want to watch it mate or you will going to the funny farm soon!'

T.J. laughed and said, 'Thanks mate I have just been thinking what an idiot I have been and it needed someone like you to take me out of it. I realise now, thank you.'

'That's alright mate the bill is in the post!' T.J. laughed for now Checker was back, work was going well and fast but he still found it hard to lift himself.

T.J. decided to take Rita off on holiday for a week, that would breathe some life back into him, to get away from law courts and painting. T.J. turned to Checker and told him, he replied, 'Good, it knackered me but boy was it worth it!'

The conversation was cut short with a lot of shouting then a groaning sound as the referee had blown his whistle for a penalty against Palace. It all went quiet as the Southampton player placed the ball, walked back, then ran forward and kicked the ball which flew straight into the right hand corner of the goal. There was a lot of booing, shouts saying the ref is a wanker and a lot of other names not repeatable, but somehow it livened up the game. The Palace players were forcing the pace, chasing every ball they were aggressive. If a Southampton player had the ball, they would run right through him. Palace could play forceful football, some would say it was dirty but it got results and it did as their centre-forward had scored, the eruption of noise was unbelievable, deafening, the shouts of 'easy, easy' echoing around the ground.

At last the cheering had abated, but the fans were still shouting for more. At half-time the score was still one- one but the expectancy of more goals was high. The four were all laughing and talking about some of the highlights of the first half, when Checker changed the subject, 'Er, T.J. is going on holiday.'

'About time', Cliff answered, 'All that paperwork in your office and the courts, then coming home to do the painting would have sent me loopy ages ago!'

Checker asked, 'Where are you going, anywhere nice?'

'Don't know yet, but abroad most likely, Spain or Morocco.'

Just then the teams started to return to the pitch. The home supporters were baying for the team to play and score goals, the noise was like a resonant tumultuous sound on the ears. T.J. could hardly hear himself speak, he was shouting at Checker who could not hear him, for he just laughed, put his hands up pointing to his ears and shook his head. T.J. had been to Palace football matches before but never heard such a noise. God help them if they score.

The game restarted. The football was fierce from end to end.

The Palace supporters were screaming, shouting, whistles and hooters were being blown, the din was unbelievable. The Palace players were responding, they were fighting for every ball. From the start of the second half Palace were in the Southampton half of the field, they were giving no quarter. Then Palace scored. Along with the rest of the jumping up and down and punching the air, shouting, laughing, T.J. forgot myself and punched Checker on his arm. Thankfully he made a playful display, imitating a boxer squaring up for a fight.

T.J. realised that was what he had been missing, a break from the humdrum of life. He thought, I will take a break and go to

Morocco, the Hotel Rif. T.J. had been there with his parents and liked it. It was in Tangiers, right opposite the beach, Churchill used to go there. T.J. thought that was why his father took them. T.J. turned to Checker and told him.

Checker replied, 'That's great, I only wish I could go with you, but my boss would not wear it, but I will do you a favour.'

Just as Checker was about to say, Southampton scored a goal, now making it two goals each. The home fans were going bananas. T.J. did not see why but Curly and Cliff were angry, evidently one of the Southampton players had impeded their goalkeeper which allowed his team-mate to score. Neither the referee or linesmen had seen the infringement, so the goal was given. The Eagle mob were going mental. They were rampaging around, the supporters nearest to them were quickly moving away but they were turning all their venom towards the match officials and Southampton players.

Curly said, 'We had better be careful when we leave, there might be a war on unless Palace can score again!'

The noise subsided. You could detect an undercurrent of impending danger. T.J. looked towards the police area, you could see the Palace security getting themselves ready. All of a sudden Palace had been awarded a penalty. The crowd stopped. There was hush around the ground. Everybody was looking towards the other end of the pitch. The Palace centre-forward placed the ball on the spot and walked back his usual six paces, the referee blew the whistle. The centre-forward ran up and kicked the ball hard towards the goal. The keeper threw himself to the right and parried the ball away. As he did so there was a groan of despair, but then the Palace winger ran in very quickly and kicked the loose ball back into the goal. He had scored! The noise from the home crowd was tremendous, the four of them were shouting and laughing, it was surreal, like unbelievable, not true, but it was.

Walking down to the café for their usual tea and sandwiches T.J. turned to Checker, 'What was you going to say about doing me a favour?'

'Ah that, well we have all noticed working on the houses was getting to you so I approached the rest of the team and asked them if they had any gripe about me bringing someone in to help with your flat? They all said no but now that you are going on holiday it will cost you about twenty-five soves, cos we will be doing your bit as well, what do you say, ay? Don't forget he will be covering for you and Rita, he is a star decorator!'

'Alright I agree, if he does our colour schemes, he does not move in and you monitor his work.'

'Right, for a best mate I'll do it but if you was a client it would cost you. I'll give shades a bell tonight alright?'

Curly interrupted, 'Who the bloody hell is shades and what's wrong with him?'

'No', laughed Checker, 'He's alright, it's just that he wears sunglasses, winter and summer, he thinks it makes him look the man.'

Cliff laughed, 'More like an idiot!'

Checker replied, 'No he is very good-looking with or without the glasses. He does narfe pull the birds, he's got the chat to go with it.'

'If he starts to chat up my Sue, he will be doing it between thick lips.' Cliff answered.

'No, he will be alright, he does respect mates birds, it's the loose ones he chases.'

Cliff said, 'Alright, are we all agreed?'

Everyone was in favour.

Cliff said, 'Right Checker, give the sunglasses kid a bell!'

They sat in the café talking about the game, suggesting what players should be dropped, who was the worst player, when Cliff turned to talk to T.J. about Morocco. 'What was it like? Can they understand English?'

T.J. said, 'Yes, a lot of them can speak many languages. Morocco was occupied by the English, French and Spanish. Their country was known as the gateway to the East, the saying where East meets West. There are, apart from the Arabs, many people of different nations who live there. I have been there three times with my parents, there are even Americans living there. My father tells me that there are a lot of villains from various countries that live there, but they don't step out of line as if they do the Moroccans, who have them monitored, deal with them severely, put them in prison for a year or two then deport them back to their own countries. My father tells me that the prisons in England are like hotels compared to theirs.'

Curly said, 'I've heard there are a lot of drugs to be had there.'

'I have heard there is a lot of smuggling of contraband, possibly drugs as well, but I can honestly say I have never heard or seen people using or selling drugs. I found Tangiers beautiful. The local people are good and I used to like walking around the covered markets. The Bazaars, mother always paid a visit to a perfumery, as I recall it was somewhere in the Medina but there is always somebody who will guide you for a small fee. Another place I used to like going to was the Kasbah. It was spellbinding. In some parts you can hold your arms out and almost touch the walls on either side of the houses and as you look upwards they seem to get closer. It's very busy with traders trying to sell you goods, it's magic!'

Checker said, 'What's that stinky stuff like, is it any good?'

'Well mother says it's the best, you see they sell the pure oil perfume and it is far cheaper than what you pay for back home, and the stuff you buy here is three times as high and is diluted by seventy-five per cent, so mother says to buy pure oil perfume.'

'Cor, I'll have some of that Dior, my Jean likes that and I was wondering what to get her for Christmas.'

Curly said, 'I'll have some of that.'

'And me!' butted in Cliff, 'What else has this place got going for it?'

'Well there are a lot of other towns, villages, seaports and markets, it's a big country. You can take a trip up to the Atlas Mountains and to Casablanca, to Marrakech that's a popular place, but my father used Tangiers as a home base. You could fly across to Gibraltar, the fare was quite cheap and it only took about twenty minutes. You could also go to Spain for the same cost, or you could cross into Spain at the border with Gibraltar. It has so much going for it. You are not stuck in one place or one country.'

'Christ T.J. you sound just like a holiday rep. If we didn't know better we would have said you was one!'

Curly asked what they were all doing that night. They looked at each other and more or less said taking the girls out.

Curly suggested, 'Look, we have all worked hard on the houses, why don't we all, as well as the girls, go to Brian's for the night. I'm sure if Checker gives him a bell he could fix it. We could pay the bill out of the fund. It will be three hundred at the most and the girls deserve it, what do you think?'

Cliff asked T.J., 'Well can we, you know what's in the bank, what do you think?'

T.J. replied, 'On the last count we had just over two thousand six hundred but Reg wants some to cover the cost of materials. I think we can afford it, plus we all deserve it, so yes!'

'Good, the banker says yes,' Cliff looked at Checker and said, 'There is a phone over there, go on give Brian a bell then.'

When Checker came back to the table he looked a bit sad and shook his head saying, 'Sorry mates but Brian said . . .' he stopped for a minute looking at them, then said, 'Yes,' and he started laughing, 'Cor, you ought to have seen your faces!'

Curly said, 'You sod, I'll get you for that!'

They arranged to be at Brian's for eight thirty.

As Checker and T.J. made their way to Wilfred Road to pick up the car and were driving home T.J. said, 'You had us all going in the café.'

Checker laughed, 'Great wasn't it, the look on your faces.'

'Don't forget Curly's promise to pay you back!'

'Don't worry, I'll keep an eye open for one of his practical jokes then after a couple of days he will forget all about it.'

As Checker dropped T.J. off at home, he arranged for him and Jean to come to T.J.'s house at eight o'clock and to leave by taxi at eight fifteen. 'See you then,' he said and drove off.

T.J. walked into the house. Mother called out from the lounge, 'Terry!'

He walked into the lounge and saw Rita. His mother started to pour him a cup of tea. Rita asked if the football match was any good and if Palace had lost again!

With a little laugh T.J. replied, 'No, it was fantastic and we won, but I was going to invite you out tonight to the nightclub, on second thoughts, mother, have you seen my little black diary. The lads have booked a table for eight people so.'

Mother replied, 'Oh I threw that out long ago, looks like you will have to take Rita!'

'Oh well I suppose so!' Mother then turned to Rita, 'You'd better telephone your parents for you will most likely stay over tonight and of course stay for dinner tomorrow.'

They both looked at T.J. who said, 'I think I have just lost, game set and match!'

They both laughed. T.J. then told mother and Rita of his plans to take time off and tomorrow go to a holiday agency to see if he could book up to go to the Hotel Rif. T.J. felt he needed a break away from work and the house painting.

Mother said, 'Good for you, I have noticed you have not been so happy of late, and always tired and that's not right for a young man. I know you like Morocco and you can get me some of my favourite perfume!'

'Yes of course I will.'

'Are you going alone or are you taking somebody with you?' Mother asked.

He replied, 'I was thinking of taking a friend but I don't think they can get the time off work or that they have a valid passport!'

Mother turned to Rita and asked, 'Can you get the time off work and you do have a valid passport don't you?'

Rita said, 'Yes, but your grumpy old son has not asked me yet, or should I say begged me to go with him!'

They both laughed and mother said, 'You lost that one.'

Then Rita came over to him and kissed him on the cheek. 'Thank you kind sir, I will go to Morocco with you, as you never know I might meet a rich Arab!'

Mother changed the subject asking what time they were going to the club. T.J. replied, 'Stanley is coming around at eight, so I want to book a cab for eight fifteen as we are all meeting at eight thirty.'

'Then the pair of you had better start getting ready, come on chop chop. I will telephone for a cab for you at eight fifteen, you'll be in your usual bedroom Rita but please telephone your parents first.'

Rita turned and said, 'Thanks mum!'

They both smiled and mother put her hand on Rita's back and said, 'Hurry along now.'

T.J. looked at them. He did not know until now how close they had become. He just stood there looking at mother and she smiled at him and said, 'Come along you two, and Terry stop standing there gawping as Stanley will be here soon!'

T.J. answered, 'Right,' then went up the stairs to get a shower and a change of clothes.

When T.J. came back downstairs mother, father and Rita were in the lounge all talking. Father appeared to have been told about the plans for he was telling Rita all the do's and don'ts of

Morocco, how to say thank you, which in their language is pronounced shookran and no is la, tea is shy. Then he turned to T.J. saying, 'You are off to Tangiers then? A good choice my boy now take good care of Rita, those Arabs can be a bit funny at times.'

Mother laughed, 'I don't know, you do exaggerate at times dear, you'll frighten Rita before she gets there.'

T.J. said, 'Don't worry mother I am sure I will get a good price for her in the covered market, you know she wanted to meet a rich Arab!'

T.J. ducked a playful punch from Rita which had everybody laughing.

At that moment the front door bell sounded, mother went to the door and T.J. heard her making Checker and Jean welcome. As they came into the lounge father greeted Stanley warmly then said to Jean, 'It is very nice to meet you, my wife and I have heard so much about you. Stanley has also told us about your boating holiday and some of the hazards you both had to overcome.'

Jean replied, 'Thank you, I am very pleased to meet you and our holiday was nice but not on a boat!'

They looked at Checker who shrugged his shoulders, 'That's a promise Duchess!'

T.J.'s father said to Checker, 'It's a pity you are not going to Morocco as well, just to keep an eye on Terry!'

'That's alright Mr B, he can look after himself, anyway Rita will keep tabs on him.'

At that moment the door bell rang and mother went to answer the door. She called to them that the taxi had arrived and said, 'Goodbye enjoy yourselves!' T.J. checked to see that he had the cheque book on him then left to go to the club.

When they entered the club Cliff and Curly were already there with Mary and Sue. Brian hurried over to make them welcome gushing over the girls telling them how pretty they looked and how nice it was to see them again. Checker remarked, 'And what about me Brian!' and he laughed.

Brian waved his hand and with a smile said, 'Hush Stanley, you naughty boy!'

This did cause a bit of merriment, with Cliff and Curly clapping their hands saying, 'Well put Brian!'

'You boys, no wonder I look forward to seeing you all, but you do tease. Now Stanley, Terry, what drinks do you want and for your lovely girls, yes?'

T.J. replied, 'I apologize Brian, Checker and I will have the same as Clifford and Gordon, the girls?'

T.J. looked to Jean and Rita who turned to Brian and told him what drinks they wanted, then as they sat at the table Cliff leaned towards T.J. and said, 'Are we to go à la carte or?'

'For food we always do! If you are referring to Champagne, that is for all shareholders to agree. For I cannot take it upon myself to lavishly be extravagant with the shareholders funds.'

Checker and Curly laughed. Curly said he would do for him if they ever landed up before the Beak. Cliff joined in the laughing, pointing at T.J. and saying, 'Right we take that as a yes.'

Brian came over with their drinks and he enquired if everything was alright. He asked if they wished to look at the menus or were they having their usual. 'I know the boys always have steak but what do my lovely girls require?'

Once again they wanted Turbot.

'And wine?' he said with a smile.

Cliff answered, 'We will have the Bordeaux.'

Brian smiled and said 'Ah! I do believe I have awakened your taste buds to a beautiful wine?'

Then looking at the girls, Mary said to Brian 'We will leave the choice to you, we are sure that the one you choose will be a good choice.'

'Mai oui, you can be assured it will be.' And with a smile and a slight wriggle of his hips he left to go to the kitchen to place the order.

Then the talk turned to the flats and the progress they had made. Checker was asked when he believed it would be completed? His reply was he believed another two weeks and that was including Reg and Shades starting next week, so that was a bonus, and the Gas Board were also starting next week. Reg was dealing with S.E.E. Board, so yes, within two weeks, three at the latest.

They were all looking at each other and Checker said, 'That is of course if you lot don't slacken off!' Everyone had a feeling of relief or of achievement to know within three weeks they would become owners of four large flats, complete and ready for use. The moment was broken by Brian returning to their table asking if everything was all right and did they want any more drinks? They looked at Brian, some of them, especially the girls started to laugh. Brian held his hands out 'Have I said something wrong?'

Cliff said, 'No, not at all.' Then Cliff explained what they were laughing at.

'Sudden realization of a project we have all been working on has more or less come to fruition, so bring two bottles of Champagne please and a glass for yourself to join in a toast with us on the success of our endeavours and we all insist you join us in this toast for we do consider you and your partner our friends.'

Brian smiled, 'I do not usually imbibe whilst I am at work, but for my friends I will take but one small glass with you all. What was your project?'

So Cliff explained in detail what they had been doing, with that Brian exclaimed, 'Ha! That's why I have not seen so much of you, well congratulations to you all! I will get the Champagne for you.'

After the Champagne toast to each other and remembering a few of the mishaps and jokes played on each other during the work, the girls all went on to the dance floor leaving their men to talk shop.

Checker said to T.J. that he wanted to accompany him when he went to the holiday agency because he knew of a mate of his that worked in one. 'You never know you could get a better deal.'

Curly laughed, 'I don't know Checker, you seem to know everybody! Wheeling and dealing, you're in the wrong game, you would make a fortune up Petticoat Lane. I can just picture you standing by your stall in the markets shouting the odds!!'

'That's not a bad idea, I could just do it on Saturday mornings.' Checker replied laughing, turning to T.J., 'Right, I'll come round your house tomorrow eleven o'clock okay?'

'Yes that will be fine.'

Cliff spoke up, 'If you do go to Tangiers you could look up an old mate of mine, well a work mate. He was good at his work but his permit run out and he wrote to us telling that he had got a job at the Hotel Rif in the bar.'

'Is that true or are you having a joke?' T.J. asked.

'No straight up, his name is, ah, now what was it? I remember it is Mustapha-La-Leky.'

'What was it?' he asked.

By this time the girls had returned to the table so everybody was listening. Cliff said, 'Look you got a pen and a note pad?'

'Yes.'

'Right, I will spell his name out to you and you write it down, ready?

Right its spelt: M.U.S.T.-A.V. - A. - L.E.A.K. got it?'

T.J. said, 'Yes.'

'Then what does it say then?'

'Must Av A Leak', he looked up and everybody was looking at him.

Cliff said, 'Go on then,' pointing, 'The toilets are over there T.J.'

All of them started laughing. T.J. just sat there for a moment, then with a little laugh said, 'You sod Cliff, I'll get you for that!'

Rita leaned to T.J., gave him a kiss on the cheek, 'They're horrible! Take no notice of them, I won't laugh!' Then looking at the others she burst out laughing which caused everybody to start laughing again including T.J.

Just at that moment Brian came to the table, 'My friends are quite happy, yes?'

Cliff answered, 'Yes, thank you Brian. Terry hopes to be going to Morocco for a holiday so I was just teaching him some of the Moroccan sayings.'

He replied, 'Oh! How nice, my partner and I go there quite often. You know it quite well Clifford?'

'No, just the once.'

Brian said, 'It's a pity, Morocco is a beautiful country, you should go there more often. But my friends, I digress, I came to tell you your meals are ready and I will serve now.'

Off he went, then it was T.J.'s turn to turn the screw by saying, 'Shall I tell Brian one of your Moroccan sayings Clifford?'

Checker said, 'Go on tell him a swear word. Say Cliff said it means please!'

'Unfortunately I don't know any!' T.J. said.

Cliff replied, 'Alright you two, don't forget Checker, you will be on your own next week!'

'Oh no I won't. Jean will be with me and Shades and Reg.' They all laughed and just at that moment Brian appeared with the heated trolley and their meals. Once they were served Brian fussed around the girls, pouring their wine.

Mary tasted her wine and told Brian his choice of wine was very nice. Brian thanked them and said 'Enjoy my friends, bon appetite.' Then left them to eat as usual, no words were spoken.

The food was sumptuous. T.J. believed that Brian's partner must have been a top chef in a big night club or hotel in London.

Not once had his cooking or presentation been below standard. He believed the cooking was equal if not better than the meals at father's club.

The table had been cleared by Brian with the help of one of the waiters; the friends started to enjoy the rest of the evening. T.J. even got up to have a dance with Rita without being asked. T.J. somehow thought it must be the lifting of the stress of worrying about work and painting or subconsciously knowing he was going on holiday. It might have been the Champagne but he did not believe so after only having three glasses.

The night went well, every one of them was happy. Whether it was the 'nigh' completion of the flats that had them all relaxed, plenty of dancing, telling of jokes and the mickey taking of each other, of the mistakes made at work on the flats but the mood of the little group was buoyant. It was nearly one o'clock when T.J. looked around the club. They were the only ones left. It was agreed that they should all call it a night. Cliff signalled to Brian for the tab. Brian came over and gave Cliff the bill. He glanced at it then passed it to T.J., turning to Brian he thanked him for a nice meal and that he catered for them once again second to none. T.J. handed him the cheque and thanked him for a lovely evening and asked could he please organize two taxi cabs for them?

'For my special friends of course and thank you.'

Sunday morning on the dot Checker arrived as promised at eleven o'clock. Mother as usual made him welcome and within five minutes Checker had her laughing. They both chatting away to each other. T.J. believed mother was fascinated by the casual way he talked, sprinkled with a few cockney sayings. Rita and T.J. were just sitting there listening. In the end T.J. said, 'Are we going to the holiday agency then?'

Checker replied, 'All right mate, ready when you are. I'm just saying hello to your mum.'

Mother turned to Checker. 'Nice to see you Stanley, you're welcome any time.'

'Thanks Mrs B, we will be back by one thirty.'

'You will stay for dinner Stanley?'

'Lovely Mrs B, lovely.' He turned to T.J., 'Got your cheque book?' He nodded. 'Come on then, see you later Mrs B.'

As they drove towards Croydon T.J. said to Checker, 'Do you know if your mate's at work today and will the agency be open?'

'Course it will. If he gets four or five punters it will be worth it and makes his day. He is the manager so he will be the only one working. The other staff will be on a day off.'

Checker parked at the back of Kennards, not far from the pub his other friends used. As they walked along the road he turned to T.J. 'There you are, come on.'

They went into the front entrance. There was a black person talking to someone on the phone. He looked up and waved his hand. Checker pointed at some holiday posters on the walls. The person put the phone down.

Checker shouted out, 'Chalkie, how are you mate? I brought a friend along to do some biz!'

T.J. looked at Checker and told him, 'You can't call black people Chalkie!' But before he could answer the man said, 'Wolfie me old China, where you been? I've not seen you for ages.'

'You know! There and back, doing a bit and that Chalkie you know what I mean aye, ducking an diving.'

Chalkie laughed saying, 'I don't know Wolfie, you don't alter, still the same! Are you married yet?'

'Leave it out, I don't want any grey hairs yet, are you then?'

'Yes and one child, a boy, he is twelve months old just.'

'Cor, you kept that a bit quiet, why did I not get an invite then or was it a shotgun one then? Cos you used to put it about Chalkie!'

Chalkie laughed. 'No nothing like that. I was going steady at the time and my Grandad died and left me his house, there you go. Anyway you come here to book a holiday then?'

'No not me, it's my mate here, he wants to go to Morocco.'

The man turned to T.J. saying, 'You want to go to Morocco, Marrakech I suppose that's the place?'

T.J. said, 'No it's the Hotel Rif, Tangiers. I have been there before and I like it. Can you get anything there please?'

'Right, hold on, I'll look it up for you. When would you like to go?'

'As quick as possible, like tomorrow, a double room, half board or full board, facing front, third floor please.'

Chalkie looked at T.J. then at Checker saying, 'You're in a hurry, don't tell me the Fuzz or Wolfie's Wooden Tops want to see you?'

179

Checker laughed, 'Don't be silly Chalkie, he's pure, it's just that he forgot to book a holiday and he is getting a bit of grief from the old trouble and strife, you know what I mean?'

He looked at T.J., 'Right let's see what we can do then.' Chalkie started to search through the files on his computer, after a while he said, 'You might be lucky, there's a flight from Gatwick eleven thirty tomorrow, looks as it's not fully booked. I'm just checking with the company that's booking. I got it, I will give them a bell to see if they got room and of course The Hotel Rif.'

T.J. looked at Checker who gave the thumbs up, then the man Chalkie was tapping away on his computer keyboard. When he finished he looked at T.J. 'Right you're booked on flight number AXL 200, leaving Gatwick eleven thirty for Morocco, landing Tangiers then going on to Marrakech.'

Checker said, 'Great, come on, we got time to say hello to Trev and John and have a swift one.'

His mate Chalkie said, 'Hold on! There's the matter of flight tickets plus the "Do-ray-me" yet?'

Checker looked at his watch. 'Well come on then, let's get on, it's nearly twelve and we got to be home for dinner one thirty.'

Chalkie laughed and said, 'Well, well, me! I would never have thought to see Wolfie under the hammer; she must be a bit tasty to have you going! The easy laid back Wolfie, frightened of nobody!'

T.J. said, 'No, you have got it wrong, it's my mother. Wolfie is staying for dinner but come to think of it she is a bit tasty.'

We all had a bit of a laugh with Checker pointing at Chalkie and saying, 'Wrong.'

Chalkie said, 'Right, let's get on with it. Name?' Looking at T.J. Passports valid?'

T.J. answered, 'Yes.' Gave him his name and Rita's full name. 'Hmm, lives over the brush then your mate?'

T.J. looked at Checker, sort of made an enquiring look who then remarked, 'Yeah, that's the second one. He likes to taste before buying, just like yourself Chalkie mate, you use to put it about, your misses must be a brammer to nail you down?'

Chalkie looked up, nodded, saying, 'She's the goods man.'

T.J. got his flight tickets and paid. Chalkie thanked him and wished him a happy holiday.

Checker looked at his watch. Come on we got about half hour to kill, let's see if Trevor and John's about. As they walked to the pub T.J. said to Checker, 'Did your mate mind being called Chalkie?'

He said, 'No! Right, what do you call a bloke with ginger hair? Ginger right? Blokes named Clarke are always called Nobby and Tony that's Chalkies first name and his surname is White and they are mostly called Chalkie, get it?'

T.J. pondered, 'But being black sounds a bit racial?'

'Might be now "but" when we were kids growing up in a rough area he was one of our gang, you know one of the lads. We would play and fight together, for what it's worth they were good times, I think racial started much later.'

They went into the pub and Checker said, 'That's another thing I've learnt you.'

T.J. could see Trevor at the bar. Checker shouted out, 'Caught you, it's about time you put your hand in your pocket, mine's a lager so is T.J.'s.'

Trevor turned around, laughed, 'Checker my old mate, glad to see you but can't buy you a drink, that was my last, I'm brassick! Course if I can nip you for a flim I'm willing to buy you one.'

Just at that moment his mate John joined them, he said, 'Glad to see you, I was just saying to Trev if none of our mates don't come in we will have to call it a day, our credit has run dry behind the bar.'

Checker turned. 'Where you just sprung from?'

'Ho! The Karsey, still now you're here mate mine's a pint.'

Checker looked at T.J., with a smile. 'See what you done, just cos you wanted to come here it's going to cost me.' He said to the barman, 'Two lagers please and what these two Herberts want.'

Trevor laughed. 'Cheers mate but how about that flim, pay you back next time you come in? Only me and Johno plan to stay a bit longer now you're here.'

T.J. said, 'We are not staying long, I have promised to be back home for one thirty and Checker's driving.'

'Yea we only come in for a swift one, say hello and go and before you ask again Trev, here you are.'

Checker gave Trevor a fiver then looked at T.J. and then John. T.J. got the strong impression he was to give or loan him a fiver also.

T.J. gave him a five pound note to which John said, 'Thanks T.J., drink up, I buy you a drink.' which caused a bit of merriment. They both declined the offer and left the pub leaving them both five pounds better off.

As they were driving home Checker laughed, 'I don't know T.J., you don't half get me into some scrapes and this one cost me as well!'

'And me.' T.J. said.

They got back home with a good twenty minutes to spare. Mother was pleased her son had managed to get two tickets, plus booked into The Hotel Rif. Father said that he would drive them to Gatwick.

T.J. said, 'Must telephone Mr Bowen in the morning to explain why.'

Father said not to worry about that as he was meeting Richard, Mr Bowen senior, at the club that night so he would let him know.

T.J. said, 'Thank you father.'

Mother asked Rita if she would have any problem with her employer? Rita answered, 'No, I will tell them a little white lie, I'll tell them I've won a holiday or I've met a rich Arab who wanted to marry me.'

Mother said, 'Rita!'

Father for once laughed.

'Don't worry mother, many a true word is said in jest. If a rich Arab wants to buy, if the price is right I might consider the offer, any bid over fifty pounds would be close.'

Checker laughed and said 'Is that all you think you're worth then?'

Mother said, 'Right Rita. After dinner you go home and pack a suitcase. Don't forget your passport and when you go to Morocco you will look after our little boy?'

Even father joined in the laughter at mother's joke. Turning to Rita mother said, 'You come back here and stay overnight, now if you will help me to serve dinner, father will do the wines and tomorrow I will travel to Gatwick with father to see you both off.'

As they both left the room to go into the dining room father turned to Checker. 'An aperitif Stanley?'

Checker looked towards T.J., he nodded and Checker said, 'Yes please Mr B.'

Father looked at T.J., he said, 'Yes.'

As father passed them their drinks he heard mother call out. 'Don't forget us girls now!'

Father smiled. 'They're all ready dear.'

After dinner they all retired to the lounge, father was in his element mainly talking to Checker and Rita about Morocco, the do's and don'ts and must visit the museums which tell you about the different nations that had occupied their country and had left their ways, one of the most spoken languages, apart from their own, is French. 'If you stop and have a cup of mint tea and sit outside at one of the tables you just sit there, hear the babble of voices and soak up the atmosphere.'

Mother said, 'Where dear? Pardon? Where do you sit having your mint tea?'

'Oh did I not say, sorry it's at the Cafe de Paris, right opposite the French Embassy.'

Later, Rita left to return home to collect her passport and clothes, Checker also left reminding them to send a card and don't forget the stinky stuff. T.J. asked him to tell Reg he did not have to vacate his flat when all the work was done, he could stay and he would see him on his return.

Chapter Nine

THE FOLLOWING DAY they left home at nine thirty to drive to Gatwick. Normally it would only take roughly thirty minutes but Mother insisted to go early as you never know at these airports. Father had told T.J. earlier that he had spoken to Mr Bowen and he was quite happy about him taking time off. Rita had also telephoned where she worked. They got to Gatwick with an hour to spare, as we made our farewells Father slipped me an envelope saying, 'Enjoy yourselves.' and they were gone.

We booked in to our flight desk then sat down and waited to be called for the flight. T.J. told Rita what Father had given me but T.J. will not open it. Then Rita tells him Mother had also given her an envelope as well, she was going to tell him when they got to the hotel.

T.J. said, 'Remind me to ask at reception for a safe key, there is a small charge but it's safe, I always get one for passports, travel documents and spare cash so if you get mugged or lose anything it's no big deal. That reminds me, do you have a Bankers card? If so put that in the safe as well.'

Rita laughed, 'You make Morocco sound more like a thieves den than a beautiful country like your Father described!'

'No I might have made it sound like a thieves den, it is not, it's just being safe than sorry. Father and I always got a key for a safety box and to open it require two keys, one is held at the reception desk and the other by yourself. There are rich people there and poor by our standards, very poor so it does not pay to encourage them. You will see a lot of street beggars. When I first went to Tangiers I gave them money here and there but when I stopped to have a mint tea at one of the cafes I had to change notes as I had given over eight pounds I had in small denominations to the street beggars. When I told father he just laughed and said well you have learned the hard way Son, begging is a trade and some of them are quite well off.'

They were called to board their flight. Once seated they were soon airborne. When the stewards started to come around with the duty frees T.J. told Rita, 'Don't worry about buying bottles of drink, get a couple of cartons of cigarettes and I will do also.'

'But we don't smoke, why?'

T.J. replied, 'It is very good, a sort of wheeling dealing, a carton of cigarettes to the Bar Manager gets you good service and the same for the Major-Domo of the restaurant area. You get a table for two plus good service, anyway I mostly go Ala-Carte so you do not have to sit at tables with other guests.'

Rita said, 'You're a snob Terry; I never would have thought that of you!'

'I am not but when you sit down to eat and other holiday makers start talking asking where you come from and then light up a cigarette, puffing out smoke when you are eating it is not nice, in a bar it's acceptable, at a footie match also but not when I'm eating.'

'No you're right love, I don't like that either.'

Just over two and a quarter hours they had landed and disembarked, got our luggage and through Customs. As they walked out to get on board the bus T.J. told Rita, 'Hang on to your suitcase, there will be about twenty or so Arabs coming up to grab hold of your suitcase and carry it for ten yards to the bus then after want money for doing so.'

Walking to the bus in bright sunshine and warm, a difference to back home late November. 'It will be a bit cold, maybe raining, just to think when we return it will be December. That reminds me we must try and get some Christmas presents.'

They arrive at the hotel, only eight people got off the bus. The people left on board must be going onto other hotels further in town. The Courier took us all inside to reception. T.J. immediately informed the Courier of his name and booking for a double room, third floor, front which we had paid for.

T.J. felt Rita tug his arm, 'Patience, she already knows.'

T.J. told Rita, 'You have to tell them, they will put you anywhere around the back and the ones that drop them a few quid get the front.'

'Do they?' Rita asked.

'Yes, they did once to Father when we was on a family holiday. He went for the Courier all guns blazing, He had paid for double rooms, one for me and one for them and they only tried to put us in a three bed room, so I have paid extra for a double room, third floor, front and that is what I want. The hotel Management don't mind if the Courier tries to get away with it because they get an extra room to rent which is already paid for.'

Our conversation was broken by the Courier calling their name, they went to her and she said that we had paid for double rooms adjoining but there's only two of you why when you can only use one room.

T.J. replied, 'Originally there would have been four, the other room for my parents, my Father is a Judge and Court hearing has taken longer but they hope to join us within the next day or two.'

She looked as though she was about to say something "but" anticipating her, I said, 'A High Court Judge!'

She said, 'Oh.' Then she walked away over to two people, talking to them the man appeared to be annoyed, very annoyed remonstrating to the Courier and appeared to be holding his hand out.

They finally got the keys to our rooms and with the help of a Porter with the baggage they were taken to their rooms. After giving the Porter a tip he left them to relax and unpack.

Rita asked why T.J. had booked two rooms when one was enough and why did he tell the Courier a lie?

T.J. replied, 'I did not tell you before but Father had asked me if I minded them joining us in three days time, sometime Thursday late morning he hoped. He wanted to treat Mother to a surprise that is why I did not tell you before, just in case you let slip to Mother.'

Rita looked at him, slowly smiled, 'You mean to say that I have only got three and a half days on our own to "shag" the life out of you now? You tell me I only got three, well don't think you will be getting off light for the only time you will be allowed out of bed is just to come up for air so we better start now, so get them off!'

T.J. was only too happy to please.

Tuesday afternoon they left the hotel. T.J. had persuaded Rita to go into town. As they walked towards the town centre, on more than one occasion they had to tell young men and boys asking to be their guides around town that they were not needed. At times they were most persistent, T.J. had to be more sharp, telling them in their own language saying La shookran! Meaning no thank you. They made their way to the Kasbar, as they walked in Rita could not get over the strangeness of the narrow streets, the many colours of the doorways into shops, their traders inviting you in to try and sell you anything from mats, carpets to brass ornaments. Rita saw a "Hookah" and asked what it was, before T.J. could say that it was a tobacco pipe, quite common in North Africa the owner stepped forward and immediately started his sales pitch.

T.J. just stood there and watched, his assistant came out with a tray of mint tea in glass cups. They were invited inside, T.J. sat down on the nearest seat and watched Rita and the salesman, it was obvious Rita wanted to buy it. She turned to him asking for help, T.J. told her what it was and asked did she still want it? 'Yes.' was the reply so then came the haggling over cost. T.J. always liked this part for they always tell you they are poor with a wife and many children and what you was offering was far lower than it cost them yet it was all carried out with smiles, plenty of hand movements all done to make you think you have won and you bought it at cost and they made no profit.

As they walked further into the Kasbar, they could smell things being cooked by street traders, the ambience of a different country and the babble of different tongues chattering away. Morocco is a place where one could lose one's reality of the pace of life back home. Just relax, smell and drink in the culture, the Moroccan way of life, the people, the different colour of their skins from pale brown and much darker, some even black as Newgate's knocker. Probably that is why so many people from many different countries live there, from all over the world, as Father says, you can bump into many just sitting outside at the Cafe de Paris.

T.J. said to Rita, 'Shall we go to the Cafe de Paris?'

The answer was, 'No! We have had enough fresh air, let's go back to the hotel, we can go to the cafe tomorrow but now you have a pressing engagement! Come on show me the way back, after all your Mother did ask me to look after her little boy!'

'I have heard that when some people go on holiday they turn into sex maniacs!'

'Are you complaining little boy?'

'No, no! It's just that when my Mother sees me again I will be a frail, dark eyed, little boy.'

Rita replied, 'Good, she will know that I have been looking after you then.'

Chapter Ten

BACK HOME IN Croydon at St James' Road there was some cause for concern. The work on the houses was really coming to an end. Checker had told Reggie he could stay at TJ's flat, Shades had made all the difference but Curly evidently had been doing a bit of shopping in Croydon on Monday and got involved in an argument with two men in the high street. One thing led into another, ending in a fight although it was two against one Curly was no slouch, he put paid to both of them but unfortunately he had broke one of the men's jaw and the manager of a shop witnessed the fraction ongoing , called the police. They arrived just as Curly was about to leave. He was arrested, charged with GBH and released on bail. He went to the legal firm that T.J. works for, for help but he has no witness and both men say he had started the argument. Checker is making enquiries around and with his friends to find out who the two men are. John and Trev said, 'If they do find them, do you want the frighteners put on or how many witnesses do you want?'

Checker laughed. 'Don't talk daft you two, any witnesses you know have got records longer than yours, they would be thrown out of court.'

John said, 'No, now what about you, have you got a police record?'

'You know I haven't.'

Then John looked at me and said see, you never been nicked, no police record and good job, see you know what I mean?'

'But I was not there.'

John said, 'Who said so? You was on the opposite side of the road, you saw these two go towards your mate and started to punch him, you know what I mean?'

Checker said, 'Alright, I know but I could not do it, I would be sure to slip up and then done for Perjury.'

'We know that Checker.'

Trevor said, 'Come on get the beer in, lets go over to that table over there I'm sure we can sort summing up.'

'Right.' Trevor said 'First of all we will put it about we want to talk to them. I don't think we will have much bother finding them, that's the easy part. I can get their names and addresses by four o'clock today.'

'You can do that, how?' Checker asked.

'Ha! Don't you worry about that, what we want to know is what do you want done to them? We can talk to them or give them a slap or John can introduce them to his friend!' With that both Trevor and John started laughing.

When Trevor stopped laughing he said, 'There is another way but that will cost! but it will work.'

'How?' Checker asked.

Trevor said, 'I know of a witness who saw it all happen, now if you want she will go into the shop and say or ask what happened to that young man that got set upon by those two yobs outside your shop Monday, now the shop owner will ask if she has told the police and if she has not, she ought to as he did not see it all. Now our witness will say Oh I don't know, my Harry would tell me off summint awful, he don't hold with the cops. It would mean going to court an all that. No I don't think so. Then the shop owner will say, hold on a minute Ma. I make you a nice cup of tea and I'll get that nice young policeman to come and see you, he won't want you to go to court, he will just ask you what you saw and that's it. Ho alright then but I'm not going to court, my Harry would not like it, so there.'

Trevor said, 'There you go Checker, do you want me to arrange it or not?'

Checker laughed and looked at Trevor, 'You can arrange some bird to tell a porkie and get away with it, comon Trev I thought I knew you better than that, we are mates man, if you want a few notes I give you some but you would not pull a scam on a mate ay?'

Trevor and John looked at Checker, Trevor said, 'On a mate, never, not one as close as you are to John and me, never.'

'Sorry mates but you made it sound so easy you know.'

Trevor replied 'Course it is and by the way not a bird but an elderly woman about fifty five never been to court, never had anything to do with the cops, as honest as the day is long but out of work. Her old man's pension is not much, for a few quid course she will do it.'

'How do you know?' Checker asked.

'Cause we know her, John and me drop her now and again that's when we are flush and a bit of meat now and again. If she knows that's all she got to do and not go to court she can't be add up for perjury see?'

'Ha, suppose she makes a cock up of her story, she can be done for wasting police time.'

'Don't talk daft Checker, the police will just ask her what she had seen then they will give those two blokes a tug, then tell them they have a witness and it collaborates with the other man's statement that they were the villains.'

Checker paused for a minute or two. 'Alright go for it, but first how much?'

John and Trevor looked at each other then Trevor said 'A ton.'

'A ton!' Checker said 'That's a bit steep ain't it?'

'Not really.' Trevor said, 'Your mate will as it stands, will get fined somewhere between two to three hundred, be a good boy for a year or two, probably on probation, have a police record and his brief will want paying and they don't come cheap!'

Checker said, 'Alright, how much you two going to make ay?'

Trevor laughed, 'Alright me and John a tenner each and Ma gets eighty, can't be fairer then that cos we are the go betweens, if it was legal and an agent was doing it, it will cost.'

Checker said, 'I wonder if the barman will let me use his phone, got to get Curly's say so, also what time it happened and what he told the police.'

John said, 'Course you can.' He called out, 'Hey Jim, my mate wants to use the dog, alright?'

The man got the telephone from behind of the bar and placed it on the bar. Checker said, 'Thank you.' and telephoned Curly, explained everything to him, told what it will cost if he is in agreement. 'Tell me everything he told the police in his statement also what time of the day did it happen?'

After two or three minutes he said 'Okay but no money passes hands Checker!'

'They will need a bit up front, sort of goodwill, don't forget they will be getting you out of the hole and it will clear your name, any way if you still use your brief you can claim costs and damages and loss of earnings. You will get it all back!'

Curly pondered for a few minutes then said, 'You're sure Checker?'

'Positive, I trust them, they would not let me down.'

Curly answered, 'Alright, fifty up front and if it works, a ton after but the most goes to the old dear, now it's one thirty now meet me at the flats three o'clock alright?'

'See you there Curly, mean while I will tell them.'

When he returned to Trev and John he told them what Curly had said also he had notes but fifty now and a ton if the scam comes off, is it a deal? They agreed.

As they were driving to meet Curly at the flats, Checker asked Trevor that he said he could get the names of the two men by four o'clock. 'How?'

Trevor replied 'Well seeing you are close I'll tell you. You know Saturdays in the pub at dinner time, you see horny ere.' Pointing at John, "Messing with a couple of young girls about sixteen or seventeen, well they think it's great hanging around with him, the great crimm and his tattoos, well he nips them into the karsey one at a time like and slips them a bit of nourishment like. They love it, mind you if his wife is around they are always talking to her as they baby sit for them, if he takes her out "well" they both work up at the courts in the offices see?'

'Typist!' Checker said, 'Bloody hell mate, you can't trust nobody these days!'

'Except us mate.' Said John. 'But mind you if I did not have to service them now and again we would not get to know anything.' Trevor started laughing, Checker joined in and so did John.

Trevor said, 'I don't know Johno! You make it sound like a penance when you know you love it, you know what the saying goes, a standing cock has no conscious and nor have you mate?'

He replied, 'Only trying to catch up with what I have missed when I was inside.'

Checker said, 'Hold on! You don't mean that old dear who is going to testify for us is also a friend of horny as well?'

They both started laughing with John saying, 'Leave it out, I'm not that desperate, bloody hell mate I thought you knew me better than that?'

'Give over Johno.' Trevor said, 'I met with an old lag who was in Brixton when you was, he said all the lags on your landing when

192

you was walking by, they all stood with their backs to the wall.'

We was all laughing and John said laughing, 'That's not true, the only ones that did stand with their backs to the wall was the ones that didn't have make up or curlers in their hair.'

Checker said, 'Alright, alright cut the jokes, I'm driving, I got to concentrate you two will get us in an accident. Anyway serious now, if the old dear is not a friend of John then who is she?'

'Well as it happens, she is a friend of mine.'

Trevor said, 'And before you say anything the answer is no, she is an aunt, my mother's sister so Ma has a different surname to me, never been nicked, lives about one hundred yards down the road from my mum's house so she is clean alright? And I know she will do it, she does not like the police cos of what they did to her younger brother.'

'What did they do then?'

Trevor continued, 'Well he used to drink in a pub just by Vauxhall Bridge, south side like, well there are a few tasty blokes that use the pub as well. It's a place, well does not pay to say anything outer the way like, no scruffs, all suited, smart, none of your catt numbers or C & A's like none of your ready to wear whistles. All tailor made for the wearer, you can smell the money and sense the awareness of respect for each other but one word out of the way and that is enough spark to create mayhem. Well my uncle, mum's younger brother was waiting for his mate when there was a ruck, about six or seven blokes givin it some! Furniture got smashed, glasses and one mirror. When the shout went up the bill. Mother's brother said it was amazing, one minute they were punching each other, the next they were talking and laughing. One of them had a cut forehead and probably the bloke who gave it to him was lending him a hanky chief when the law came in asking questions. The landlord said everything is alright now Officer; we had some young tearaways come in and started trouble and arguments with some of my regulars. One of them hit young Tony there with some weapon, cut his head. Just as the Police were leaving one of the men pointed at my uncle and said to the Police Sergeant, he's a stranger I think he was one of them. They arrested him and he got time and had to pay for all the damage.'

'After he had done his time he learnt after that they thought he was an undercover cop but he was invited back to the pub by the lads, free drinks all night then they had a whip round for him and he ended up with twice what it had cost in fines, but, the police did not believe him when they nicked him so now he has got a crim record. That's why Ma don't like police.'

Checker pulled up outside the flats, he said to John and Trevor, 'Now behave as Curly is a serious type of bloke, likes a laugh and football but this is outer his depth, no messing keep it straight, reassure him everything will be alright and there will be no come backs on him alright?"

John said, 'Don't worry, he's got nothing to worry about if he got the gelt the job is done, all wade and paid, right lets be having it then.'

'Come on then.'

They all got out of the motor. John and Trevor followed Checker into the house. Curly was there, he seemed nervous but John was quick to see and held his hand out to Curly saying, 'Hello Mate, got a bit of agg? Don't worry will sort it, the way Checker says you been lumbered? Those wooden tops will stitch anybody who looks a bit green. Some of them are all right but those looking for a pro-mo will have anybody as the saying goes, even their own mothers. Right let's be having the story right.'

Curly told them exactly what had taken place. Monday, roughly eleven thirty he thinks they were after the shopping bags he was carrying. As they approached him one of them pushed into him and the other tried to take one of the shopping bags. 'So we had a fight and because they lost the argument, when the Police arrived they both blamed me.'

John said, 'Right don't worry, if it goes to Court you'll get off and don't forget to ask your brief to get your record and prints destroyed.'

Curly answered, 'As easily as that?'

John replied, 'Don't worry it's done, got the gelt?'

As Curly gave them the money John said to Trevor, 'Will see the girls for their address, best safe.' He turned to Curly. 'Don't worry mate, we won't let you down, seeing your a mate of Checkers.' Then to Checker, 'Come on, take us home, me and Trev have got some work to do.'

Saturday: Palace were playing at home, Checker met up with Cliff and Curly in their usual place in the ground while they were waiting for the game to start the topic was asking Curly if he had heard anything more about his forthcoming trial hearing and had a date been set. He said that his solicitor told him there have been some news, that the police were carrying out investigations but that's all he could tell him.

He looked at Checker saying, 'What do you think?'

'I think that could be good news mate, I will try and find out for you.'

Cliff said to Curly, 'What you asking him for? Your solicitor can't tell you, how can he?'

Curly said, 'I don't know I just said it, you know Checker he always seems to know anything and everything.'

Cliff laughed, then said, 'Next you'll be telling me he's going to be the Judge hearing the case!'

Checker laughed saying, 'You never know mate, I could have a part time job on the bench!' As he said that he looked at Curly, gave a wink, then thought! Curly could not have told Cliff, he always believed they were close?

His thoughts were interrupted with the roar of the crowd as the teams came out on to the pitch with Cliff saying, 'This is more like it, there's nothing like a good game of football, it sort of clears the mind. You sort of forget everything else.'

He turned to Curly saying, 'Right mate?'

'I hope so.'

Checker interrupted by asking, 'What do you think the score will be then?'

Cliff answered, 'I don't know but I would not like to put any money on it, Coventry have been doing well of late, winning both at home and away.'

The teams had lined up, the ref blew on his whistle to start the game. It seemed that both teams were showing a bit of respect for each other. After about twenty minutes or so the crowd was starting to shout out loudly, urging them to attack. Checker was being very vocal, shouting at the team when all of a sudden he noticed this bloke with a Palace woollen beret pulled right over his head and ears, also covering his forehead and a scarf wrapped around his neck also covering his chin. The person had his back to the game and appeared to be looking for somebody, looking to Checker's left side and right every now and again. The man sort of cuffed his nose with the back of his hand and sleeve.

Checker sort of smiled and thought the cuffs on the blokes coat will be a bit stiff. He could not see all of him as there were people in between them. Then all of a sudden the man pushed the woollen beret back on his forehead and more or less was standing on tip-toe looking over the heads in front of him, looking straight at Checker. All of a sudden Checker realized it was Trevor. Checker looked at him and thought he wants to see me on the quiet. Trevor cuffed his nose again but his forefinger was pointing towards the main stand. Checker winked at him to let him know he understood as Trevor walked away, still giving the impression he was looking for somebody in the crowd.

Checker thought that Trevor's actions could mean there might be somebody watching. He thought for a minute, it would be no good following right away. He decided to wait a few minutes. He turned to Cliff, 'Bloody hell mate, looks like both teams want to play patter cake than play football! Come on you wankers I didn't pay good money to watch you play footsie!'

Cliff laughed, 'Now, now, Stanley it's called being cagey. You wait, it only needs one goal then it will be game on.'

'Bloody hell I'm going for a leak, you coming?'

'What's up Checker you want me to hold your hand? You're a big boy now, you can manage on your own.'

That remark had both Curly and Cliff laughing, Checker joined in and saying, 'No you dickhead, it's me cock I wanted you to hold!'

All three laughing and Checker ducking a playful punch from Cliff as Checker left to go towards the stand Curly shouted out, 'Mind how you go sweetie.' Checker gave him a two finger salute.

As Checker passed through the gate to under the stands he saw Trevor drinking from a small bottle of drink bought from the small stall under the stand. As he walked towards Trevor he smiled. 'Hello mate, long time no see, you alright?'

Trevor replied. 'Yes, John and me thought you might need a bit of news. Ma has done her party piece, it went down a treat. They swallowed the bait, they wanted her to go to Court but she refused and being elderly they did not want to hassle her so they thanked her and let her be. John and me was coming to let you know when

John noticed them two blokes are in the crowd, not far from where you and your mates are standing. They are about fifteen yards to your right, a bit further down but standing behind them about six to eight feet are two plain clothes cops. John recognized one of them, he is the station Sergeant at the Croydon nick, names Parmer he thinks.'

'Any way John is waiting in the cafe for me but he did say Parmer's a bit nasty and he would nick you for anything so if them two blokes see Curly again and try to make waves, ignore them cos Johno thinks one of them might be a nonse, a grass, one of Parmer's team so it might be a set up alright. I'm off now, see you down the pub Wednesday night.' With that Trevor left.

Checker stood there for a minute thinking of what action to take, at that time he heard a big roar of noise from the crowd. He thought bloody hell somebody's scored and I missed it, sod you Trevor. As he made his way back to his mates, still trying to think of a way to tell Curly without letting on to Cliff, he thought tell them both a little lie but also the truth, saying it was himself that recognized the blokes and the wooden tops. Curly would know the real truth but Cliff would not, he hoped?

As he got nearer to his mates he looked over to where Trevor had indicated. It was easy to see the two blokes as Curly had given him a good description of them but what Curly did not know was they were part of the Eagle Mob. They were in amongst them talking and laughing. Checker then tried to see if he could pick out the wooden tops, then he saw them. It wasn't hard to pick them out, they stood out like sore thumbs. You could see they were not your norm of football supporters. As he got to his mates Cliff laughed and turned to Curly. 'Look who we got here mate.'

They both looked at Checker with Cliff saying, 'Did you find anybody to hold your cock for you?'

Checker joined in the laughing then said, 'Who scored?'

Curly said, 'Nobody, we thought it was a goal but it was ruled offside.'

'Right mates, I got something to say now so let me stand in between you both so you can both hear without me shouting.'

Cliff said, 'Aha do you want me to hold your hand?'

'Cut it out this is serious, right now what I am about to say is keep your heads and don't start looking around alright? Well Curly gave me a good description of the blokes he hit. Well they're here.'

Cliff looked up. 'Where?'

Checker replied, 'Don't look, I'll tell you why in a minute, standing about six feet behind them are two wooden tops. One of them is a Police Sergeant, I recognized him from when I had to take some of the firm's papers up to the Croydon nick for he was the one who signed for them. Now there might be some standing behind us. It might be a coincidence or a set up or it could be nothing, mind you if one of them blokes is a nonse they might be trying something. So as much as I would like to stay and watch the match, when it gets to half-time I think we ought to leave.'

Cliff laughed, 'Leave half way through a game of football, you're having us on or have you lost your marbles? Come on Checker we all play jokes on each other but it's December not April fool's day.'

He looked towards Curly who was not smiling, Cliff said, 'Do you believe him? Have a look, see if you can see the blokes you had some agg with. If they are there then we will give them some.'

Curly said, 'I did and they are there in the mix of The Eagles, I believe him, I agree with him, I think we should leave. I don't want no more trouble. If Checker says there are police nearby it could mean something or nought, just a coincidence but if it is not? Don't forget I got a business I worked hard to build and I don't want to throw it away.'

The whistle blew for half-time. As they made their way to the exit Checker could not deny the temptation of looking behind them but no one was following, he though better to be safe than sorry. They went to their usual cafe.

The owner said, 'Hello lads, you're in early, what the game not any good?'

Cliff answered, 'It wasn't.' Looking at Curly and Checker. 'I bet it is now?'

'Right lads, what you having?' said the owner.

Checker replied, 'One bacon sarnie and a cup of rosey for me, Cliff and Curly concur?'

'The same please.'

They sat at their usual table and started to talk to Curly about the case. Curly was at a loss, he had no idea, he had faith in his solicitor. In the past he has heard T.J. say good things about him, says that he has not lost a case, 'Anyway when he told me that the police were investigating some other news about the case he seemed quite upbeat and assured me that he was confident and told me not to worry.'

Checker said, 'There you go mate, I would say your home and dry. Don't forget to ask your brief to claim for cost and loss of earnings.'

Cliff said, 'Hark at him.' Laughing. 'You sure you're not sitting on the bench?'

Curly looked at Checker and asked, 'Are you sure mate, are you really?'

'As sure as eggs are eggs.'

Cliff once again asked, 'How do you know?'

Checker laughed and said, 'I met a little old lady selling lucky heather, I bought some and the old lady wished me luck and said my friend has no problems. See I believe in fate, don't you? I thought it was an omen?'

Cliff laughed, 'I heard some fairy tales but that beats them all.' At that moment their tea and sandwiches arrived.

Just as they were eating Curly said, 'I wonder how T.J's getting on, I wished that he was here. He could have taken on the case and told us a bit more.'

'You have no problem, trust me. As the bishop said to the actress.' Checker laughed.

Cliff turned to Curly. 'See what I mean 'what' does he know?'

Checker answered, 'Sorry Curly, I just could not help it 'but' believe me, I had a visit.' Winked at Curly and for Cliff's sake said, 'Or a vision and they said everything is alright.' Looking at Cliff, 'Don't you believe in fate then?'

Curly asked Checker, 'Did you really have a visit?'

Checker answered, 'Yes, and if you had kept your peepers open you would have seen it as well.'

Curly looked at Checker. 'You mean here? Is that why you went to the toilet at the match?'

Checker nodded his head.

Cliff asked, 'Am I missing something or have you two gone effing mad, him saying he's had a visit and you believing him. If it carries on like this I will be joining you two at bedlam!'

Curly and Checker started laughing and Cliff joined in saying, 'I don't know why I'm laughing, maybe I'm going mad like you two nutters?'

Curly said, 'Right Cliff, I will tell you. Checker told me he had a friend who could point the police into investigating a little bit further into the characters of the persons claiming that I was the person guilty when I was the owner of a respectable business.'

Cliff said, 'We know that and your brief would point that out in court.' He looked at Checker. 'Alright, who is this mate of yours that's got an in with the bill?'

Checker replied, 'That's private.' Then turning to Curly, 'See! I told you he wouldn't believe us.' Then saying to Cliff, 'I'll bet you ten notes that Curly will be found not guilty before it goes to Court or in Court and them two blokes will get done for wasting police time and telling porkies and if the police let it go to Court they will be done for perjury as well.'

'Done, I risk a tenner and if Curly gets off it will be worth it. I know you have got some funny mates Checker, but in Court?'

Curly said, 'I hope you have lost, Cliff . I believe Checker and anyway lets change the subject, when's T.J. likely to be back?' Looking at Checker, 'I don't know but he's only going for a week most likely Tuesday and I hope he has brought the stinky stuff back with him, that will make a nice Christmas pressie for my Jean.'

Cliff laughed, 'You're an old cheap skate Checker, what about you then Cliff, you ask for some as well?'

Cliff's reply was, 'It's only a make up present to go with the big one I have bought.'

Curly cut in by saying, 'Well I will be pleased to see him, stinky stuff or not.' Turning round and looking towards the cafe owner, 'Can we have three more teas please?'

The man waved his hand but appeared to be listening intently to his radio. The boys carried on talking, wondering what the score was at Palace and about the flats. The only thing outstanding was the confirmation and certificates passing the electrical and gas work. The Health and Safety would then give their confirmation of the flats being fit for habitation.

Their conversation was interrupted by the cafe owner bringing over the teas and also saying, 'You missed out today lads, they had a bit of trouble at the Homesdale end. The bloke on the radio said the police were expecting trouble today and they were there in force. The bloke on the radio says they have arrested a lot of them, gang called The Eagles, evidently they picked on some other blokes and it turned out they was the old bill in plain clothes.'

Checker said, 'It's funny how fate works annit? We always go to the Homesdale end, we thought the game was rubbish and walked out, if we had stayed we might have seen it or got mixed up in it.'

Curly said, 'Yes I'm glad we left, that mob ought to be barred. They get the game a bad name.'

'Too right.' The cafe owner said as he walked away.

Checker looked at Cliff who in turn looked at Curly then back to Checker. 'Alright, Alright, so you saw the old bill there. That does not mean they were there because of us does it?'

Checker replied, 'No it's just luck or fate mate.'

Cliff sarcastically replied, 'I will believe that the day you are made Prime Minister!'

'If they do mate, one of the first things I would do is bring back the stocks and the ducking chair.'

Curly added, 'And conscription.'

Cliff said, 'Yes they ought to bring a Penal Regiment, like France had way back.'

'What was that?' Checker asked.

Cliff answered, 'As I have read it was an Army type regiment that was made up of volunteers, people/criminals that had been caught and convicted had a choice, join the Penal Regiment or go to jail and the jails in those days were very bad so they join up.'

'Well! That will be a piece of cake.' Checker said.

'No.' Cliff replied, 'It involved hard labour, working on Government work and in times of war they were the first ones in the front line. They were supervised by officers and N.C.O.'s, the N.C.O.'s were made up from criminals that have been given life sentences, hard men, who if anybody did a runner they would be the first to go back inside.'

Curly said, 'Sounds like the French Foreign Legion then?'

Cliff said, 'Yes in a way but the Foreign Legion they got paid whereas the crims did not.'

Tuesday morning Checker had a site visit to make at Liverpool Street Station. As he was leaving his place of work he thought that he will be going past Norbury. He would call in on Mrs Bond, see if she knew when T.J. would be returning from holiday. He had tried phoning but did not get any reply. As Checker turned into the road where they lived he could see Mr Bond's motor in the drive. He pulled up outside. As he was getting out of his car he heard his name get called out. He looked up it was Mrs Bond, she waved and beckoned to him to come into the house.

As he walked in he said, 'Hello.' And started to apologize for not telephoning first but Mrs Bond cut him short by saying, 'Terry will be pleased to see you, he has not long taken Rita home. He should be back shortly.'

'I did try to telephone last Friday but you and Mr Bond must have been out as I could not get a reply.'

She smiled then said, 'Did not Terry tell you? Father and I joined them in Morocco Wednesday, it was lovely, just a few days but nice.'

Checker said, 'Great, I'm glad he's back, we need a few things to tidy up at the flats. A couple of bills to be paid and Terry holds the company cheque book and accounts. Apart from that the flats are finished, just a bit of paperwork, but how is he? Has he recovered from the grumps?'

She laughed, 'I have never heard it called that before but yes he is much happier now, he is more his old self. Would you like a cup of tea while you wait Stanley?'

'No thanks Mrs B., I must be off. I only called round to see when he would be home. I have an urgent appointment at Liverpool Street Station. Can you tell Terry I will meet him at the Norbury eight thirty tonight Mrs B. please. I'll have Jean with me so tell him not to fetch the pressie with him, he will understand.'

She laughed, 'I'm sure he will.' As he left she waved and called, 'Take care.'

Rita and T.J. had decided to walk to the Norbury Hotel, as they approached the main London Road, turned right towards the Norbury, holding hands talking about the holiday and how great it will be to see Checker and Jean, T.J. saw two men walking towards them.

As they got nearer T.J. and Rita moved to one side to allow them to pass but the two men also stepped aside standing in front of them. T.J. apologized and Rita gave a little laugh and her and

202

T.J. stepped to one side to carry on but the two men once again stepped with them. T.J. said, 'Do you mind and let us pass please.'

The smaller of the two men said, 'Did you hear what he said mate?'

The taller of the two men said, 'Yer and he said it so nice, do yer fink he's one of them? Yer know a powder puff?'

The other one answered, 'Could be.'

The taller of the two laughed. 'If he is he's yours, I'll have the bit of skirt, I'm not into iron-hoff.'

But Rita cut him short by saying, 'Get out of the way you ignorant lout.' And went to push passed them but he pushed her back.

T.J. said, 'Take your hands off her.'

'Ho yer, an whose gonner make me?'

'Gorn, hit him, Gorn give him a bit of muscle!'

The big one laughed, 'I save the best bit of muscle for his crumpet so you make sure she don't run off after I finished.'

Just at that time an elderly couple were standing nearby, the woman shouted, 'Leave them alone you bullies!'

The taller of the men said, 'Don't worry girl, I'll save some for you, I don't mind a bit of old!'

Her husband shouted, 'You cheeky bastard! If I was younger I'd tear your head off.'

'Shut up you old git or I'll set my mate on to you.'

While all the talk was going on T.J. was weighing up his chances what to do but he only had one option, that was fight and as Checker has always said, get in first, make it count. He looked at the man saying to himself, on the jaw, the point or button. He clenched his fist and as the man turned to him he hit his jaw as hard as he could. The man fell to the ground.

He turned to the other man who was holding on to Rita, telling him to let go of her, he swung punches at the man hitting him again and again, shouting at him. 'You filthy bastards!'

In his madness he was elated, punching the man in front of him. He'd taken on two men and beat them. He heard Rita shouting at him, it sounded in the distance, then all of a sudden the side of his head seamed to explode, it hurt. He turned standing in front of him was the man he had knocked down and then he felt another blow to his chest. The man standing in front of him was saying, 'Comon, little hero.'

He was hurting, the man was goading him by saying, 'When I've finished with yer I'm gonner give your bit of skirt a going over, she'll love it.'

All of a sudden Rita swung her bag at him hitting him saying, 'You filthy bastard!'

He back handed her.

T.J. seemed to galvanise new strength. He started to fight, once again he aimed for the man's jaw but this time he was ready for every punch T.J. threw. He got two back he was being punched in the back. T.J. knew the other man was also hitting him.

T.J. was hurting, he was screaming and crying. He felt himself falling, falling, tired, falling asleep. He no longer felt pain. Rita was screaming at the two men to leave him alone. The man grabbed hold of her. 'Now it's your turn bitch, I'm gonner spread your legs open wide, you won't want anybody else after.'

All the time his mate was shouting, 'Gorn Larry give it to her, make her suck it first.'

The man laughed, 'I let her do that after.'

Rita said, 'You Filthy Bastards!' The man pushed her hard against a wall, she spat in his face.

The elderly woman was shouting at him saying her husband's gone to phone the police.

'Leave her alone!'

The man shouted, 'Archie give that old cow a bit of cock, she's only jealous.'

His mate said, 'I'm not like you, you would shag anything.'

The other man laughed as he pushed Rita hard against the wall grabbing her by the throat with one hand, the other hand roughly tearing her knickers away. Rita was screaming and crying. He was shouting, telling her to shut up.

Larry did not hear a motor pull up. The car door flew open, a man got out of the motor, fast, leapt across the pavement and kicked the man hard up the backside. Larry's knees gave way, he half turned to see who had hit him.

Checker hit him hard again. Checker then grabbed hold of Archie the other man, he held him by the shirt collar and hit hard once in the face while still holding on to him. Checker shouted to Rita and Jean to get Terry into the car.

The elderly couple started to shout, encouraging Checker. 'Give them some of their own back! Go on hit him!'

Checker could not hear them, he was aggressive beyond reason. He was just punching hard and fast at the man's face who was unconscious. His face was a blooded gore. Checker was screaming, 'You bastards, you touch my blood brother you're dead!'

Checker let go of the man who just crumpled to the ground. The elderly couple had gone quiet. They were witnessing an act of brutality. Checker turned to the other man named Larry who was just rising to his knees, Checker grabbed his hair, shouting, 'Let me help you bastard!'

Then he slammed Larry hard against the wall grabbing him by the throat with his left hand squeezing hard, saying, 'Do you like it ay?' as Larry with both hands tried to pull at his hands. Then Checker started punching Larry hard in the body also kept kneeing Larry hard into his groin, shouting at him, 'It'll be a long time you use that on a girl you fucking bastard!'

Then through the fog of rage he heard Jean screaming at him. Checker turned and saw Jean crying, telling him to stop and drive Terry to hospital. He let go of Larry who fell to the ground then he walked to the car. They both got in. He started the engine and started to drive to Croydon to Mayday Hospital.

The rage had left Checker, he was crying and asking how T.J. was. Jean was trying to pacify him, telling him not to worry.

'The Doctors will see him right, you will see.' Jean then told him, 'When we get to the hospital you stay in the car, I'll get help from the hospital staff for if anybody sees you in the state you are in they will think it was you who hit Terry.'

Checker started to protest but Jean was calm and adamant, 'We will tell people you gave us a lift alright? We do not know you, for what you done to those two men you could go to prison right? You go to Terry's mum and dad, tell them, then go home. I'll let you know later. That's right Rita?'

She replied, 'Yes of course and thank you Stanley.'

When they reached the hospital Jean went into the hospital, within minutes a nurse and porter came running out pushing a wheelchair. When they got T.J. out of the car to take him in Jean called out, 'Thank you very much for your help.'

Checker then drove away to go to T.J.'s mum and dad.

Back at Norbury the Police were on the scene, also an ambulance. The crew were kneeling beside the two men administering first aid. There were two policemen questioning the two elderly people.

'You tell them mum,' said her husband, 'You saw it all as I went to phone the police, you tell them Alice.'

The woman told them pointing, how the two men were stopping a young man and his girlfriend from walking past them.

'That big one there was threatening to punch the young man, knock him out then he was going to rape his girlfriend. Well the two of them set about the poor lad, they beat him to the ground. The poor lad tried to put up a fight but for every punch he gave he got half a dozen back. Then him, that big one started on the girl, he slammed her against that wall there. He had one hand around her throat, the other hand was pulling at her knickers. I shouted at him to stop but he laughed and told that other man to rape me, Dad here stepped in front of me and warned him not to try but bless him he would not have lasted long.' she continued, 'But then out of the blue a car pulled up, just there.' The woman pointing, 'The car had hardly stopped when a man jumped out and kicked that man.' She said pointing, 'Yea, right up the jackcy.'

'Cor his bollocks must have flew right to his eye balls.' said her husband, then he laughed, 'I bet they said tilt.'

The Policeman said, 'Yes, alright Dad, what happened next?'

'Well he just set about the two of them, he took no prisoners. Me and Mum cheered him on but after a while the man was in a rage and it got 'orrible to watch. Then he left.'

'But what about the first man, the one them two supposed to have beat up?' the policeman asked.

'No another car picked them up, ask them lot over there,' pointing to across the road. 'They watched it from the start, Mum called out to them for help, the yellow bastards.'

The other policeman started to cross the road to question them but as he approached them they started to disperse. When he got to them the remaining people said that they did not see anything, had only just arrived and stopped to look when they saw the ambulance.

He returned saying, 'Nobody saw anything.'

The first policeman asked, 'Could you give us a description of the man who attacked these men?'

Alice and her husband looked at each other. There was silence.

The policeman said, 'Well, what did he look like? Was he tall, small or what? What colour hair, was he white or black?'

Alice looked at her husband.

The first policeman said to his colleague, 'Look I will ask Mum here, you take Dad over there and we'll try and get some description from them.'

As Checker knocked at Mr and Mrs Bond's house door, he was trying to compose himself. Mrs Bond opened the door, recognized him and started to tell him Terry had left; she saw the mess he was in. She called out to her husband at the same time taking Checkers arm and taking him into the house towards the kitchen.

Terry's father looked at him, 'Good God boy what's happened? Have you had a car accident? Was Terry with you?' He turned to his wife saying, 'Get a large brandy for Stanley. As she went to the lounge he called, 'Make that two, I might need one!' Then gently asked Checker, 'What has happened?'

Checker then started to tell them how he was driving to meet with Terry and Rita and saw them being set on by two men. 'By the time I stopped the car I saw Terry fall to the ground. One of the men had Rita by the throat up against the wall and trying rape her. I'm sorry sir, I lost it, I just jumped out of the car and went for them. I just kept hitting them. Terry is like my brother to me, I shouted to Jean and Rita to get Terry in the car, I know I was crying, screaming, I saw Terry on the ground and I just kept hitting them.'

'It was Jean who stopped me. I drove to Mayday Hospital. Jean, Rita and the hospital staff took Terry in, Jean would not let me go with them, she said the mess I was in the police would have arrested me. She told me to come and tell you, anyway I don't know what damage I did to those two men? Rita said I might have killed them.'

Mr Bond said, 'Good.'

Mrs Bond said, 'Father!' He looked at her.

'I know my dear but what have they done to Terry?'

'Drink up Stanley then Mother take Stanley upstairs, Stanley get a shower, Mother put all his clothes in the washer. Lay out some of Terry's clothes, dinner suit, white shirt, bow tie then you put an evening dress on. I will put on the same as Stanley then we will all go to the hospital. Meanwhile I will telephone the hospital.' Just as he was about to phone he said, 'Stanley, can I have the keys to your car?'

Checker gave him his keys. Mr Bond got the keys for the garage, left the house and drove Checker's car into the garage.

On returning he telephoned the hospital for some news of his son but all the nurse could tell him was that the doctors were carrying on investigations. After he had got dressed in his dinner suit he telephoned Whitehall, introduced himself and requested transport plus police protection, stating it could mean nothing or more as his son has tonight been attacked and hospitalized. When he put the phone down Checker and his wife were standing there in the lounge.

He looked at them saying, 'Stanley has been with us all night, now when the car comes to pick us up! Mother you had better make a flask of coffee for you know who, now Stanley you are our nephew and been with us all evening and we were just about to go out for dinner when we got the news. Is that clear?' Checker and his wife agreed.

After about five minutes there was a knock at the door, Mr Bond went and opened the door, a policeman. 'Alright your Honour?'

'Come in Constable.'

As they came back into the lounge the policeman said, 'Good evening mam.'

She replied, 'Hello James, nice to see you but I wish on a better occasion.'

'Too true mam.' He turned to Checker and held his hand out.

'Good evening sir.' Checker replied.

Mrs Bond told the policeman, 'We were just about to go out for a meal with our nephew.'

The policeman replied, 'I can see that you were not dressed to go to the hospital.'

As they left the house Mrs Bond told the policeman, 'There's the coffee and a tin of biscuits, you know where the switch is for the heater.' As they closed the door on the entrance porch the policeman sat down on the bench seat. Mrs Bond said, 'Is the inner front door locked?'

Her husband replied 'Yes.'

Back at Norbury the two policemen were comparing notes of the description the elderly couple had given them. One of the Policemen said, 'It looks like they both saw a different fight.'

The older of the two said, 'Well I do not think we should push it any further, they have had a nasty shock tonight and they do look frightened. Ask one of the ambulance men to have a look at them and if they're alright we will take them home.'

The ambulance crew agreed, they were safe to take home but had reservations about the two men, one of them has a fifty percent chance of full recovery, the other one whose face is in a state has far less. 'We have radioed in and Mayday at Croydon can take them.'

The policeman replied, 'We will see you there but have you been able to establish who they are?'

One of the ambulance crew handed the policeman a driving licence. 'That was in the pocket of the bigger one of the two, a Mr Larry Barker.'

After the police had taken the two elderly people home they proceeded to drive to Mayday Hospital. On route they radioed in to give the address and name of Mr Barker taken to Mayday Hospital, Croydon to inform any relatives.

Mr and Mrs Bond and Checker on arrival at the hospital made their way to accident and emergency area. As Mr Bond was about to go to reception the policeman with them indicated that he would enquire after Terry's well being and whereabouts. After two or three minutes he returned to say that Terry had suffered severe injuries. X-rays show some internal damage. The doctors are with him and carrying out operations. The policeman said that the Sister on duty says that you could use her office to wait in if you so wish as one of the nurses showed them to the Sister's office.

Mrs Bond asked the nurse if she could tell them anymore, of which she could not. Then Checker noticed Rita and Jean walking into the waiting room. Before he could say anything, Mrs Bond had also seen them and hurried over to them, talked to them for roughly five minutes then they all returned to the Sister's office.

They were a bit tearful. Mr Bond went into the waiting room to talk with the policeman who had come with them. Checker went partially into the waiting room when there was a commotion, nurses hurrying to the entrance, there were ambulance men and hospital porters walking quickly in, pushing stretchers in with male patients. They looked terrible; Checker did not need telling who they were. He overheard somebody saying, 'Bloody hell! Two more from Norbury, there must be a maniac loose up there.'

Mr Bond and the police were looking on at the patients on the beds. Just then some more police came into the hospital. Mr Bond turned towards Checker and slowly came over, put his arm around Checker's shoulder and whispered, 'Don't worry Stanley, I would have done the same, now don't forget you were with Mother and I all night.'

An hour had past, Rita, although her face was bruised, her neck also, told them what had happened. Also how they were saved from further savagery when a man came to their rescue. She did not know of him but she was grateful for what he had done, saved her from further savagery and only wished the man had came earlier to save Terry.

The policeman said, 'I believe the two men in question that attacked young Mr Bond and yourself are here in the hospital and they are being transferred for surgery. Young Mr Bond is soon to be transferred to intensive care unit.'

Mrs Bond said, 'I will ask Sister if we can see him?'

The Sister informed Mr and Mrs Bond that only immediate family can visit, i.e. themselves only as he is sedated so only a short visit. As Mr and Mrs Bond followed the night Sister, Checker asked Rita and Jean if they wanted anything. He only said it as he was at a loss and did not know what to do. Then as they just sat there the policeman had gone to join the others, then there sounded like an argument which got louder and louder. A man was shouting, wanting to see his brother, demanding to see him.

Checker looked out to the reception, the man had his back to Checker and he saw two policemen trying to calm him. Then Checker heard the man shout, 'I am Mr Raymond Barker and somebody from the Police Station telephoned to say my brother is here, a Larry Barker and I want to see him!'

One of the policemen told him that his brother was in the operating theatre, Raymond Barker went quiet. Then after one minute started swearing, 'Alright you fucking coppers, which one of you bastards done him? Aye don't try and palm it off, which one of you done it?'

One of the policemen was trying his best to calm him and tell him his brother had been brought in by ambulance and they were there to try and find out who had done it and why?

Checker turned to Jean and Rita and whispered to them. 'That bloke out there, making all the noise is called Hookey and leads the Eagles mob at Palace. You know Jean, the geezer that tried to mix it with me and T.J. at Norbury, you know.'

Jean replied, 'I only know what you told me, if it is, you stay here. Don't let him see you, we have enough problems with Terry.'

He started to say, 'He's no problem I.'

When Jean remarks, 'Ho yes, go on play the big man, get yourself arrested!'

Checker looked at Jean and Rita, 'Sorry, maybe one day I'll grow up and think first.'

Jean said, 'Don't you worry Stan, I will do all the thinking, you stay as you are, I would not want you to change. We are a pair, but sometimes!'

Checker smiled, 'Yes we are and I did let you drive the boat on holiday.'

Jean was about to say something but was interrupted by Mr and Mrs Bond coming back into the room, you could see that both had been crying. Rita asked, 'Is Terry alright?'

Mr Bond replied, 'Terry's on life support, he is in a coma! The hospital staff are doing their best, let's all go home. I need to think and get him transferred to another hospital. Stanley could you please find the constables that brought us here? Tell them we are ready to go home.'

Checker looked towards Jean who nodded her head.

Checker turned and walked into the main area of Accident and Emergency department, he saw the policemen talking to two others. Also out of the corner of his vision he saw the person called Hookey staring at him. He did not react, he carried on to the group of policemen.

Then Hookey shouted, 'Oi! Don't I know you?' Checker carried on. 'Oi, you wanker I know you don't I?'

Checker stopped, half turned to look at Hookey but before he could say anything the policeman that came with him and Mr Bond had come up to him and said, 'It's alright sir, is everything alright?'

Checker looked at him and told him that Terry was on life support and in a coma. 'We would like to go home now please.'

The policeman turned and signalled to the other policeman who came over. He informed them of Terry's medical condition. In turn they looked at Checker then at Hookey saying to Checker, 'Has he been giving some grief sir?'

Checker by this time was near to tears, muttered, 'Don't worry, we just want to go home.'

The policeman who came with them put his arm around Checker's shoulder saying, 'Come on son let's go home.' Then looking at the other policeman saying, 'See to that bastard.'

When they got home the policeman called James asked about Terry. When told he appeared at a loss, he just nodded his head as he went to the porch. Mr Bond said, 'I don't think it will be necessary for you or any of your colleagues, it appears they have caught the men. I hope it is not a retribution from some criminals of the past but I and my family are very grateful for the expeditious way of yourself and your department. While you James and your colleagues are with us we can rest assured, thank you.'

The policeman bid them goodnight and left. They were all in the lounge, Mrs Bond asked, 'Tea anyone?'

They all said yes. Jean got up to help her and Rita followed into the kitchen. Mr Bond went to the drinks cabinet, did not say anything and poured two generous glasses of brandy, came back to the chairs, handed a glass to Checker. Nothing was said as they both drank.

When the others returned from the kitchen Mrs Bond placed the tray on the coffee table. The atmosphere was sombre. She started to pour the tea as she did so looked towards her husband. He held out his hand to her saying, 'Yes please.' And put his glass of half finished brandy down saying, 'Tea will be fine dear, I am not going to pour my sorrows into that yet, I know all we can do is wait for news and never give up hope.' Then with a forced smile, said, 'Well you youngsters if you are all staying for the night we had better get you sort of bedded down and I and my wife would very much like you to stay. Your company will be most helpful to us all I believe.'

Mrs Bond said, 'Yes, I would like that so if you want to telephone your parents to let them know, you are welcome.' She looked at them.

Jean spoke first saying, 'Thank you, I would like that.' Then Rita, then Checker.

Mrs Bond said, 'Good, when we have finished with our tea us girls better rustle up some dinner for us all and as Rita knows, we have enough rooms for you all and if you girls want to be in the same room you can have the large spare room with two single beds. Stanley can have your old room Rita.'

Mr Bond said, 'I have almost forgot, I had best telephone Richard to let him know about Terry, as it would help him to arrange Terry's work to be passed to others.' Then as an afterthought said to them all, 'You can stay as long as you like here, I know my wife and I would find it most helpful.' Then left to telephone Richard Bowen, Terry's employer.

The next morning around the breakfast table everybody was having breakfast, the mood was sombre, everyone appeared to have had a restless and fitful night. They were quiet, all thinking with their own thoughts. Mr Bond had telephoned the hospital and was informed that there was no change in Terry's medical condition. Checker in his own thoughts had made up his mind that he would seek revenge on Hookey and his brother because he believed it was no coincidence that Hookey's brother was at Norbury last night. Mrs Bond broke the silence by saying that they were going to the hospital later and if anybody wanted to join them they would be welcome. Checker answered that he would like to join them but he had to telephone his employers first, Jean and Rita said likewise.

When they all returned to the hospital they were informed that Terry's condition had worsened, that he was not responding. Mr and Mrs Bond were by his bedside. Checker, Jean and Rita were seated outside the ward in the waiting area. Roughly half an hour had past when their waiting was interrupted by Mr and Mrs Bond coming out of the ward, both were crying. A nurse was holding Mrs Bond, speaking to her softly. Mr Bond was ashen faced his tears running freely. He held out his hand towards Checker who he and the girls went to them both, holding and hugging them. It was a forlorn group of people, all holding each other and crying, nobody wanting to let go. It was obvious to Checker and the girls that Terry had died.

After about ten minutes had past Mr Bond said to them all, 'I won't be but a few minutes, it will be alright dear!' Then saying to Checker, 'I want you to come with me Stanley, if you don't mind?' He turned and walked back into the ward.

The Sister in charge came to them. 'Can I help Mr Bond?'

He answered, 'Yes, my son's body, I do not want it touched by anybody, no doctor's, anybody! I will have him collected by the Police Coroner's office, Whitehall. As you might or might not be aware, I am Judge Bond, High Court. My family and I are under the Police protection office and they will determine what killed my son! My nephew here is witness to this conversation so I suggest that you better make sure that not one piece of tissue is missing from my son's body. So if some over zealous doctor has tampered? I will sue the culprit, and your name Sister?'

She stammered, 'Er, Sister Clarkson, night Sister.'

Mr Bond said, 'Thank you.' Turned and walked away with Checker following.

When they returned to his wife he said, 'Come on lets all go home, this is a depressing place, I also have some urgent telephone calls to make.'

When they had returned home, Mr Bond excused himself and retired to his study to make his calls he had intimated earlier. The calls to Mr Bowen to make quick reservation of his wishes to the hospital not to tamper or contaminate Terry's body, one to the Police Coroner's to make them aware of his wishes and lastly one call to the police to let them know and that he believed the persons who murdered his son are at Mayday Hospital, one of them was a Mr L Barker.

When he returned to the others in the lounge Mrs Bond proffered him a cup of tea and asked if he wanted anything to eat? He declined, he then asked Checker, saying, 'You had better get in touch with your other members/owners of the flats. I know Terry drew up papers covering the selling of one flat and the other members have first refusal but Terry has made a will, I do not know of the contents but Richard Bowen, his employer, tells me Terry had recently made a will which Richard witnessed. He says part of the content referred to some flats and asked if I could contact them all for the reading of the will?'

Checker said, 'What, Terry made a will? He's too young to have done that.'

Mr Bond replied, 'No Stanley, I have always insisted that my wife, Terry and myself, in case of any eventuality, such as now.'

Checker looked at Mrs Bond who nodded her head. He said, 'I s'pose I better tell them then.'

Checker, after telling Cliff and Curly of T.J.'s death and of his will, to be ready for reading, he made his way to the pub used by his mate's Trevor and John. On meeting them he told them of T.J.'s death and would they help him to catch who had caused T.J.'s death. But when they had caught them he would ask them to leave because he did not want them to be involved with what he had planned to do to them.

'What are you going to do then?' asked John.

Checker replied that he would not kill but make them physically in pain for the rest of their lives so they will always remember why.

'I'm not a sadist but I want them two to suffer for the rest of their natural.'

John looked at Trevor who nodded then told Checker, 'We are with you mate.'

He laughed saying, 'Anyway if you get caught you would be lost without us inside! That's what true mates are for!'

Trevor said 'Yes, I did it for Johno once, I would do it for you.'

Checker replied, 'Thanks, it won't come to that, I hope.'

Thursday: seven days had passed. T.J. was buried.

There was quite a big affair, Checker did not count but he guessed there were about sixty to seventy people there, about twenty five of them returned to Mr and Mrs Bond's house afterwards, Cliff and Curly also. It was at that time Mr Bond tells them the reading of Terry's will would be on Friday at eleven thirty at Mr Bowen's offices.

Clifford, the most inquisitive, inquired if Mr Bond had any idea of the contents?

He replied, 'No.'

Checker, with his inner thoughts did not tell anybody that when at the graveside throwing some dirt onto the coffin, he swore a solemn oath to T.J. that he would get the Barker brothers.

Friday as arranged they met at Bowen & Bowen Solicitor's offices. When they were all seated in Mr Bowen's office he started to open and read out to all.

'T.J.'s Will, it states that he had not left anything to his fiancé Rita as he was well aware his parents would look after her as they more or less consider her their daughter and she would not want for anything.'

'To Stanley Wolf, he gives him the deeds and contents of his flat at St James Road, as this is a gift, it does not cause any inconvenience to others but if Stanley wanted to sell he would still have to give first refusal to Clifford and Gordon. "All and lastly I give all monies and savings accounts, plus bonds to my parents to do as they will, after all that is where most of it came from, I do believe! However, my father will close the company accounts, pay outstanding debts, including the mortgage to the flats. Good bye to you all and thank you."'

As everybody left the solicitor's, Terry's father invited all of them to return to their home for a small repast in memory of their son. As they all made their way back to Mr Bond's house, Checker had travelled in Gordon's car, along with Clifford, the silence was broken with Cliff saying to Checker, 'You done alright! You have copped his flat, meaning you own the whole house!'

Checker turned and said angrily, 'You might have been pleased if it was you, I'm not! I rather him to be sitting beside me now, not in a box, so shut it. Gordon stop the car, I'll make my own way and I promise you I'll get those bastards.'

As Checker slowly walked, in deep thought, he muttered to himself, vowing that he would avenge T.J.'s murder. He slowly looked to his left, he saw and felt T.J.'s presence, he was walking beside him saying nothing, just smiling and as T.J. faded away Checker called out, 'I promise T.J., I promise.'

The End